"What Are You Doing Up So Early?"

he asked. His hastily donned plaid shirt gaped open, exposing an expanse of muscular, tanned chest and a mat of thick, curling black hair. Andrea moved her gaze from his bare skin to meet his eyes as he continued. "I know. You got up early because you wanted to surprise me with breakfast in bed!"

"Dreamer," she laughed back. His lighthearted tone had chased away her restless doubts. "You can't be serious."

"But I am. I always awaken ravenous . . . or don't you remember?"

Her voice caught. "It's been a long time," she murmured.

"Too long," he agreed.

Dear Reader:

There is an electricity between two people in love that makes everything they do magic, larger than life. This is what we bring you in SILHOUETTE INTIMATE MOMENTS.

SILHOUETTE INTIMATE MOMENTS are longer, more sensuous romance novels filled with adventure, suspense, glamor or melodrama. These books have an element no one else has tapped: excitement.

We are proud to present the very best romance has to offer from the very best romance writers. In the coming months look for some of your favorite authors such as Elizabeth Lowell, Nora Roberts, Erin St. Claire and Brooke Hastings.

SILHOUETTE INTIMATE MOMENTS are for the woman who wants more than she has ever had before. These books are for you.

Karen Solem
Editor-in-Chief
Silhouette Books

Dark Side Of The Moon

Lisa Jackson

Silhouette Intimate Moments

Published by Silhouette Books New York

America's Publisher of Contemporary Romance

Silhouette Books by Lisa Jackson

A Twist of Fate (SE #118)
Dark Side of the Moon (IM #39)

SILHOUETTE BOOKS, a Division of Simon & Schuster, Inc.
1230 Avenue of the Americas, New York, N.Y. 10020

ISBN: 0-671-49381-7

First Silhouette Books printing February, 1984

10 9 8 7 6 5 4 3 2 1

*To Mom and Dad,
with love, Susan*

Chapter 1

THE HEAVY DOOR SWUNG VIOLENTLY OUTWARD, LETTING THE late afternoon sunshine pour in to the stark marble building, filling a small space of the gloomy interior with the warmth of late Indian summer. A moist Pacific breeze full of the promise of the ocean met Jefferson Harmon as he strode out of the turn-of-the-century courthouse, and his near-black hair ruffled in the wind. His jaw was set squarely, and his hazel eyes glinted with fierce determination. He paused only slightly as he noticed the swarm of newspaper reporters and television cameramen that were milling along the steep cement steps of the building. A dark look of savage anger crossed his aristocratic face, but was quickly, professionally disguised. Damn that Lara, he thought to himself; summoning the reporters must have been her idea. She knew how he hated facing the press when it came to issues involving his personal life. The oath that had been forming in his mind never made it to his lips.

From habit, Jefferson shifted the deep-set scowl his features formed into a pleasant, though restrained, smile. Although he squinted against the bright glare of the rapidly lowering sun, he presented a poised and self-assured image. All of the anger that had been threatening to overcome him in the last few hours was well hidden behind his hazel eyes. Only those who knew him well would notice the dangerous gleam of determination in his gaze and the square angle of his jaw that remained rigidly set in proud resolve.

To appear more at ease than he actually felt, Jefferson casually pushed one hand into the pocket of his navy-blue suit pants. Repressing the urge to loosen the knot of his expensive silk tie, he grinned at one of the reporters that he knew from his days in politics. Jefferson appeared every bit the successful man that he was—or had been—as he descended the steps under the hazy California sun.

"Hello, John," Jefferson called to the reporter, and flashed his famous smile. He mentally braced himself for the barrage of questions that his affable greeting invited.

The press took their cue and converged upon their subject. Reporters shoved and elbowed their way closer to Jefferson, and traffic along the palm-lined street slowed to watch the spectacle. Questions, some louder than others, were tossed in his direction, and he fielded them with the ease of someone accustomed to being in the public eye. Microphones, wielded almost like weapons, were shoved into Jefferson's outwardly calm face as he smiled into the cameras.

"Mr. Harmon?" The portly, middle-aged reporter who had been greeted by Jefferson earlier began to speak. "Is it true that your divorce from your wife, Lara, is final as of today?"

Jefferson's smile faded slightly as he answered the bespectacled man with the bushy, graying moustache and homey grin. "That's right, John," Jefferson admitted, deciding it was time to end the hastily convened press conference before the questions became too personal. With a wave, he pressed through the throng of reporters and headed toward his parked car. Jefferson hoped that his gesture would dismiss the crowd. He was wrong.

"What about the custody of your daughter, Megan, Mr. Harmon?" This time it was a shrill woman's voice that called out to him. "What about her? Has Mrs. Harmon retained custody?"

There was a hitch in Jefferson's long, easy stride, and he felt every muscle in his body tense at the mention of Megan. Relax, he told himself, trying to retain his escaping composure. He whirled to face the smartly dressed young woman with the cold, calculating eyes.

"We're still working on that," he offered politely, flashing her his most disarming smile. The smile still intact, he muttered a mental oath at his scheming ex-wife, Lara. She was probably still in the courthouse, watching him from the window, enjoying the scene that she had created —at his expense. A muscle in Jefferson's jaw twitched at the thought, and once again he turned toward his silver Mercedes. If he could just get to the car before his temper took complete control of him, he would be all right. The sporty car was parked near a palm tree, not more than a hundred yards away. He walked briskly toward the auto.

"But, Governor!" The insistent young woman with the brassy blond hair relentlessly pursued her story. "Won't you please tell us a little more about the divorce?"

In his pocket Jefferson's fist clenched, but he willed it to uncoil just as he reached the waiting Mercedes. He leaned against the silver car casually, and his gaze traveled over the faces of the reporters that had followed him en masse from the courthouse steps. "I'd prefer not to comment about the divorce at this time," he responded crisply. There was just the slightest edge to his voice, and he hoped that the commanding tone of his voice would dissuade the asking of any more impertinent, personal questions. Why, he wondered, after two years, would anyone still make the unpleasant mistake of referring to him as governor?

"Then—" a new voice beckoned him, and he turned to face a young, and obviously green newspaper reporter "—could you comment on the rumor that your wife has a drinking problem?" The young man was anxious, and hungry for a story. Jefferson could read it in the eager brown eyes and nervous twitch of his cheek.

Jefferson's deep, hazel eyes turned the color of tempered steel and impaled the young man that had made the mistake of asking too private a question. "No." He jerked the car door open and began to slide into the soft leather interior. As the next barrage of questions assaulted him every muscle in his body froze.

"What about the rumor that both your divorce *and* Mrs. Harmon's drinking problem were caused by your affair with that girl before you were married. Is it true that you really never got over her? If so, why did you marry Lara Whitney? Do you still see that woman?" Jefferson's eyes darkened and narrowed as he glared at the impertinent young man. The reporter sensed a change in his subject's attitude and, smelling a story, pressed his advantage. "Mrs. Harmon publicly claims that you never really forgot that *other* woman, and that you married Mrs. Harmon on the rebound. Is there any truth to your ex-wife's accusations?" Jefferson looked away from the interested eyes that were watching his every move and quickly settled behind the wheel of his car. The young man continued to badger him. "You know the woman that I'm talking about, Governor Harmon. She . . . was a Conscientious Objector to the war . . . or something. . . ." The hard, condemning voice trailed off, as the reporter hurriedly scanned his notes. The young newspaperman knew that he'd made some trivial mistake . . . a vague error about the girl and the scandal of ten years past. What was it? Didn't he have that woman's name?

Jefferson's response to the inquiry was to slam the car door shut, flick on the ignition and roar out of the parking lot. His anger got the best of him, and he ripped the gears of the Mercedes mercilessly. His calm exterior dissolved into a contemptuous frown as he left the anxious reporters behind him. Perhaps his ex-wife, Lara, would be so good as to offer her opinions to the press about the farce that she had called marriage.

As he turned the wheel of the car he thought involuntarily of his young daughter. If it hadn't been for Megan, he wouldn't have continued the charade that his marriage to Lara had become. Jefferson's face softened as he recalled his five-year-old daughter and all of the suffering that the child must have borne in her life. As his fingers tightened around the steering wheel, Jefferson promised himself that he would fight Lara tooth-and-nail for custody of the only bright spot in their otherwise grim sham of a marriage.

The afternoon in the office had stretched longer than Andrea had expected. As the hours in the confining cubicle slowly ticked by, she felt her stomach tighten into a knot of anxiety and uncertainty. That morning, after the Nielson ratings had come out for the previous week's shows, the president of Coral Productions had immediately informed the office staff of an emergency personnel meeting, slated for four thirty.

Andrea shifted uncomfortably in her desk chair and eyed the clock. Four fifteen. The waiting would soon end. Now, as she sat staring vacantly out of the window toward the hazy hills in the distance, she could see the writing on the wall, she could almost envision the headlines: Coral Productions loses three shows; bankrupt company closes its doors. The tension that had been building in the small suite of offices had been charging the air. Everyone involved with Coral Productions was on edge, because each person understood that his job, along with the operation of the company as a whole, was on the line.

An early edition of the local paper sat folded on Andrea's desk. While passing the final minutes until the meeting convened, she opened the tabloid in an effort to occupy her worried mind. Her misty green eyes scanned the columns on the front page: the economic recession was still waging war with the American people, and unemployment had jumped another percentage point for the month of September. She pushed an errant lock of blue-black hair behind her ear and lifted her eyes from the disturbing news. Never in all of her thirty years had she considered that the state of the economy could affect her. Not personally. She pursed her full lips tightly and rubbed the back of her neck with her fingers. That was the problem with being born rich, she decided, one never expected the money to run out.

To avoid thinking about the pressing problem of her potentially uncertain employment, she quickly flipped past the national news. She took a sip of her cold coffee and nearly choked as her eyes met the headlines in the social section: HARMON DIVORCE FINAL: CUSTODY OF CHILD STILL UNDECIDED. Beneath the bold, black letters, Jefferson Harmon, his jaw square and determined in the dull image of a black and white newsprint photo, stared back at her.

"No," she whispered to herself. "Not again." She regarded the image of the tall, broad-shouldered man and fought the urge to toss the newspaper into the trash basket. Ten-year-old emotions ravaged her body—the same emotions that tore at her each time Jefferson's famous face reappeared in the public limelight. She willed the tears that were burning the back of her eyes to dry as the memories of pain and suffering, guilt and betrayal, love and deceit, came flooding back to her. "I can't go through this again—not again," she said to herself as her small palm slapped the disquieting article. Memories, wild and fanciful, brimming with love and the taste of salt air, began swimming in her mind.

How distant those warm, enticing summers seemed now. While she was lost in thought, her fingers reached out to touch the flat, cold image of Jefferson's face and traced the familiar line of his jaw. The picture didn't do him justice, she mused distractedly as she remembered a younger man, dashingly good-looking, with a smile that was slightly off-center and eyes that were intelligent, kind, disturbing—eyes that could darken to stormy gray when he became challenged or angry. How many times in the past had she witnessed the darkening of his deep-set, hazel eyes?

Ignoring the time that was passing, Andrea skimmed the article. Her throat became dry, and she bit her lower lip as her eyes touched on the printed words. Familiar phrases, some that haunted her nights, leapt up at her to scorch her mind: brilliant young lawyer . . . marriage to prestigious wealth . . . short term of governor . . . controversial resignation . . . scandalous past . . .

"Hey, Andrea!" Katie's soft voice called through the door of Andrea's small office and broke into her reverie. "Better get a move on. The meeting's in five minutes!"

Andrea's startled green eyes broke from the article to her wristwatch to confirm her friend's announcement. "I'll be there. . . . Save me a seat," she managed to say at last.

"Sure," Katie answered, a confused look in her clear, blue eyes. She shrugged her slim shoulders and hurried off down the hallway toward the conference room.

Hurriedly Andrea folded the newspaper and set it on the corner of her desk. Although the evening tabloid was not normally a scandal sheet, the article on Harmon read like a vicious gossip column. His famous life, dissected anew, was splashed before the public eye with short, explicit references to his personal and political career. The newspaper story left Andrea feeling naked and vulnerable. Would the pain never end? Would the past never stop chasing her?

"Dear God," she whispered almost inaudibly. "Will I ever get over him?" For several long moments, she stood gazing vacantly at the newspaper, remembering endless lost hours of making love in the warm Pacific rain. She felt the grit of sand scrape against her bare feet and heard the lonesome cries of marauding sea gulls over the relentless pounding of an angry, northern surf.

With difficulty Andrea swallowed the tears that threatened to spill and forced her thoughts to turn to the present, and the immediate problems with her job. She couldn't—*wouldn't*—let herself fall victim to the past. Never again. Her fists balled at her sides as she regained her composure, and defiantly she willed her feelings to retreat to the past. She quickly picked up her pen and note pad and hurried down the hall to the conference room.

The small central room where the meetings of Coral Productions were held was thick with the haze of blue cigarette smoke and the scent of stale coffee. Nervous chatter buzzed around the table as Andrea entered the room and slid into a vacant chair. The other employees of Coral Productions, a secretary, the bookkeeper, and three other scriptwriters—the "office personnel"—were already seated or sprawled around a small table strewn with Styrofoam cups of tasteless black coffee and half-full ashtrays. In the middle of the table was another copy of the newspaper that Andrea had just read. Again Jefferson Harmon's face stared blankly up at her, and Andrea had to force her eyes away from the unsettling photograph.

Andrea was relieved that Bryce Cawthorne, one-time character actor and now president and owner of Coral Productions, hadn't yet arrived. So far the ax hadn't fallen, and all of the talk about closing down the company was pure conjecture. She managed a thin, encouraging smile at Katie Argus, the other woman on the scriptwriting team, but the furrow of Andrea's dark brows, and the shadow of anxiety in her large, sea-green eyes belied her outward equanimity.

"Are you okay?" Katie asked, her bright blue eyes searching Andrea's delicate face. "I didn't think that you'd make it before Bryce got here. Is anything wrong? You look a little pale."

"I'm fine," Andrea replied with a faint smile. "Just a little concerned."

"Aren't we all?" Katie observed, almost to herself,

while her long, brightly polished fingernails tapped against the glass tabletop. Her full lips pulled into a pouty frown of concentration, and even her deep tan seemed to have paled against her sun-streaked golden hair.

"Not me," a well-modulated male voice announced from a distant corner of the room. "I'm not worried." Jack Masters shrugged his shoulders with indifference and slumped into a chair opposite Katie. An anxious line of concern etched his forehead and belied his casual exterior. "It isn't my fault that Nicole Jamison can't act her way out of a paper bag."

"I don't see that Nicole has anything to do with shutting down production," Katie snapped back irritably.

"It's simple," Jack explained, lifting his palms skyward. "She should never have been cast as the virginal do-gooder bride in *Pride's Power*. The character of Justin Pride would never have fallen for and married a woman like Nicole. She's just not right for the part of Angela. Justin would want a strong woman, proud and yet vulnerable, virtuous to the point of self-sacrifice—not some scheming bitch like Nicole Jamison. She's about as innocent as Mata Hari!" Jack pronounced sarcastically.

"And just about as old," Katie murmured, half to herself.

"It doesn't matter," Andrea pointed out, trying to be heard over the snicker of laughter at Katie's dry attempt at humor. Andrea examined each of the faces surrounding the small table. As senior writer she had a small edge of influence over her co-workers, and the fact that she had worked the most closely with Bryce Cawthorne gave her better insight into some of the problems that the small production company faced. "At this point we're only second-guessing ourselves. Whether it was a case of poor casting, a lousy time slot or anything else, the fact is that *Pride's Power* has continued to slip in the ratings. Last week it was polled in the bottom twenty. Who knows why?

Maybe the public has become saturated with nighttime soaps."

At that moment the door to the room flew open and banged against the wall. Bryce Cawthorne, his perennial frown in place, strode into the room. Under his arm was the latest dismal set of Nielson ratings. Ignoring the captain's chair that had been reserved for him, he hoisted his small, wiry body onto the lowest filing cabinet. From his perch he looked over the tops of his bifocals at all of the anxious eyes that had followed his dramatic entrance. He pulled the ratings sheet from under his arm and began listing the current shows produced by Coral. It didn't take long.

"*Night Sirens*, our latest police production . . . and our newest hopeful, climbed to number 42. *Dangerous Games* fell off another three ratings points to 46. And, our feeble attempt at nighttime drama, *Pride's Power*, tumbled down to 57." After an audible groan from Bryce's captive audience, there was an unsettling silence as the weight of Bryce's somber announcement settled like lead on the shoulders of everyone in the room. Bryce continued. "From what I understand all three shows will be canceled at the end of the season." Bryce tossed the disturbing ratings sheets up in the air. The assembled staff watched them land with a smack in the middle of the table, next to the newspaper article on Jefferson Harmon.

Andrea's eyes stopped for a moment on the picture of Jefferson before returning to Bryce's furrowed face. He shook his head in confusion. "I don't know what to tell you. . . ." His eyes moved around the table. "I don't understand it. I thought we had a winner in *Pride's Power*." He rubbed the back of his neck with his hand and attempted to uncoil the tension in his shoulders. "We just can't afford any more flops . . . not even one!"

Andrea bit at the corner of her lower lip. She was probably the person in the room closest to Bryce, and yet even she had trouble asking the question that was uppermost in everyone's mind. "What exactly are you saying, Bryce?"

Andrea could feel the sting of tension in the air as all eyes focused on the owner of the company. Bryce rubbed his palms on the knees of his worn designer jeans. "I don't know," he admitted, shaking his balding head. "I came up with a couple of ideas for new shows, but most of them were scrapped immediately by the Powers That Be in the broadcasting company. It seems that they're not interested in airing any more situation comedies, detective shows and, least of all, night soaps."

Bryce was depressed. Andrea could tell by the droop of his usually straight shoulders. "They didn't like any of your ideas?" Andrea was amazed. Since his retirement from acting, Bryce Cawthorne had become something of a Hollywood legend when it came to creating new and interesting ideas for television. Until two years ago, when the ratings had begun to sour, it seemed as if Coral Productions could do no wrong.

"The only real possibility is with an independent cable network. I've been talking to some of the sales people at ITV, and they are very interested in presenting a weekly special about an interesting, controversial public figure. . . . It might work . . . it definitely has possibilities. . . ."

"Like who?" Katie asked, eyeing her boss with interest.

Bryce leaned backward and stared at the ceiling, lost in speculation. "Oh, I don't know . . . I've just been kicking the idea around a little, but it should be someone who is a household word, who creates a bundle of public interest . . . someone that people like . . . or hate, I suppose. For example, there's Sondra Wickfield . . ."

"The wealthy philanthropist who allegedly shot her lover?" Andrea asked.

"Right, or, I don't know, maybe that country singer who had an affair with the Spanish nobleman," Bryce continued, warming to his subject.

"You're talking about the people that grace the front

pages of the scandal sheets," Andrea observed, and her eyes flickered from Bryce to the picture of Jefferson Harmon and back again.

"No, not necessarily," Bryce countered. "Think of it as human interest stories." His tone was placating, and Andrea began to feel a coiling uneasiness grip her.

"I don't know," she began, but Bryce's stern look of challenge halted her argument.

"We're talking about saving the company, Andrea! Face it, we're fighting for our lives . . . *your* job! I'm only attempting to give the public what it wants, and right now there's a barely tapped gold mine in revealing the intimate lives of the famous."

Andrea knew that the argument was going in Bryce's direction, and she wisely withheld further comment. She realized that to push Bryce when he was this desperate, would only make him all the more adamant.

"That's right," Jack chimed in, siding with the boss and eager to get in on the conversation. "There are a lot of personalities that the public is dying to hear about. Take, for example, Jefferson Harmon," Jack continued, pointing his finger at the newspaper. "Now, there's a guy that we all want to know more about!" Andrea's heart leapt to her throat as her green eyes, wide with concern, moved from Jack's finger on the newspaper back to Bryce.

"Exactly!" her boss stated, and Andrea felt her heart sink. "Harmon is a perfect example of the kind of interview and examination that the cable company wants. Andrea, what do you think?"

Vaguely Andrea heard her name. "What?" she asked, and she could feel the color rush to her cheeks.

"About the new show, what do you think?" Bryce prodded, his gaze pinioning her.

"Ah, well, I guess it's a good idea," she managed to say, hoping to get a grip on herself and avoid angering Bryce any further.

"But you have some reservations?"

"No, I was only questioning the choice of guests. It . . . it would be important that anyone we cover be an interesting, powerful personality. Someone who is newsworthy today. . . ." Was she rambling? She wondered, forcing herself to smile stiffly at Bryce.

"That's why I think Jefferson Harmon would be a perfect choice. Perhaps his should be the first story in the series," Jack continued. "Have you seen the headlines this afternoon?" Jack asked the group around the table. He flagged the newspaper in the air theatrically. "How about all of this interest in his divorce and the custody of his kid?"

Andrea knew that she had to stop the speculation about Jefferson, before the pain and embarrassment of ten years past caught up with her again—just as it always did whenever Jefferson Harmon's name was splashed across the headlines.

Andrea cocked her head to one side and calmly looked Bryce in the eye. "Don't you think that Harmon is yesterday's news?" she inquired, and though her voice was even, she could feel her stomach fluttering. The color drained from her face, but even so, she hoped that she was masking the disturbing sense of dread that was climbing up her spine.

"Not this guy!" Jack asserted. "He's been in and out of the papers ever since he began his political career. Remember all of the ruckus about him and that college girl, back, when was it, about ten years ago?"

"That's ancient history!" Andrea snapped, and an unguarded defiance lighted her light green eyes. Andrea's angry tone wasn't lost on Bryce.

"Not necessarily," Bryce interposed, ending the simmering argument. It was obvious to her boss that Andrea was upset, though she attempted to mask it. Her usual sparkling complexion was drawn and wan, and there was a disturbing look in her eyes. Was it fear? Bryce wondered. It seemed impossible. In the eight years that Andrea had worked for him, she had proved herself to be unafraid of any challenge he offered. And yet, something was definitely wrong with her. She was nervous, stiff. And from time to time her gaze would wander to the newspaper that Jack held in his hands. Bryce puzzled for a moment, but decided that her anxiety stemmed from the fact that, like most of the employees, Andrea realized how desperate the situation had become for Coral Productions. Everyone was on edge. "Okay, people," Bryce sighed, "the bottom line is this: I've got to find a way out of this mess, and if it means taking a chance on a new program, then we'll do it!" Bryce surveyed the group of people around the table. All of the eyes that met his severe gaze seemed in agreement with his statement. "All right, that's it, then. Let's go home."

The group began to head out of the door. Andrea slid out of her chair, but before she could leave the room, Bryce's hand on her sleeve held her back. As she turned to face him he released her arm. When they were alone, he asked, "Is there something wrong—something that I don't know about?" His gaze had softened, but his dark eyes still probed hers.

"Nothing," Andrea replied, but even to her ears the words didn't ring true. Yet how could she tell Bryce, or anyone for that matter, about the lie that she had been running from for ten long years.

"You're sure?" He seemed unconvinced.

"Well, I am a little worried about the company," she hedged, hating herself for her deceit.

"Don't be. It will work itself out."

"You didn't sound so sure of that in the meeting."

"It was all just part of the show to keep you writers on your toes," he retorted with a fatherly smile.

"Convincing show, I'd say."

They walked out of the room together and, for the first time, Andrea noticed the deep lines of age that had crept up on Bryce Cawthorne over the past eight years. The corners of his eyes were ridged with a webbing of crow's-feet, and lines of worry were etched irregularly across his forehead and neck. His voice was sober as he stopped at the door of her small office.

"You were planning a vacation for the next three weeks?"

"That's right, but if it's inconvenient and you'd prefer me to stay, I can take the time off later, after everything is ironed out."

His hand, raised like a flag of surrender, stilled her. "No, no, by all means, go. I think it would be better for all of us if you got away between the seasons. If we do go ahead with the new program, I'll need you back here to help with the nuts and bolts." He shook his balding head as he leaned, cross-armed in the hallway. "Go, and don't give the rest of us a second thought. You look like you could use some time off!"

"I look that bad, do I?" she asked with a grim smile.

"Of course not! But I think that it would do you some good to get away. You worry too much."

"I've had a good teacher," she pointed out.

Bryce raised his finger and scored an imaginary "one" in the air as his dark brown eyes twinkled. "Take care of yourself, Andrea, and get some rest. Just be sure to leave your number with Carol in case I have to reach you."

"I will," Andrea promised to Bryce's retreating figure as she snapped out the lights to her office, reached for her purse and tucked the newspaper under her arm. The article on Jefferson Harmon was hidden deep in the society pages, and Andrea almost tossed it into the trash. But then she thought better of it. Something inside her forced her to take the article home to reread in the privacy of her apartment, to think about the times she and Jefferson had shared, long before their lives had become complicated, long before they had bitterly parted ways.

Chapter 2

THE RINGING OF THE TELEPHONE STARTLED ANDREA AND interrupted her pensive thoughts. She had been sipping a rare blend of tea and gazing through the leaded glass windows of the red brick town house at the gray, threatening sky that seemed dark against the hills of Queen Elizabeth Park. It felt good to be home again; even the somber, overcast skies of bleak November didn't dampen Andrea's spirits, and she felt more at ease than she had in the past few weeks. Her vacation to her parents' Canadian home was exactly what she had needed.

At the second ring of the insistent phone Andrea turned to face the intrusive instrument. She had only been on Vancouver Island for six days, and expected no calls. Her parents had telephoned just last night from Hawaii, and the only other person who might call was her sister, Gayla, who lived near Seattle. Buoyed by the thought that the caller was probably Gayla, Andrea hurried to the telephone.

"Hello!" she called cheerfully into the receiver.

"Hi! It sounds like your vacation has brightened your mood," Bryce's voice boomed to her over the wire.

Andrea felt a little deflated, but tried not to let her disappointment show. "I suppose it has," she agreed distractedly as she leaned against the wall and twisted the telephone cord nervously. Bryce Cawthorne wasn't the kind of man to waste time or money on long-distance phone calls merely to pass the time of day. There had to be a reason for his call. Perhaps, after all, he had decided to close the doors of Coral Productions. Andrea was sickened by the thought, but rather than wait for the bomb to drop, she took the offensive in the conversation. "What's up?" she asked.

"Good news, I hope," he replied.

"That I could use," she said with a rueful smile.

"Remember the new show that I brought up in the meeting?"

"The interviews with celebrities?"

"The very same!" At his words Andrea experienced a sinking sensation. There was something in Bryce's voice that triggered her unease. He continued, "Well, I think I've sold it to ITV. It's somewhat tentative. They've agreed to air five shows, and if the public likes those, ITV will broadcast an additional ten shows."

"Sounds good . . ." Andrea murmured, still twisting the cord of the phone and waiting for the forthcoming hitch. She had a gut feeling that Bryce was holding something back . . . some piece of information that she might not like.

"It's the break we need," he continued fervently in a lowered voice.

"So . . . do you want me to come back to California to work out the details?"

"No." He paused. Here it comes, Andrea thought. "But I was hoping that you could help me out a bit."

"You know that I'd be glad to." What did he want? Already she knew that she would regret her agreement to help him.

"Okay," Bryce said with a sigh. "Here it is: We have to make sure that every one of the shows is a hit—we don't dare miss with one."

"I understand that. What do you want me to do?"

"We've come up with a few possibilities for the interview, and for the most part, the people concerned have agreed—with only a few reservations."

"But . . ." Andrea prodded, biting her lower lip.

"But the one man that we really need for a lead-off story hasn't been available to us."

Andrea couldn't sustain the suspense any longer. "You're talking about Jefferson Harmon, aren't you?"

There was a surprised snort on the other end of the line. "How did you know?"

"Why else would you call?" Andrea retorted. "I'm up here in Victoria, and you've learned that Harmon has a retreat on a private island nearby. Right?" Andrea's stomach was twisted more tightly than the phone cord.

"Yeah. . . . You know, it's just kind of a coincidence, you're being so close to him."

Andrea drew in a long, steadying breath. "So what exactly do you want?"

"The problem is we can't reach the man. I've talked to his ex-wife's secretary, his one-time press agent, even the incumbent governor. But it seems that they can't, or won't, give me a number where he can be reached. I was hoping that you could talk to the phone company up there, see if they could contact him—or maybe go see him personally."

"If the man has taken so many precautions to ensure his privacy, don't you think he might be a little upset to have me knocking on his door?" Andrea replied in what she hoped would seem a reasonable tone of voice. "Why don't you just get someone else? Harmon obviously doesn't want to be bothered!"

"Precisely my point! He grants no interviews, avoids the press at all costs, wraps his privacy around him like some God-given cloak and the public eats it up! They can't get enough of him. It's his penchant for secrecy that works against him. It makes the public want to explore him. . . . Get to know him; just get an inkling into the psyche of the man. What made him renounce his governorship? How does he feel about his ex-wife, his kid, American politics today?"

"And you expect me to persuade him to agree to the interview?" Andrea asked, shocked.

"No. Leave that to me. All I want is a chance to talk with him. If you can somehow find a way to get in touch with him and have him call me—that's all I need."

"You make it sound so easy."

"Are you with me?"

Andrea swallowed. Her mouth was dry. "Of course I'll try," she agreed hesitantly, "but I doubt if I can do anything."

"You might be surprised," Bryce commented enigmatically. "We're just lucky that you're up in Victoria, so near to him. Boy, that's one helluva break!"

As Andrea hung up the phone Bryce's parting words began to echo in her mind: A *coincidence* . . . a lucky break that she was so close to Jefferson Harmon and his private isle. If Bryce only knew, she thought wryly to herself as she picked up her cold cup of tea and sipped it slowly. Was it coincidence that she was here, alone, less than ten miles from Jefferson's summer home? Or did she come of her own will, hoping to meet him again? Although it was early November, she had suspected Jefferson might retreat to the island after the news of his divorce hit the papers. Was it fate that lured her to him, or was it her own free will that tempted her to find a means of communicating with him? Though she loathed the idea, she knew in her heart that she had never really stopped loving him. And, although she had maintained her distance from him since his marriage, she had never stopped thinking about him. Did she secretly hope that she would get just such an opportunity to see him again? Was the reason that had prompted her to arrange this hasty visit to her parents' Canadian home, because she suspected that Jefferson might be nearby? God, she hoped not. She wanted to believe that the reason she had come to Victoria was expressly to get some sorely needed rest from the hectic pace of Southern California and her job. But try as she might, she couldn't shake the feeling that she had secretly wished for an excuse to see Jefferson again.

It seemed so wrong. While Jefferson was married, Andrea had wished only for his happiness, and when the rumors that the marriage was foundering had surfaced, Andrea grieved for him and his wife. No matter how much pain she might have suffered in loving Jefferson, Andrea had sincerely hoped that he had found happiness with Lara Whitney. Andrea had no illusion that Jefferson would ever be able to love her, and she prayed that Lara Whitney would prove to be the woman that Jefferson could cherish.

Or was Andrea kidding herself? How many times had she seen pictures of the strikingly beautiful Lara on the arm of Jefferson and inwardly wished that she could trade places with his wife? How many empty nights had she lain in the loneliness of her bed and longed for him, while hating herself for the thought. Though outwardly she had told herself that she had only wished for Jefferson's happiness, hadn't she cried for hours in teary anguish the night his child was born? Hadn't she lain awake trying to understand why she felt ripped to the bone in her desperation? It wasn't that she was not happy for him; it was good to know that he had a child, a little girl of his own to love. But she couldn't banish the feelings that somehow she had been betrayed, and she felt painfully envious of the woman who had borne his child. Hers was an intimacy Andrea could never share with Jefferson.

Over the years Andrea's pain had lessened, and when confronted with pictures of Jefferson's famous child, Andrea was forced to smile. Megan was thin and fine-boned like her beautiful mother, but had the same haunting and piercing eyes of her father. She was a beautiful girl and seemed to carry herself with a maturity that extended far past her five years.

So now the opportunity to see Jefferson presented itself

again, if only Andrea was strong enough to accept the challenge. It was a difficult and emotional decision. Although it had been over ten years since she had talked with him, she was still nervous at the thought, as evidenced by her suddenly perspiring palms. Could she face him again?

With sudden decisiveness she set down her teacup and dialed the number that had lingered, stagnant, in her mind. She slammed the receiver down as the recorded message told her that the number she had dialed was non-working. Quickly she dialed the operator. But she couldn't get through with the operator's assistance either. After nearly half an hour of frustration, Andrea hung up the phone. She realized that there was no way for her to hide behind the impersonality of a telephone conversation with Jefferson. He had apparently pulled all of the right political strings to ensure his privacy, and if the telephone company did have a number where he could be reached, Andrea had been unable to coerce it from any one of the four operators that she had spoken with.

The question loomed before her, as threatening as the purple clouds that hung over the city; could she face Jefferson Harmon again, after all of the bitterness and suspicions of the past? Would he agree to see her? Or would she again feel the rejection and pain that she had suffered at his hand? Was she strong enough to accept his rejection? Could she contend with a door slammed in her face?

Andrea didn't bother to change her clothes; instead she reached for her raincoat. Armed with the frail excuse supplied by Bryce Cawthorne and Coral Productions and the naked truth that she had to see Jefferson again, Andrea ignored the winter gales of the sea squall that whistled through the city streets. She set out for the marina, hoping to find some money-hungry sailor who was crazy enough to take her to Jefferson's private retreat. Though the wind had picked up considerably in the late afternoon, Andrea was fortunate enough to find one young sailor foolhardy enough to fight anything the stormy sea had to offer—for the right price, of course. She was reluctant to take the brash young man up on his offer, but could find no one else willing to ignore the storm warnings and take her to the island.

Andrea's conscience argued with her judgment, telling her that it was dangerous to sail in such rough water, and that it was ludicrous to knock on Jefferson's door after ten long silent years. Her mind reasoned that he might not even be on the island, and that the terrifying journey would all be in vain. Despite the logical arguments that her mind put forth, Andrea knew that she had to see Jefferson while she still had the courage to look into his dark, arrogant eyes.

What seemed more ridiculous than any of her arguments against the short sea voyage was the fact that she was anxious, almost eager, to see him. Once more she wondered if she had subconsciously willed an excuse to seek him out.

The rain was pelting down furiously, and she nearly slipped as she stepped onto the tiny, pitching motor boat. As she tied her hair back from her face with a leather thong, the sailor of the small craft eyed her speculatively.

"Not dressed for sailing, leastwise not in a storm the likes of this," the bearded young man observed while unleashing the moorings that held the rocking boat to the dock. His watery blue eyes traveled up the length of her calfskin boots, across the heather-colored tweed of her skirt, over the ribbing of her cashmere sweater, to meet her steady gaze.

"This trip was a sudden impulse," she responded with an innocent shrug of her shoulders.

"An impulse? To weather this storm? You've got to be kidding!" He rolled his eyes toward the dark heavens.

Andrea smiled patiently, reticent to give the prying sailor any other information about herself. He adjusted his stocking cap and started the engine of the boat. With a lurch they were off, and after maneuvering past the other docked vessels of the marina, they were out of the harbor. Andrea hiked the collar of her coat up further on her neck to block the chilly rain from her face and shoulders.

The dull gray clouds continued to pour rain, and the boat pitched recklessly in the leaden water. Rain and salt spray moistened Andrea's face and curled the wispy tendrils of hair as they slipped from the thong that was intended to hold her long, ebony tresses away from her neck. Anxiously her tongue rimmed her lips and tasted the salt of the sea.

"This Harmon fella. He expecting you?" the sea man asked.

"Why do you want to know?"

The sailor shrugged his shoulders and sipped from a thermos that Andrea suspected held brew stronger than coffee. "Oh, I don't know, but from what I hear, he's the kind of guy who likes his privacy."

"Doesn't everyone?"

"I suppose so, but with him, it's different. Takes it all real personal, if you know what I mean. I don't know how he'll react when he finds a stranger dumped on his doorstep."

Andrea chose to ignore the remark and instead squinted her eyes against the rain to search the darkening horizon for the island. She knew that it would look different from her faded memory of it, as she had only visited the isle in late summer, long ago. Daisies and rhododendrons had been in bloom, the sand had been warm, and a lazy, caressing sun had warmed her bare skin. But now, in bleak November, as her destination loomed before her, a rocky mountain rising from the sea, she felt a chill of apprehension skitter down her spine. Andrea experienced a dry, tight knotting in her stomach that couldn't be explained solely by the rocking of the small craft on the stormy sea.

Vivid memories flooded her mind, trapping her. Memories flavored with the romanticism of the passing of time.

Memories that had drawn reality out to the abstract and distorted the events of a much younger, happier time in her life. Where were the fields of daffodils and clover that had scented the air? Where were the lush, verdant oak trees that stood imperially on the island? In the gray of winter, with the wind howling and the rain beating mercilessly down on her, Harmon Island looked far more foreboding than welcoming. *What am I doing here?* she wondered crazily, and for a moment was sorely tempted to tell the young man guiding the vessel to take her back to the safety and warmth of the town house in Victoria.

It was nearly dusk by the time the sailor had managed to settle the boat against the mooring of the wooden dock near a shallow, rain-drenched strip of beach. It took some convincing, but Andrea made the man promise to wait for her, at least for an hour. He was reluctant to stay because of the increasing tempo of the storm, but at the prospect of a little extra money he agreed to wait. He hoisted his Thermos in the air as a salute to her before heading into the shelter of the boat's cabin.

Andrea drew in a long, deep breath of cold air and started to climb the wooden staircase that led from the tiny beach up the face of the cliff toward the interior of the island. The gray sky and dark waters of the sea added to the early onset of evening, and Andrea was careful as she ascended the slippery steps. It was difficult to remember clearly, but she hoped that upon reaching the top of the slick steps, she would be able to see the house. It occured to her that the last thing that Jefferson might want on this stormy night was to confront her. She remembered their last bitter quarrel. Andrea grimaced at the thought, and hoped that she hadn't made the precarious voyage across the rough waters of the sound for nothing.

Once she had mounted the stairs, and the face of the cliff no longer guarded her from the force of the gale, the wind angrily whipped her wool skirt against her thighs. The wet, rough fiber added to her discomfort, and she vaguely chided herself for not wearing her more practical jeans. But, then, she hadn't expected that the storm would rage so severely, nor did she remember that she would have to hike so far to get to the immense house.

She looked back for a moment to survey the wild, crashing sea below her. The frothy white waves thudded against the small stretch of beach near the dock, and the tiny boat rocked crazily against its moorings. Why had she come here? Her rational voice reprimanded her. Ignoring the doubts that crowded her mind, she continued to pick her way carefully down the sandy path. How would Jefferson react to her intrusion of his private refuge? A shudder of apprehension darted up her spine and lingered, but she tried to repress the feelings of trepidation that began to capture her with the oncoming stormy night.

The rain continued to beat down on her in gusty sheets of water as she hurried onward. Once around a bend in the path, Andrea stopped, her pale green eyes caught in fascination at the sight of the regal house that guarded the island. It was more impressive and stately than she had recalled. A mansion by Andrea's standards, it seemed to rise out of the very ground that supported it. From its spectacular appearance, Andrea guessed that it had been built over a hundred years ago. The foundation was hewn from the stone of the cliff, carved from the smooth, solid rock of the island, and the imposing two floors that stood over the foundation were masoned of stone, the color of a dove's underbelly. Only the arches and the roof were composed of darkened, weathered timbers.

The roofline was immense, fitted with wooden gables and turrets that stretched upward to the dreary, nightlike sky. Large paned windows of leaded glass winked from almost every angle of the house, glass eyes that watched the turbulent sea. The warmth of fireglow illuminated the otherwise somber manor, and after a moment's hesitation, Andrea hurried to the broad double door of the house and knocked deliberately against the ancient wood. She felt cold apprehension grip her and wondered vaguely if she could be heard over the whistling gales of the wind.

Jefferson Harmon looked up from the newspaper article that he had been studying intently. He gazed into the red, dying embers of the fire and listened to the sounds of the night. His dark, near-black eyebrows drew together in concentration. Was it his imagination, or had he heard a faint rap on the front door? Impossible. He paused for a moment, and then decided the noise must have been a tree limb knocking against the walls of the house in the storm. He chided himself at his own case of nerves. He was upset, and he knew it, ever since the phone call from Lara only hours ago. Damn that woman for making such a mess of the divorce and dragging Megan into the middle of it all.

After straightening the newspaper, he once again became absorbed by the article about his ex-wife that recounted her late-night dancing date with a wealthy young European and the subsequent automobile accident that had put both of them, as well as a few innocent motorists, into the hospital overnight. Luckily it appeared that no one was injured seriously . . . a fact confirmed by Lara only a few hours before on the phone. The newspaper reporter was sympathetic to Lara Harmon, driver of the ill-fated vehicle. Jefferson was not. His scowl deepened as he continued to read.

The knocking began again, and this time, instantly alerted, Jefferson pulled his long body from the comfort of his favorite leather chair and quickly made his way to the front door. Who could possibly be here, in the middle of a Pacific tempest? He discounted it being anyone he knew— all of his friends respected his privacy and would have called in advance. Who then? The only logical explanation was that some poor fool had stupidly been caught in the storm and landed on the island rather than attempt the rugged journey inland. It had happened before, but Harmon was in no mood to try and make small talk with anyone, much less some idiot who didn't even have sense to stay on dry land when a storm was brewing. Jefferson was in a foul mood, and he knew it, but found it impossible to dispel. Reading the article on his ex-wife had made him irritable, and talking with her only served to make him feel tired and frustrated. The last thing he needed at this moment was a stranger on his front porch. It would be difficult to keep his anger in check, especially with some inexperienced blow-hard sailor.

Jerking the door open roughly, Jefferson was stunned by the sight that met his eyes. A woman—young, near thirty he guessed—was standing, straight as an arrow, on his front porch. The fact that rain cascaded over her, and that cold, Northern winds had obviously tousled her hair and chilled her body as well, didn't seem to concern her. The collar of her raincoat, which was fashionable and totally impractical, was hiked around her neck, and she was clearly soaked to the skin. Still, she held her head regally high, as if she anticipated his hostility. An image of another woman, another time, began to form in his mind.

As the light from the house spilled into the evening and touched upon her face, Jefferson drew in a long, steadying breath, for not only was she the most intrinsically beautiful woman that he had ever laid eyes upon, but she was a vision of the very woman who had haunted his nights and fired his blood: Andrea Monroe. Jefferson had all but forgotten the depth of her femininity.

It wasn't that she was gorgeous in the classical sense— quite the opposite. Her features were perhaps a bit too large for her small, clear face. But the combination of round, deep-set sea-green eyes, surrounded by thick, black lashes, her short, straight nose, and the wide, voluptuous curve of her mouth, gave her a look of sensuality coupled with an innocent vulnerability that instantly captivated him. Perhaps it was the sparkle of raindrops in her tangled hair, or maybe the startled look of hesitation in her intelligent green eyes, but whatever the reason, Jefferson Harmon suddenly realized that she was the most strikingly provocative woman that he had ever had the misfortune to meet. Her guarded gaze locked with his, and he saw in her eyes an unmistakable, proud defiance.

Oh, God, Andrea, Jefferson thought inwardly. Why now? Why, just as he was trying to pull his life back together, had she come to complicate things?

The shock of the door opening had startled Andrea, and for a moment she hesitated, awestruck. The man in the doorway was certainly the object of her quest, and yet, confronted with the powerful physical presence of Jefferson while touched by his memory, Andrea faced those nagging doubts that had been working on her ever since she had first read the article about his divorce, over a week ago. The man standing before her was just as foreboding as she remembered. Even dressed casually in faded western jeans and a wool work shirt, he exuded the strength of his personality. He was taller than she recalled, and he carried himself with a proud authority that hinted of arrogance. His face was stern and commanding, but roguishly handsome. Severe hazel eyes, shielded by thick, ebony brows and dark, straight lashes, bore down upon her with inquisitive but uncompromising dominion. And in the depths of those glaring eyes a flash of recognition gleamed.

The mutual silence between them was broken only by the sound of the wild surf pounding relentlessly on the shore, hundreds of feet below them. He looks older and somehow more vulnerable, Andrea thought as she stared past his indifference and delved into the private depths of his soul. He's been scarred.

"Jefferson?" Andrea asked, her voice rough from the cold wind. She attempted to look him squarely in the eye, and hoped she appeared outwardly calm. The mixture of the tempestuous storm, the blackness of oncoming night and the strong virility of the famous man before her had shattered her poise. It's been so long . . . too long, she thought. Deliberately, she refused to be intimidated by the force of Jefferson's physical presence.

"Andrea? What in God's name are you doing here . . . in this storm?" he inquired, his dark gaze dropping from her face to study the rest of her rain-drenched frame. Although fully clothed, Andrea felt suddenly naked, as if the man she was addressing could see to the very core of her being, into her mind and through her soul—just as he had always done.

His dark eyes lifted. "Did you come here looking for me?"

"Yes . . . I . . ."

"Why?" he demanded tersely. "Are you a reporter now, searching for the latest scoop on my life? If so, the interview is over!"

Andrea felt herself inwardly cringe. "I'm not with the press," she stated evenly, and knew in her heart that if she mentioned Bryce and Coral Productions, she would get no further with him. Besides which, now that she had seen him, she wanted to see more. She hadn't exactly lied—she wasn't a reporter.

"But you did come looking for me?" Serious questions shadowed his eyes.

"Yes." She stared deeply into his probing gaze and wondered how she would ever be able to broach the subject of the interview. It seemed almost petty, when she considered all of the love and hate that had bound Jefferson and her together and thrust them fatefully apart.

Jefferson's face softened slightly. "I'm sorry," he murmured quietly. "Please come in. You look like you could use a good, strong drink and a warm fire." A smile lit up his harsh face, and for an instant Andrea remembered the charismatic young governor who had used the flash of his slightly crooked smile or the edge of his razor-sharp wit to lure hesitant voters to his party.

"There's a fire in the den," he remarked, leading the

way through the large, exquisite marble vestibule toward
the rear of the house. Andrea nodded in mute agreement,
remembering the intimate evenings alone with him in just
that den, and knowing the way to its cheery interior
without his direction. She followed him as he led the way,
and smiled uncomfortably to herself at the alluring enigma
he presented. If only she could touch him again, talk to
him the way that she once had. . . .

She snapped her mind back to the present and tried to
focus her thoughts on the house rather than the man. The
old manor was filled with classical, formal antiques, beautiful and yet cold. Jefferson Harmon himself held that
same formal, cold wariness in his eyes, but also exuded a
warm, comfortable country charm that seemed to reach
out and grasp her. She noticed that he was clad in stocking
feet, and yet he carried himself almost loftily as he walked.
The man still intrigued her, and frightened her just a little.
Perhaps she had made a very serious error in judgment in
coming here to meet with him face-to-face. She had
suffered his rejection once already in her short life—could
she face it again?

"Take off your coat," he commanded, "and lay it over
there." He pointed to a worn leather chair near the fire.
"I'll get us a drink, and you can explain just what it is that
made you brave that god-awful weather to come and visit
me after nine, make that ten, years. Somehow I don't
expect that you're here asking for contributions to your
latest crusade for mankind and against the violence of
war."

Andrea smiled in spite of herself, ignoring the bite in his
words. She took the proffered drink and set it on a corner
table. After removing her coat, she warmed her palms
against the coals of the fire and then took a long swallow of
her brandy. "You're right, Jefferson. I'm not here solicit-
ing anything . . . not really."

"Oh?" Once again he flashed her the charming, off-
center smile.

"No. I—I came here because I wanted to see you," Andrea admitted with a sigh, her voice uneven.

He stared for a moment into the amber depths of his drink, and his smile faded into a scowl. "Why now, Andrea? After ten years, why now? Is it because of the divorce?" he asked, his hazel eyes touching hers. "Here, let me help you with that," he continued, and set his brandy on the table near hers.

Andrea had been struggling with the leather thong that had restrained her hair. But her fingers, stiff from the cold, wet weather, fumbled at the rain-swollen knot. Jefferson came up and stood behind her, his strong, sure fingers working against the leather.

"Damn," he swore under his breath, and the warmth of the air that had passed from his lungs brushed Andrea's chilled neck. "When you decide to tie a knot, you really do a job of it, don't you?"

"I didn't realize that it would get so wet, or swell so much. The storm was more severe than I had imagined," Andrea attempted to explain.

"Obviously," was the dry retort. "You still don't look like a lunatic, and if I remember correctly, you're far from it. But only a madwoman would attempt to brave that storm!"

Andrea couldn't disagree with his logic, and she found it difficult to think of anything other than the strong fingers that brushed against her neck as Jefferson worked at the thong. Although he didn't outwardly acknowledge the intimacy of his touch, Andrea could feel her skin warming when his hands seemed to linger against her neck.

"Ah, well, we really don't have much of a choice here," he began, admitting defeat. "This calls for drastic action."

"What do you mean?"

From deep in his pocket he pulled out a silver jackknife, and in one swift stroke, cut the confining cord. Involuntarily Andrea's hands flew to her throat, and she whirled to face the man she had once loved so much.

Her quick reaction and the startled look in her eyes arrested Jefferson. There was something about Andrea that was alluring, captivating, and yet distant and wary. Who had she become during the last ten years, and why was she here?

"I didn't mean to frighten you," he asserted as he snapped the knife closed and put it back in his jean pocket. He returned the brandy snifter to her slightly trembling hands.

"You didn't."

Doubtful, he cocked a black eyebrow. He took a long swallow of his drink, and Andrea watched the fluid movement of his throat as he swallowed the smooth liquor.

Jefferson stared at Andrea in the deepening silence. Even the wind from the storm seemed to have become a distant, vague memory as his eyes took in all of her. "Well," he finally said, breaking the heady, thick silence, "I could start out the conversation with something like, 'Long time, no see,' or 'Gee, Andrea, what have you been up to for the last ten years?' or even something as inane as 'I certainly didn't expect to run into you tonight,' but I've never been one for small talk, and I realize that you didn't come here to apologize . . . or just to check on my health. . . ." His smile was affable, but there was an underlying determination to his words. "What is it that brings you here?"

"I told you that I wanted to see you again."

"All right, I'll buy that, but why tonight, in this storm?"

"There is a reason," Andrea admitted, unable to look into his eyes. "I told you that I wasn't a reporter, and I'm not. But I do work for an independent production company, Coral Productions, and, to make a long story short, we've run into a little financial difficulty—"

"And you're looking for additional capital?" he guessed.

"No."

Again silence. All of his attention was directed at her. He regarded her pensively over the rim of his glass, and the warmth of his gaze steadied her.

"Coral Productions is promoting a new show for cable television. It's about faces in the news . . . in-depth interviews with people of celebrity status, like you. Coral Productions would like you to be the lead interview."

Andrea's declaration stung the air, and the warmth in Jefferson's eyes cooled as his face hardened. "Pardon me?" he whispered.

Andrea took in a deep, sharp breath. "I said that the company wants you to be the first feature story in our series."

He stepped farther away from her, as if to regard her entire body with his condemning gaze. Jefferson's jaw clenched, and Andrea could tell that every muscle in his body had tightened. His legs, dark silhouettes against the scarlet embers of the fire, tensed, and his fingers clutched the empty brandy snifter in a death grip. "That's why you're here?" he accused.

"That, and the fact that I wanted to see you again."

He snorted derisively. "You expect me to believe that you purposely stayed away from me for ten years, and just coincidentally you want me to go public with my life. . . . You can't be serious, Andrea. I thought you knew me better than that! What do you take me for, a fool?"

"Oh, no . . . you don't understand."

"I think I do. Let me get this straight. Isn't Coral Productions responsible for that piece of trash on Saturday nights—*Pride's Passion?*"

"*Power,*" Andrea corrected. "*Pride's Power.*"

"No wonder you're in trouble."

Andrea attempted to protest, but his sharp gaze cut her off. "It doesn't matter; whatever the reason, Coral is in trouble, and wants to do an interview show. And I assume

that your boss, Bryce Cawthorne, right?"—Andrea nodded in confirmation—"knows about our past relationship
and hoped that you could persuade me to talk to him."

"He doesn't know anything about us!" Andrea shot
back at Jefferson.

"Sure he doesn't. He just happened to send you up here
to find me, and he doesn't know that we knew each
other . . . intimately? You expect me to believe that?
Come on, Andrea, give me a little credit."

"Bryce thinks it's a coincidence that I came to Victoria."

"Was it?" Jefferson asked, his hazel eyes pinioning hers.

"I don't know," she admitted honestly. "I knew about
the show before I came up here, but I tried to dissuade
Bryce from considering you."

"I'll just bet you did," he mocked.

Andrea stiffened, and her green eyes darkened in rage.
"It's not important whether you believe me or not. That's
the way it was. You have to know that I don't want this
interview any more than you do! I don't want all of the
scandal about you and me and Mart dug up again! It's over
now! Dead and gone!"

Andrea could sense Jefferson appraising her, mentally
calculating everything about her. "Okay, Andrea, you've
got my undivided attention, so why don't you explain
what, exactly, brought you here, and why you expect me
to believe that you're not in cahoots with Cawthorne." His
voice was brittle, and Andrea could feel the anger simmering beneath his words.

"I came to Victoria, to my parents' town house, for a
vacation, to get away from the pressures at work and just
to think. I didn't expect for Bryce to call me with orders to
contact you, but he couldn't get hold of you. You're not
listed in the book, you know. Anyway, he called me, and I
told him I'd talk to you."

"That's it?" he demanded.

"All of it."

"All right, let's just say that I believe you," he agreed affably, and Andrea was reminded of his infamous courtroom charm. "Let's assume that you don't think that Bryce knows of our past friendship," he suggested, caution underlying his smile.

"You don't have to assume anything. It's the truth!"

"You're sure?"

"He couldn't." Why didn't she sound convincing?

"Why not? The man can read, can't he? Your name and mine were linked very closely in the press, weren't they?"

"But that was ten years ago," she protested feebly, suddenly realizing that he knew something that she didn't.

"And Bryce Cawthorne has the memory of an elephant." Jefferson saw the first traces of doubt cross Andrea's face.

"What are you saying?" she demanded.

"I'm stating that your boss lied to you, pure and simple. He called me yesterday with his ridiculous idea, and I hung up on him."

"But he told me that he couldn't get hold of you."

"Did he?" Jefferson laughed mirthlessly. "He's more conniving than I suspected."

"But how . . ."

"I don't know. Lara probably gave him the number. That sounds like something she would do." A grim smile twisted his lips into a thin, uncompromising line.

Embarrassment and confusion flooded over Andrea, and she could feel the stain of color on her face. Tears of frustration burned at the back of her eyes, but she refused to cry. If Bryce had lied to her, he hadn't much cared for her feelings, and if Jefferson was lying to her now, well, it didn't much matter. "Look, I'm sorry if I've inconvenienced you at all, Jefferson. Here's my card . . . Bryce can be reached at the number on the left, if you reconsider." Her voice began to waver, but she continued bravely on. "I'm sorry about everything," she whispered, and her throaty voice trembled with emotion.

"Don't be."

"I . . . look, it was probably a mistake for me to come here in the first place," she admitted.

"I don't think so," Jefferson argued, condemning himself mentally. What was he doing, what was he hoping for? Why did he feel so attracted to Andrea, just as he had in the past. Had he forgotten all of her lies, the disillusionment he had suffered at her hand? Then why, in God's name, did he feel an urge to comfort her, to touch her, to make love to her until dawn?

From her position sitting on the couch, Andrea pulled her eyes upward to meet the unwavering gaze of the man standing determinedly before her. She wanted to apologize and hurry out of the room to hide in the night. But something in his eyes made her linger. Was it tenderness or wariness, passion or loathing? Andrea was too tired to guess. She stood up and reached for her coat.

The warm, gentle touch of his hands on her shoulders surprised her. "Don't go," he suggested huskily.

"I have to go."

"You can't think that you can find a boat to take you back in this storm."

"No, there's someone waiting for me." She started to turn, suddenly feeling the warm, delicious pressure of his fingers near her throat.

"Who?" he challenged, his voice growing rough.

"A sailor, I don't know his name. He said he would wait an hour," she glanced at the bold, Roman numerals on the clock face over the fireplace mantel. "I've really got to go," she whispered breathlessly, but remained standing in the inviting den, allowing Jefferson's warm fingers to caress the light fabric of her sweater and promise higher, more intense sensual delights.

"Stay," he persuaded, his dark eyes deepening with passion.

"I can't," she persisted. "Please, don't touch me. I can't think when you touch me. I've never been able to."

"Don't think," he advised, while his thumbs touched the silken skin of her throat. "Just listen to the wind."

Andrea closed her eyes and concentrated on the whistle of the northern gale. She felt as if her entire body were beginning to melt in the heat of his hot, persuasive touch, and when his lips descended to find hers, she let herself fall into his arms and returned the passion of his kiss with an intensity that had lied dormant for ten years. Her heart fluttered wildly in her chest, and a warm, moist heat coiled within her body. She found herself willingly trapped in the velvet touch of his embrace.

His hands, large, strong and sensitive, kneaded warm circles of moist desire against the small of her back, and she felt her skin quake when his fingers tugged at the hem of her blouse and touched her lightly, tentatively, flesh to flesh. The passion that was seducing her took her swirling backward in time, and she knew that if she didn't stop him soon, she would be lost to him forever.

"This is crazy," she sighed into his open mouth.

"I know."

She felt her knees collapsing, and his weight, gentle but sure, forced her onto the soft mat of carpet before the fire.

"Oh, Andrea," he moaned, "it's been so long . . . so long." His lips, warm and inviting, brushed over her neck, and his hands, eager with long-denied passion, wound themselves in the thick, wet strands of her blue-black hair.

She let her arms move upward to encircle his neck. It all felt so right: the hungry possession of his body over hers, the radiant heat from the dying fire, an inner glow inspired by the brandy and the stormy wind whistling far in the distance.

His lips whispered promises as they swept over her face and touched her cheeks, her eyes, her throat. And his tongue, with a claiming passion long hidden, traced the outline of her lips, the length of her jaw, the lobe of her ear. Without thought she felt her body arch up to meet his, to invite him boldly closer.

With a moan of surrender Jefferson let his hands slide upward over the soft, silken texture of her abdomen to slowly, erotically, caress a breast. Instantly Andrea felt her nipple stiffen and her breasts strain against the lacy bra that held them confined. "Let me love you," he whispered into her hair.

"Please . . . please . . ." she begged, gasping for breath. "Oh, Jefferson—I need you."

Her plea was as desperate as the feeling of renewed, torchlike passion that was blinding him. He knew he should stop and control himself. He knew all too well his vulnerability where Andrea was concerned, and yet he couldn't resist what he had dreamed of, longed for, and yet denied himself because of her lies . . . all of her lies. Blood thundered in his temples as he pulled the sweater off her body. For a moment he hesitated, studying her perfect body in the shadowed fireglow. If it was possible, she was more beautiful than he had remembered. And as he gazed into her eyes, heavy with awakened passion, he felt a damnable urge to make love to her endlessly. But he stopped himself.

Rational thought took command of his body. Why had she come here tonight? What did she want of him? Was she really as willing as she seemed . . . or was she using her body as a means of getting him to do what she wanted—be it the interview or anything else. Jefferson knew only too well what he could be talked into doing just for the sake of Andrea Monroe.

His desire ripped savagely through his body, but the fact that Andrea had lied to him in the past, and had waited ten long years to resurface, gave him pause. Don't do it again, his reason told him. Don't let her use you.

Andrea's eyes watched Jefferson's face. As surely as the tide went out to sea, he willed his passion to subside. She could read it in the straight, hard angle of his jaw, the glint of determination in his eyes. Slowly he rolled away from her to lie on his back and stare at the ceiling.

"You and I have a lot to talk about," he said with a sigh. "And I think it's time that we ironed out some of the problems of the past."

"Do you think it's possible?" she asked, suddenly feeling empty.

"I don't know," he admitted, pinching his lip between his teeth and drawing his brows together. "I just don't know."

Chapter 3

"I'VE GOT TO GO," ANDREA STATED AFTER A FEW HEAVY moments of silence. She had pulled her sweater back over her head and disappointedly noted that Jefferson hadn't attempted to stop her from getting dressed. Furtively she looked at him, seeing his long, lean torso and the taut muscles that strained rigidly in the shadowed fireglow. He stared vacantly up at the cross timbers of the ceiling, lost in thoughts of the past.

"You're not going anywhere," he advised.

"I have to."

"No, you don't. You may have been foolish enough to brave that storm once, but I'm not letting you attempt it again. If something should happen to you, I don't want it on my conscience."

"You don't have to worry about that."

"Look, Andrea." Jefferson's voice was cold and emphatic. "I wasn't the one who came knocking on doors in the middle of a raging tempest." He propped himself up on one elbow and stared down at her, his eyes narrowing as he surveyed her. "Now that you're here, I think we should talk. It's long overdue!"

"But I told that sailor I would be back within the hour."

Jefferson's eyes slid to the clock face. "You've already missed that appointment by about twenty minutes."

Andrea curled her legs beneath her as if to rise. "Really,

I have to go. I gave you Bryce's card, and I would appreciate it if you would call him—as a favor to me."

Jefferson's hand reached out and manacled her wrist. "I don't see that I owe you any favors to begin with, and I think you're being foolish. Let the seaman go. Stay with me."

"I . . . I don't know," Andrea murmured, and bit at her lower lip. All of her senses begged her to stay, to listen to him, but something in her conscience told her that staying with Jefferson would only make it more difficult to leave later.

"We could use some time together," he coaxed, and his hand over her wrist loosened enough to let his thumb slide seductively up and down her forearm. "Admit it, Andrea. You really would like to stay with me."

"Of course I would, Jefferson. I'm not foolish enough to try and hide that fact. But I don't know if it would accomplish anything. I was hoping that, at the very least, we could become good friends again."

"And at the very most?" he asked, his hazel eyes twinkling.

She pulled her eyes away from his gaze and stared into the fire. "I don't know," she admitted in a rough voice.

"Let's find out," he coaxed. "Stay."

"I can't!" she admitted with a finality that even he understood. His thumb abruptly stopped its intimate caress of her arm and pulled away.

"Have it your way," Jefferson agreed, icily. Still, his dark eyes challenged her decision. She felt at once angry and helpless. He knew she didn't want to go, but he was willing to let her make her own choice.

He watched her as she silently slid into her wet raincoat, and he mentally chastised himself for the burning longing that still lingered in his mind. It was impossible not to mistrust her. Although she had seemed vulnerable, perceptive and incredibly drawn to him, he had to remember that she had left him without so much as a look over her shoulder after all the publicity of their affair had become front-page news. And that brother of hers, Martin, with his left-wing ideals and underhanded scruples, had used both Jefferson and Andrea to his own best advantage; to champion a cause that had nothing to do with them. Jefferson's jaw squared at the thought, and his eyes darkened in quiet rage.

Was it possible that Andrea would attempt to use him again? Would she be so bold? It seemed incredible that after ten years of silence she would come to him again, unless she wanted something in return. Even after ten lost years, she didn't seem to be the kind of woman who would give herself so easily to a man, and yet she had yielded to him with no protest. Did she actually think that he would believe that she might still care for him? When he had halted the passion of their lovemaking only moments before, he had seen the unmasked look of disappointment surface in her intent green gaze. And her face, caught in relief against the onyx color of her hair, was as quietly reproachful as he had remembered. Damn her for her beauty, and those haunting eyes that seemed to pierce right to his soul.

Andrea gave an embarrassed pull on her raincoat and cinched the belt tightly over her slim waist. She felt the dark, inquisitive probe of Jefferson's eyes on her body, but she avoided his gaze. She wondered fleetingly how she could have let things get so one-sided and out of hand. It was true that she felt the same attraction for and fascination with Jefferson that she had as a college girl, but she had matured since then and, hopefully, learned from her mistakes. Then why had she felt a welling sense of disappointment when he had forcefully pulled away from her?

Without a word Jefferson led her out of the stone manor and escorted her down the path toward the steps. In the time that had passed, evening had set in, and it was difficult for Andrea to find her way. Twice she stumbled on an exposed tree root, and only Jefferson's strong, aloof touch kept her on her feet. The wind raced over the ridge of the island, blowing cold, salty spray and minute particles of sand against Andrea's face. Her hair, dark as the stormy night, streamed out behind her in windswept tangles.

The stairs had become treacherous in the darkness, and Andrea picked her way carefully down the steep steps, grateful for the wooden railing that gave her a modicum of balance as she descended. At last she fumbled on the lowest step and felt the soft, wet sand of the beach crunch beneath her boots. In the darkness Andrea could barely make out the small boat that was tied securely to the dock. Shuddering from the cold, she hurried to the craft.

Jefferson was at her side, and although he hadn't uttered a word since they had left the den, Andrea could feel his simmering anger and imagine the square outline of his determined jaw.

Although Andrea was walking within inches of him, Jefferson had to shout to be heard over the crashing of the sea. "You really expect to make it back to Victoria in this?" he shouted incredulously. "You'll never make it!"

"I've got no other choice," she shouted back.

"Sure you do. Wait until the storm dies down!" She began to shake her head, and Jefferson caught hold of her forearms, gripping them tightly and shaking her. "For God's sake, Andrea, just this once use your head. Stay with me—at least until it passes."

Andrea hesitated, and at that moment a large wave crashed against the dock, sending white spray up in the air and down on Andrea. The icy, frigid water drenched her in its wet, cold plume.

"That does it! You're not going!" Jefferson swore emphatically. "I was going to let you have your bullheaded way again, but not now. It's just not safe!" Andrea began to protest, but Jefferson continued. "I'll tell the skipper, you wait here. I'll only be a minute."

Before Andrea could argue, Jefferson stepped onto the boat and slipped into the cabin. He was back in a matter of seconds, and Andrea could see the look of disgust that crossed his features. "Come on, let's get out of here," he advised, taking her arm and nearly pulling her down the weathered wooden planks of the dock. "Your friend was in no condition to go anywhere."

It took nearly twice as long to climb up the staircase as it had to climb down. Andrea felt chilled to the bone from the Arctic winds that pressed cold fingers through her clothing and propelled her upward. By the time that she got back to the house, she was exhausted and nearly frozen.

"You know, Andrea," Jefferson said, after slamming the broad wooden door of the house, "I gave you credit for more brains than this."

"What do you mean?" she shot back at him.

"I mean, not only do you tempt fate by challenging the worst storm of the year, but you do it in one of the poorest excuses I've ever seen for a boat. To top matters off, you hire a drunk!"

"The choice was restricted."

"To a drunken madman?"

"Yes!"

"And you couldn't wait for the weather to clear?" he accused, tossing his wet poncho on a hook near the door.

"I . . ." She sighed, her voice catching. The long day and the strain of seeing him again were taking hold of her. "I was afraid."

"Of what? Certainly not the storm—or that questionable excuse for a skipper!"

She drew a long breath into her lungs to steady herself. "That wasn't what I was concerned about."

"What then?" he thundered, grabbing her elbow and leading her back toward the den. She ignored his question, aware only of the strong persuasion of his touch at her elbow. Through the light fabric of her raincoat and the thin sweater, she imagined his fingers against her skin.

Once back in the warm den, with it's cherrywood walls, deep, plush burgundy carpet and comfortable leather furniture, Jefferson strode over to a closet near the bar and pulled out a large, rust-colored terry-cloth robe.

"Change into this," he commanded, tossing the robe at her. "You can put your clothes over the fireplace screen for now. We'll wash and dry them later." His eyes skimmed over her body in a quick head-to-heels appraisal. "I'll try to find you some slippers that fit while I'm changing into dry clothes." He strode to the door of the den and stopped short, as if a sudden thought had occurred to him. "There's a telephone on the desk, in case you need to inform someone of your whereabouts." His hazel eyes regarded her intently. "I mean, in case someone is waiting for you." There were questions in his gaze, but he didn't bother with them. "And if you need another drink, you know where the bar is." His face softened slightly. "Fix me one, too: bourbon."

"I remember," she murmured with a hesitant smile as Jefferson's footsteps retreated in the long, dark hallway of the ancient, Tudor home.

Andrea tugged off her wet clothes and hung them carefully over the screen. She pulled on the long, warm, comfortable robe and cinched the belt around it tightly. The sleeves were much too long, and she rolled them upward in order to free her hands.

Taking Jefferson's advice, she padded barefoot to the bar and poured them each a strong, neat bourbon. Her eyes traveled over the leather-bound editions on a nearby bookshelf, and her fingers encountered a light covering of dust on the books—proof of their disuse. A pity, she thought to herself. So grand a home used as a hermit's refuge. So large a library idly gathering dust. So alluring a man wrapped within himself. If only things had turned out differently for them, perhaps Jefferson would be as she remembered; softer and warmer somehow, free of the mistrust that she could sense in his quiet gaze. What had happened to him, to her? How had something so wonderful gotten so tangled in bitterness?

Andrea felt the winter's chill climb up her legs, and she hurried back to the chair near the glowing fire. She tossed another moss-laden log into the flames and heard the hiss and pop of the fire as it reignited against the new wood. She settled into the worn ox-blood leather of the antique chair. Carefully she tucked her feet beneath her and buried them in the soft folds of Jefferson's robe. A faint scent of his aftershave tingled in her nostrils, and bold, vivid memories began to overtake her. Absently she swirled the amber-colored liquid in her glass and gazed into its clear depths, trying to piece together the memories that assaulted her . . .

It had been a long, hot spring; a spring rare even for Southern California, and Andrea had found herself hoping to go home to her parents' summer town house in cool, well-groomed Victoria as soon as the term was over. She was restless, as were many of the local students, not only from the incredible heat, but also with the bitterness and unease of a war that no one seemed to want, and somehow was impossible to end. Her older brother, Martin, was graduating soon, and he would be eligible for the draft when his student deferment had run out.

It was nearly June when Andrea and a few friends, Martin included, had gone to the political rally. Several politicians who had succeeded in the primary had come to speak with the students in the open arena of the outdoor amphitheater. It wasn't intended that the rally become a heated debate, but the two candidates had immediately squared off and verbally attacked each other.

That was the first time that Andrea had seen Jefferson—from a distance, as one of the spectators in a crowd of nearly two thousand. He was a young lawyer at the time and was considered a dark horse candidate for the California State Senate—the youngest man ever to have won his party's nomination in the primary. The moment Andrea had seen him, she had sensed in him a difference from the other, blander politicians. She knew of him only what she had read—his reputation as a brilliant corporate lawyer preceded him. It seemed that he had just the right combination of charm, looks, savvy and ruthlessness to propel him quickly up the ladder of success. Although only twenty-six years old at the time, Jefferson Harmon had become a household word in California. The young lawyer with the tanned, masculine face, graced with a comfortable flash of a smile and thick, neat hair, had wooed the public, especially the young, female voters, over to his camp. Even from a distance Andrea had felt his magnetism. When he smiled at the crowd, she felt that it was a message sent to her alone.

When the topic of the debate began to encompass the Vietnam war, a few hecklers in the crowd began to shout obscenities at the raised podium. The shouts calling for an end to the war interfered with the debate. Martin, himself a Conscientious Objector, yelled pointedly at the politicians, urging them to stop the war.

Jefferson's principal opponent, a rotund, white-haired gentleman, ignored the remarks thrust in his direction. He was the incumbent, and as such, he was accustomed to the antics and catcalls of a young crowd of restless college students. His feathers remained unruffled as he attempted to swing the argument away from the topic of the war and on to safer, more stable ground.

Jefferson, however, was distracted by the audience, and more than once his keen, hazel eyes surveyed the crowd to sort out the leaders. Often, while searching for Martin, who was shouting at the top of his lungs, Jefferson's gaze found Andrea's—or so she imagined.

The rally continued in the relentless sun, and the

audience quieted. Jefferson's concentration fell neatly back in place, and he managed to come out a victor in the debate, at least in Andrea's estimation. Sometime during the heated discussion he loosened his tie, tossed off his jacket and rolled up his sleeves, never once missing a point in the debate. Andrea was mesmerized as she watched him talking, arguing, blasting shrewdly at his opponent, seemingly unaware of the sweat that trickled down the length of his throat, past his open collar. Andrea wondered just how far the beads of sweat traveled, and found herself blushing at the thought.

When the debate ended, Andrea felt disappointment spread through her as she watched Jefferson Harmon take a long drink from a cup near the podium, sling his coat over his shoulder, and hurry down the steps to the back of the amphitheater.

"Come on, Andie," Martin was saying to her. "Let's go see if we can talk to those guys personally."

"What guys . . . the politicians?" she gasped as her heart fluttered.

"Sure, why not? They're the ones pulling all of the strings in the country. Let's just see if they'll talk to us."

"Right on!" a friend of Martin's agreed. "They owe it to us. Those are the guys that are sending all of us to the front lines."

"But I don't think that state senators have much influence about the war," Andrea objected. "You should be talking to someone in Washington."

"You've got to start somewhere," Martin replied. "Let's just go see what these guys have to say for themselves."

Martin and a few of his friends headed out in search of the politicians, and Andrea followed. It wasn't so much that she approved of what Martin's friends were doing, but she was intrigued, and hoped to catch a closer glimpse of Jefferson Harmon.

Although the crowd hurried toward the politicians, a

long, black limousine carrying the incumbent was already heading out of the winding road of the campus.

"Too bad," Martin said roughly under his breath. "I really wanted to corner that guy."

"We're still in luck," Martin's friend Dave had rejoined. "That Harmon guy is still here . . . over there!" Dave pointed a long finger at Jefferson. "Wouldn't you know it, he's talking to the ROTCs."

Somehow Andrea felt a compelling need to defend the young political newcomer with the intense hazel eyes. "There's nothing wrong with that, Dave," she shot out unexpectedly. "Some people want to become officers in the military and the Reserve Officer Training Corps, and others, unlike you, need the money to help them get through college. Not everyone is born with a silver spoon in his mouth!"

"How would you know about that?" Dave goaded, pulling on the strands of his thin beard. "You've never had to work a day in your life!" His dark, condemning gaze moved from Andrea back to Martin. "You'd better watch out, my friend," he cautioned Martin, "it looks like little sister is becoming a warmonger!"

"Cut it out," Martin shouted, ignoring the simmering argument between his sister and his friend. "Let's go see what Harmon has to say."

Jefferson was just moving away from the crowd of would-be young officers and heading toward his car. He was still holding his jacket over his shoulder, and in the other hand he held a bottle of cola.

"Hey, Harmon," Martin said, accosting Jefferson, and Andrea visibly cringed. "Why don't you cut out all the double-talk and let us know how you really feel about the war."

Jefferson smiled affably and tossed his empty bottle into a nearby trash can. "Personally, I don't like war, *any* war," he stated while casually throwing his jacket into the back seat of his old BMW. His broad shoulders strained against the cotton of his light blue Oxford shirt, and a smear of sweat pasted the fabric against his back.

"And so what do you propose to do about it?" Martin asked. "That is . . . if you're elected."

"Whatever I can," Jefferson admitted. "But I don't think I'll have a helluva lot of influence. The California State Senate is a far cry from Congress."

"Cop-out!" Dave muttered, and Jefferson's hazel eyes snapped. He began to open the door to his car, and his eyes rested on Andrea's embarrassed face for just a moment. He seemed to hesitate, but then, as if thinking better of a betraying thought, he settled comfortably behind the wheel.

"What about your old man, Harmon?" Martin persisted. "Wasn't he an officer in the army?"

"A major," was the clipped reply. Jefferson's eyes darkened.

"So you grew up living off the backs of enlisted men—draftees. From what I understand, your old man made quite a fortune in his time! How does it feel to know that he made the bucks, while other men died?" Martin taunted, leaning against the door of the clean black automobile and sticking his face nearly inside the open window.

"Cut it out, Martin," Andrea whispered loudly as she tugged on her brother's arm and attempted to pull him away from the window. Once again Jefferson's penetrating gaze encompassed her.

"Listen to your girl friend," Jefferson advised Martin as he started the car and his charming grin faded. "You don't know what you're talking about."

With those final words Jefferson jerked on the steering wheel and maneuvered the car out of the parking lot, past the blooming cherry trees, in the direction of the intricate mass of freeways of Southern California.

"Bastard!" Martin shouted at the car, and kicked at the

dusty ground in his frustration. "Damn bastard politician! He's supposed to be different, but they're all the same!"

Not so, Andrea puzzled to herself, as she shielded her eyes against the glare of the sun and watched the sporty black car drive past the campus gates.

It was later that summer when Andrea chanced to meet Jefferson again. The incident on campus had lingered in her memory, and she couldn't quite seem to forget Jefferson Harmon and his winning, intimate smile. And although Martin seemed to hold a personal grudge against the man, Andrea attributed it to the fact that Martin had a chip on his shoulder when it came to politics. Martin blamed all the politicians for the Vietnam war. He had applied for another student deferment, hoping to enter graduate school and avoid the draft. But he had been refused, and unless he reported to the draft board within the next two weeks, he would be considered guilty of draft evasion. Even his hastily acknowledged status of Conscientious Objector to the war fell on deaf ears, as far as the military was concerned. And although his parents had the town house in Victoria, on Canadian soil, Andrea's father was adamant that his son do his national duty and join the armed forces. Martin was, after all, an American citizen, as were his younger sisters, Andrea and Gayla.

Andrea was torn. She didn't much care for Martin's political leanings, and yet she understood his concern and resentment. She didn't think of him as a coward, as did her father, but thought of him as what he was: a young man anxious about his future and his country's commitment to a foreign war that seemed fruitless and painful. Besides which, at the time, Andrea was barely twenty and somewhat naive.

Martin had been gone for several days on the pretense of meeting with the draft board. It was early September, and Andrea's mother and father had already moved back to California to enroll Gayla in her last year of high school.

Andrea had stayed in Victoria, feeling restless. University studies didn't start for another three weeks, and she preferred swimming in the calm waters of Deer Lake during the Indian summer days on Vancouver Island to the heat and mayhem of the outskirts of L.A.

It was while browsing in the Granville Island Public Market, looking over the vast array of fresh fish, vegetables, shellfish, fruits and meats, that Andrea noticed she was being watched. At first she didn't see anyone staring at her and tried to shake off the feeling, but it persisted.

The open-air market was bustling with activity: shopkeepers in white aprons displaying their wares, curiosity seekers and tourists browsing over the interesting produce and exotic samples from the ocean. And everywhere was the smell of the salt sea from English Bay.

Andrea carried a small basket over her arm and was gathering a few groceries to sustain her until she had to leave Vancouver Island later in the month. Already she had picked up a loaf of fresh-baked sourdough bread and a brick of cheese. She was studying a display of razor clams when the distinct feeling that she was being watched again climbed up her spine. Instinctively she raised her eyes. They clashed with hazel eyes she had seen only once before, but immediately she recognized the face of Jefferson Harmon.

He was studying her as if attempting to place her face in some distant cog of his memory. She found the power of his gaze mesmerizing, spellbinding. He was dressed casually in faded, low-hanging jeans that showed signs of age and a simple cotton pullover that hid none of the tense muscles of his chest. Yet dressed in comfortable, worn clothes, a pleasant smile on his face, he still retained the same commanding presence that he had so forcefully demonstrated while speaking to the college spectators in California. Andrea guessed he stood no taller than six feet, but somehow he seemed to tower over and stand out from the crowd of shoppers in the busy fish market.

Andrea could hear the quiet noises of the city, but they seemed to be droning in the distance. The occasional honk of an automobile horn, the busy chatter of merchants displaying their wares, the familiar sound of a large ferryboat plowing slowly through the salty sea—all the sounds that normally commanded her attention were subdued when Jefferson spoke to her. She felt as if she were alone with this commanding man who stared so intimately into her widened eyes.

"You're Andrea Monroe," he surmised, to Andrea's amazement as he gave her a quick head-to-heels appraisal. She was surprised, but tried to stifle the urge to shrink under his studying gaze. Instead, she angled her face upward to meet his arrogant gaze.

"That's right." Though she tried vainly to hide the fact, she felt awkward and incredibly young in the presence of such a famous man. Although he could only be a few years older than she, he seemed light-years ahead of her in maturity. She managed a feeble imitation of his warm, knowing smile.

His hazel eyes darkened. "You were with your brother last May in the amphitheater at U.C.L.A."

Once again Andrea was surprised, and it must have registered in her large, green eyes, because when Jefferson noticed her reaction, the severity of his gaze appeared to soften. How did he know of her and Martin? *Why* would he know them?

"How do you know who I am?" she asked, lines of concentration etched across her smooth forehead.

"Your brother isn't one to just lie back and take things sitting down. He makes a lot of noise. Especially about his feelings on Vietnam. It doesn't go unnoticed," Jefferson observed with a dismissive shrug of his shoulders.

"What do you mean?" Andrea asked, a trickle of fear running in her blood. Was Martin in some sort of trouble because of his left-wing ideals? "Is someone spying on Martin?" she asked indignantly.

Jefferson's smile broadened. "You've been seeing too many movies about secret agents. Nothing as sinister as spying against your brother is going on . . . at least not that I know of." He picked up two tart, red apples from a stand, paid for them, handed one to Andrea, and polished the other against his jeans.

"Then how do you know who he is?" Andrea persisted.

"Aside from the fact that he's written nearly a dozen letters to me—not exactly fan mail, mind you—and the fact that he's made the local news on campus, I made it my business to find out about him."

"You were spying!"

"You've got an overactive imagination." A twinkle of amusement lighted his eyes.

"Then what would you call it?"

"Curiosity," he said with a lift of his broad shoulders.

"Why?" she demanded, not sure what to believe. He seemed to be toying with her.

"Come on," he directed, with an affable, off-center grin, "and I'll tell you all about it. Then you can fill me in; tell me what a beautiful girl like you is doing up here."

"Don't you know why I'm here? If you've been checking up on Martin, certainly you must know about me also," she tossed out with a touch of sarcasm. What was it about Harmon that tempted her so? she mentally asked herself. No matter how hard she tried to deny it, she was attracted to him. Was it his looks? His infamous courtroom charm? His teasing hazel eyes? His fame? *What?* No matter the cause, Andrea realized that she was more strongly bewitched by the roguish man standing before her than she had been by any man before. She sensed that he was compassionate and warm, but yet she felt that getting to know him might somehow become dangerous. It galled her to think that Jefferson Harmon, just because he was a political contender, had the *nerve* . . . the *influence* . . . the *power* to check up on Martin. Perhaps Martin was right all along. Perhaps Jefferson Harmon was just another scheming politician.

"Your folks live up here in the summer, don't they?" he prodded, touching her bent elbow, and guiding her through the tight, noisy throng of shoppers.

"You've been doing your homework," she replied frostily.

A smile, oozing with country-boy charm, illuminated his face, just as he intended it to. Once out of the confining marketplace, and back in the bright, near-blinding sunshine, Jefferson bit into his apple and watched her as he swallowed. A warm breeze, flavored with the tang of the ocean, blew across English Bay. It pushed Andrea's long, wavy black hair away from her face and pressed the lightweight cotton of her pastel halter dress against her bare legs.

"So, it seems that you know why I'm here," Andrea pointed out, shielding her eyes with her hands to ward off the glare from the sunlight reflecting on the water. "What about you? What is it that brings California's favorite son up to the northern beaches of Victoria?"

"Vacation," was the simple reply. His eyes moved from her innocent face to skim the clear, blue water.

"From politics?" she asked, pressing to find out more about him.

"And everything else."

"But I thought that you, along with the rest of the contenders, would be campaigning hard and heavy. The election is in early November. That doesn't give you much time."

Jefferson nodded vacantly, as if his mind was on something other than the conversation. "Everyone, including a politician, needs some time to himself—to relax."

"So you decided to find the quiet life in Vancouver?" she inquired dubiously. One black, sculptured eyebrow raised to show her disbelief.

Jefferson pulled pensively on his lower lip, and his thick, near-black hair ruffled in the breeze from the sea. "Not exactly. My family owns an island up here, complete with a large house. I came up to spend a quiet weekend."

"Alone?" she asked, feeling her breath become tightly constricted in her throat.

"Does that surprise you?"

"No . . . I suppose not, but I do think it's strange that a person who came to the northern Pacific seeking solitude would come down here to this madhouse at the market."

"One has to eat," he pointed out. His smile was as gentle as the mild summer's day, and when he looked down upon Andrea with his commanding dark green eyes, she felt for a moment as if she might melt into the liquid warmth of his gaze.

Her voice faltered, but boldly, she continued. "What I do find surprising, almost incredibly so, is that up here, in all of these people," she waved theatrically to include the milling crowd of the market, "you bump into me. It seems highly unlikely."

"And suspicious?"

"I didn't say that."

"But you thought it," he perceived, noticing that her lips seemed to be trembling slightly. He tossed his apple core into a nearby trash can, and seemed to weigh his next words. "There's really nothing strange about it at all. I found you today because I wanted to. I don't leave a helluva lot to chance, and I wanted to meet you. I followed you here."

"What? From the town house? Why?" Andrea was incredulous.

"I wanted to see you alone, and I wasn't in the mood to make small talk with your family, especially that brother of yours. Just as I got to the town house, you were leaving. So I followed you to the market."

"But *why* did you want to see me? I don't even know you!"

"That's the mystery, isn't it? I can't even tell you for certain. Maybe it's because I find it hard to believe that your brother, Martin, could have such a beautiful and bewitching sister. And because, when I first saw you on the campus, I did you a disservice by thinking that you were just one more face in a crowd of angry young students bent on heckling me. I made a mistake, and I'd like to apologize by offering to take you to dinner."

"You don't have to apologize. It was an easy mistake," Andrea managed to say feebly. "But, thanks anyway." Andrea heard the polite words passing her lips, and crazy thoughts that she would like to take them back crossed her mind. In her heart she wanted nothing more than to spend some time alone with Jefferson Harmon. It was an insane idea, and she was intelligent enough to realize it.

"You're going to pass up a dinner and a sunset horseback ride on Harmon Island?" he asked, his dark eyebrows rising. Andrea sensed that Jefferson Harmon was not often discouraged.

"I . . . I think it would be best." Still, she hesitated, and he sensed it.

"Do you?" His voice was soft, seductive.

"Look, Mr. Harmon—"

"Jefferson," he persuaded, touching her naked arm with his sensitive fingertips. Andrea felt a ripple of heated blood climb up her arm to beat erratically at the base of her throat. Jefferson's eyes lowered as he watched her pulse, and a deep, scarlet flush spread up her neck and cheeks.

"Jefferson," she managed, his name catching in her throat.

"Do you have other plans?"

"No."

"Then you must be afraid of me," he challenged.

"No, but . . ."

"But what?"

"I don't even know you!" she blurted out.

"And you never will, unless you make the effort. What do you say?"

"All right," she agreed breathlessly, wondering if she was thinking at all. It wasn't like her to be so bold. After all, what did she know of the man?

The quick drive to the red brick town house, with its elegant two stories and imposing, formal facade, was a blur in Andrea's mind. And the fast motor launch to the private island seemed to take no time at all. She had the uneasy feeling that she was making the worst mistake of her life, and yet she also thought that perhaps she was taking the most wonderful chance that opportunity had ever presented to her. There was something magical and spellbinding, tantalizing perhaps, in the feeling of adventure and romance that surrounded her. The ride over the clear blue water in the speeding motorboat was exhilarating, and in those moments while they crossed the shimmering stretch of water toward the island, Andrea felt as if she had known Jefferson all of her life.

Chapter 4

IT HAD TAKEN ANDREA SOME TIME TO FEEL COMFORTABLE IN the large stone house that commanded the island. Although her family had never been poor, she was unprepared and unaccustomed to the gracious display of wealth and power that dominated the mansion Jefferson called a summer retreat. She found it impossible not to linger over the elegant, formal antiques or the magnificent view of the sea that almost every window of the manor revealed.

The meal, prepared by a middle-aged live-in housekeeper, was excellent. Andrea had ravenously eaten the broiled Pacific salmon and steamed rice, all the while being charmed by Jefferson. His low voice, soft and seductive, vibrated in her ears, and his eyes seemed to follow her every move, as if touching her. The delicate meal, along with two glasses of clear, dry Riesling wine, and the low, enchanting conversation, seemed to wrap Andrea in warm, seductive folds of intimacy.

After the meal, without words, Jefferson took Andrea by the hand and led her to the rear of the house, and then to the stables. A large bay gelding, with a blaze of white that tapered to velvet pink at his nose, perked up his ears at the sound of Jefferson's entrance.

"Do you ride?" Jefferson asked, cocking his head in the direction of the large bay.

"A little."

"Bareback?"

"Never!" she gasped, eyeing the large horse dubiously.

"Then it's high time that you learned," Jefferson decided as he placed a bridle over the bay's broad head. "It's really very easy, and I can guarantee you that there's no better horse to practice on than old Monarch here." Jefferson gave the horse a good-natured slap on its rump before gently leading him from the musty stables and out into the clear air of the paddock that bordered the back of the manicured estate.

"I don't know," Andrea hedged, staring at the gelding with mounting uncertainty. She had ridden several times in her life, but always with a saddle, and on a considerably smaller horse. Monarch's imposing frame and heavily boned stature made Andrea's confidence waver.

"Don't worry about it. Just hang on to me," Jefferson instructed with a gleam of amusement in his hazel eyes. Andrea noticed something else in his gaze. Although it was hidden, she was aware of his smoldering desire. Unexpectedly she felt an answering passion igniting her blood.

She tried to keep her wandering mind on the conversation. "You aren't really serious; you don't think that he can hold both of us?" she asked, motioning to Monarch.

In answer, Jefferson smiled devilishly and, hoisting himself onto the bay's wide back, he swung his leg over the horse. In one lithe movement, he was astride the horse. Monarch's only response was to stamp one foot impatiently and give an inappreciative flick of his pointed, dark ears. Jefferson patted Monarch's shoulder, leaned down and offered his outstretched hand to Andrea in an invitation to mount the horse. Andrea couldn't help but suck in her breath as she extended her hands to Jefferson's and their fingers entwined. A tingle of apprehension darted across her shoulder blades. Was it fear of the horse—or the man?

With a strength that Andrea found astonishing, Jefferson lifted her onto the horse. The only movement that the bay made was to swish his tail against Andrea's slim, bare leg; naked because her dress was hiked daringly up to the swell of her hips as she sat astride the horse.

"Aren't we too heavy for him?" Andrea asked, tugging at her hem with her free hand, and trying to ignore the tension and excitement that she felt building in the air. Her bare legs were pressed against the horse's flanks, and she could feel his warm, soft coat move against her thighs and calves.

"Not for Monarch. He's a draft horse, part Belgian. That accounts for his size and strength," Jefferson explained as he loosened his grip on the reins and urged the animal forward. In his other hand, he pressed Andrea's fingers against his hard stomach. He let the bay walk slowly, letting Andrea get a feel for Monarch's steady, lumbering gait. They went past the paddock and into the wooded, unkempt portion of the island. The path through the stands of Douglas firs angled sharply downward, but the horse proved surefooted. Andrea's body was forced to hug Jefferson's as the pull of gravity pressed her, muscle for muscle, against him. Her arms were wrapped securely around his lean, hard torso, and her legs outlined his. Andrea couldn't ignore the warmth and rigid power of Jefferson's abdominal muscles as they tightened against her touch, nor could she deny that her own breathing, pulsating against the back of Jefferson's neck, had become as erratic as her thudding heartbeat.

The woods seemed to wrap both horse and rider in its intimate folds of darkness. Filtered light, the last, ghostly rays from a rapidly lowering sun, permeated the branches of giant firs and shaded the forest in a dusky, ethereal glow. Shadows lengthened against the cracked bark of the trees and hid the wildflowers that scented the air.

As the bay picked his way carefully down the stony path, the crashing of waves against ancient rock echoed against the wooded hillside. All too quickly the dark intimacy of the woods gave way to the open air and roar of the surf against the beach. Monarch pranced sideways nervously and raised his head proudly in the air. He paused for a moment, twitching his ears, his muscles tensed in anticipation, and his pink nostrils flared into the wind. The signal from Jefferson came swiftly; he compressed his legs against the bay's broad shoulders and urged Monarch into a gallop. The long, powerful strides of the horse made short work of the narrow strip of dry land. Soon Andrea felt the sting of cold seawater against her legs as the horse found more stable, wet sand near the frothy edge of the tide.

Jefferson guided Monarch in the direction of the setting sun, letting the horse race on the surf's undulating edge. The animal thundered down the beach, his strong legs plowing through the cold water of the sea. Andrea lowered her head against Jefferson's shoulders for protection, and her long, ebony hair streamed out behind her, unfurling in the wind. She felt an exhilaration entering her lungs with each breath of salty air that she inhaled.

Monarch continued on his murderous race until the strip of sandy beach disappeared into the hillside. Only as he began to climb the steep path at the opposite end of the beach from where he had entered did the horse begin to slow down. Monarch seemed to know the path by instinct, climbing steadily upward, his labored breathing disturbing the solitude of the oncoming night.

And then Jefferson finally pulled upon the reins and let the horse pause.

"Come here," he commanded her as he slipped from Monarch's dark back and helped Andrea do the same. His arms slipped around her waist, and for an unsteady moment brushed against her breasts. She felt the air whisper in her lungs at his light touch, and quickly he released her to touch only the tips of her fingers with his.

They left the horse to nibble at a few blades of grass that had surfaced in the sandy soil. Jefferson led Andrea to the edge of the cliff. He stood next to her and let his arm drape loosely over her shoulders as he pointed out the winking lights of a passing ship on the horizon.

"I used to stand here . . . in the summer, on this very spot, and watch the ships against the sky," he admitted roughly.

"Why?"

He snorted in self-derision, as if he hated to answer. "I was always hoping that my father would be on the next ship. He never was." Seemingly embarrassed, he shrugged his shoulders as if to dismiss his thoughts.

Andrea felt her heart turn over, and involuntarily she leaned closer to Jefferson. Never would she have imagined that he had ever felt the pain of loneliness. The sun had settled into the clear waters of the calm Pacific, and vibrant colors ranging from deepest amethyst to brilliant orange illuminated the night sky and reflected against the sea.

Andrea felt a strange tremor pass through her body as Jefferson's hands, gentle but persuasive, rotated her shoulders, forcing her to face him. In the depths of his gaze she found smoky passion. "Andrea," he murmured against the night before letting his head dip lower to hers. His voice was rough with an emotion that was foreign to him, and his fingers nearly trembled as he reached up to cup her chin.

Her eyes, full of innocence and longing, looked deeply into his, pleading to understand him. Her lower lip quivered in anticipation and fear, and she wetted it unconsciously with her tongue. Her provocative gesture made him close his eyes for a moment and hesitate slightly. And then, tenderly, expertly, with a flaming passion that he thought had been lost with his youth, he pulled her tightly against him. His lips, tasting of salt, brushed tentatively against hers, teasing her with a promise of higher, more savory delights. She answered by letting her head fall backward in surrender. Her long thick hair tumbled over his arm as his lips pressed desire and possession upon hers. As if by instinct she let her mouth open to him in a shuddering sigh.

"Oh, God," he whispered, pulling his mouth from hers and holding her breathlessly against him as if nothing could make him take his arms away. "I must be out of my mind."

Gently he released her and took a step backward, as if to put distance between their aching bodies.

"Is something wrong?" she asked, wide-eyed and innocent.

He seemed almost angry as he kicked at the sand and ran his hand roughly against the back of his neck. A breeze ruffled his hair, but couldn't erase the grim, determined set of his jaw or the blazing passion in his gaze. "No . . . nothing's wrong," he snapped back sarcastically. "Here we are, all alone on the island, and you couldn't be more than twenty, and all I can think about is seducing you. Now what could be wrong with that?" he asked rhetorically and added a contemptuous curse, aimed violently at himself.

"Nothing," she answered honestly. "There's nothing wrong with it."

"I don't think you understand, Andrea," he replied, coming more closely to her. He touched her arms with his warm fingers, at first lightly, but suddenly possessively. "From the first time that I laid eyes upon you, back in that amphitheater at U.C.L.A., I've *wanted* you, needed to make love to you. All my interest in your brother was only an excuse to find you, to *have* you. God, Andrea, I thought I would go crazy with wanting you." He closed his eyes with his confession, and his fingers dug into the soft flesh of her upper arms. "It's as if I can't rest until I make love to you—forever."

Her smile was wistful, knowing, and it seemed to antagonize him further.

"Don't you hear what I'm saying?" he demanded,

giving her a short shake. "I'm trying to tell you that I followed you up here with the express purpose of seducing you. I . . . I want to sleep with you!"

"I know."

His eyes rolled upward to the heavens, and he shook his head in frustration. "Then why did you come with me?" he asked. "Do you enjoy torturing me?" His breath, laced with the sweet flavor of wine, fanned her face, and she let her eyelids droop as she leaned against him.

"I'm not torturing you."

"Oh, God, Andrea," he moaned, slipping his arms gently around her small waist and holding her breathlessly against him. "If you only knew." His words, spoken in a prayerlike manner, ruffled against her hair. The purple shadows of twilight began to settle restlessly against the hillside, and only the shimmering half-moon kept darkness at bay.

"I understand," Andrea murmured.

"You couldn't possibly. You don't know what you're saying."

Oh, yes I do, she thought to herself, but you're not listening, Jefferson. *I'm saying that I love you.* Andrea felt her heart hammering wildly within the confines of her rib cage, and she knew that her blood was coursing through her veins more heatedly than ever before. She experienced a warm melting sensation curling within her, struggling to be set free.

"I do know. . . ." The air rang with her honesty.

The space between them became thick and heavy with unspoken words. Andrea could hear Jefferson's heart thudding, pounding deeply in his chest, and she felt the rigidity of his self-control begin to melt as it slipped from him.

His lips, burning with need, found hers. His tongue, tasting of sweet maleness, rimmed her lips and tenderly probed the warm invitation of her mouth. Andrea's thoughts began to swim, and she felt her knees weaken as

Jefferson pulled away from her. He watched her face in the silver moonglow, his questioning gaze driving into hers, searching for any shadowing of doubt that might flicker in her trusting eyes. He found none.

"Andrea, I want you so desperately," he groaned, closing his eyes and gritting his teeth against the rising fire in his blood. "But"— his eyes opened with renewed resolve —"I need to know that you want me, and that you understand what this means to me, to us."

She hesitated only slightly, and then, while her misty green gaze was still woven with his, she disengaged herself and stood. Then she drew her hands upward to rest at her neck. With quivering fingers she slowly loosened the small satin ribbon that held the loose bodice of her halter in place. Her gaze never left his eyes as the thin fabric dropped and she felt the cold embrace of the sea air against her bare skin.

Jefferson stiffened and took a step backward to gaze at her. Her skin seemed pale and innocently soft in the silver moonglow. The dress had fallen to her waist, and her breasts, softly rounded and unrestrained, tightened in the cool air. The wind swept her long, raven hair away from her face as she stood on the ledge over the blackened Pacific.

"You don't know what you're doing," he muttered through tightly clenched teeth.

The blush that started at her neck colored her cheeks, but her eyes met his calmly. "I do."

Jefferson swallowed with difficulty. "Andrea," he whispered, casting her name over the waves, "I don't think . . ."

"What?"

The innocence of her question reached to the deepest core of him. A tortured expression clouded his face. "Look, Andrea, I'm sorry, I should never have brought you here. I don't know what's gotten into me. . . ."

The color drained from Andrea's face when she finally

understood what he was saying. He was rejecting her. He had brought her up to the ledge to tease her, nothing more. He probably had lots of women, much more sophisticated and mature than herself. All his tender words had been empty and meaningless. As the realization hit her, a look of horror widened her eyes and tears began to burn behind her eyelids. She lowered her gaze in order to avoid the direct intensity of his eyes, and her fingers fumbled with the bodice of her dress. Her movements were unsure as she tried to retie the satin ribbon around her neck.

Jefferson's voice was husky but calm. "Let me help you with that. . . ."

"No!" He had started toward her, and she wrenched away from the touch of his fingers against her neck. She tried to muffle a sob and failed.

"Andrea?"

She turned her back to him and closed her eyes, vainly willing her tears to stop. She didn't want to cry, but the pain of his rejection was as sharp as a knife twisting in her heart. Her small shoulders shook in her attempts to control the sobs that were threatening to explode.

"Oh, God, Andrea," Jefferson sighed. She stiffened. The last thing she wanted was his pity. "I'm sorry."

"For what?" she tossed out shakily. "For bringing me here to your lonely retreat? For trying to seduce me? Or . . . for failing?"

"What?" He seemed sincerely confused.

"You know what I mean," she accused, astounded at the bitter sound of her words. Her ragged emotions and anger finally got the better of her. "This was all some sort of game to you, wasn't it?"

"Andrea, no. . . ."

"And I was stupid enough to fall for it. You brought me up here just to embarrass me, didn't you?"

"What are you talking about?" he asked, clearly stunned.

She spun to face him, swallowing back her tears. "I'm talking about the fact that I'm Martin Monroe's younger sister, and you're using me to get back at him!"

"I would *never* use you, don't you know that?"

"Then I guess I don't understand what's happening between us. I thought—I thought that you wanted to make love to me," she whispered, her voice catching.

"I did. I *do!*"

"But then why?"

Jefferson's voice was thinly patient. "Andrea, I was trying to control myself."

"That much was obvious. It wasn't very hard, was it?" she countered angrily, and hating the spiteful sound of her voice. Her emotions began to overtake her, and she wanted to lash out at him for rejecting her. She knew that she was being unfair, but she didn't care.

"It might have been the hardest thing I've ever done in my life," he admitted in a hoarse, self-condemning whisper.

"Don't," she cried, trying to stem the flow of tears down her cheeks. Why was he torturing her so? "I . . . I don't want to hear it!" As if to escape from anything else he might say, Andrea turned and began to run down the path that was parallel to the ledge. She knew that she was being irrational, but she had to get away from him. She needed to put some space between them, to think and sort things out for herself. She heard the thudding sound of her own footsteps in the sand, the pounding of her heart, the crashing of the waves along the shore, and from somewhere nearby Monarch's soft nicker. There was another sound as well. Jefferson was following her. Her feet skimmed over the sandy trail until they caught on an exposed root. She started to fail, but Jefferson's arms, strong and powerful, caught her as she stumbled. Together they fell to the ground.

"Dear God, Andrea," he whispered, "what do you think of me?"

Her voice was raspy and breathless both from her sprint and the intoxicating nearness of the man holding her. "I don't know what to think."

One of his fingers reached upward and brushed a silvery tear from her cheek. His face twisted into a frown of repentant pain, and with a moan of surrender he buried his head in the tangled strands of her hair. His hot breath against her bare shoulders warmed her flesh and forced a sigh from her lips. "Dear Andrea," he murmured, "what am I going to do with you?"

Love me, she pleaded silently as his lips moved down her forehead to her eyes. He tasted the salt of her tears, and once again an unknown anguish contorted his features.

"Don't cry, sweetheart," he pleaded, and the hot persuasion of his lips found hers. "Don't ever cry for me." He kissed her again on the lips, and his tongue gently eased into her mouth. Sparks of liquid fire leaped through her as his tongue found hers and molded against it. She felt the weight of his torso against her breast, the crushing ecstasy of his arms around her and the soft, cool sand against her back.

She wound her arms around his neck, enjoying the warm sensations flowing through her. She didn't resist when his hands found the ribbon supporting her dress and untied it. He pulled his lips from hers as he slowly, seductively lowered the bodice to once again expose the full ripeness of her straining breasts. As his eyes seared a path over her skin and down her throat to gaze at the beauty of her nakedness, she felt her nipples respond. A blush of excitement and shyness tinged her skin, giving it a rosy glow in the twilight.

With a groan of pleasure Jefferson surveyed her. His lower body lay across hers, and his stiff arms held him away from her, enabling him to embrace her with his eyes. If he had any doubts about the sanity of the situation, he cast them aside, secure in the excitement and surrender he found in her mystifying gaze. Still supporting himself with one hand, he lazily reached forward. One strong, male finger drew an imaginary line from the hollow of her throat down to linger on her breastbone. The movement was slight, but Andrea felt as if he were controlling her entire being in the tiny, slow circles he drew against her skin. Just when she thought she would cry out with her aching need, his fingers traveled up the swell of her breast to tease and fleetingly touch her nipple.

A soft moan came from somewhere in the deepest reaches of her, and she knew that her hands were working on the bottom of his shirt, tugging it out of the waistband of his jeans. He pulled the shirt over his head and cast it somewhere in the night. Her fingers moved up his silky arms, revelling in the taut, corded muscles of his shoulders. She touched him boldly, as she had never touched a man before. Her palms were flat as she rubbed the firm muscles of his chest and traced the outline of hair around his male nipples.

In response he lowered his head and captured one of her nipples in the warm, soft cavern of his mouth. Involuntarily Andrea sucked in her breath, and dizzying sensations of pleasure swept through her entire being. She held on to his head, pressing him ever more close to her. Her thoughts were distant and vague, and she was aware only of the warm, glowing sensations he was creating within her. She wanted the magical moments never to end. *I love you,* she thought desperately to herself. Dear Jefferson, if only I was brave enough to tell you that I love you.

She felt his hands move over the fabric of her dress, kneading pleasurable circles of passion against her bare legs. The light cotton fabric that separated her flesh from his added to her bittersweet torment as it was pushed and molded against her hips.

"Love me, Jefferson," she pleaded into the night. He paused only slightly, and that was to look into the pale green depths of her eyes. He saw no fear, only honesty and simmering, undeniable passion.

"Oh, yes, little one. Let me love you as no one has before."

His hands, which had crept up the hem of her dress to lovingly touch her thigh stopped their seductive motion at her response.

"No one has ever . . ."

"What do you mean?" he asked quietly, pressing a gentle kiss to her temple.

"I mean that this is the first time," she sighed. "Does it matter?"

He regarded her silently, but the passion remained in his eyes. "Are you sure?" he asked. "Are you sure this is what you want?"

"Oh, yes, Jefferson, oh, yes." She pulled his head back to hers and opened her mouth in sweet invitation.

"I must be out of my mind," he said aloud, but the passion of the girl lying seductively on the sand and the warm, late-summer night overshadowed his reason. His hands resumed their enticing exploration, and Andrea felt a white-hot lava begin to burn in her.

She reached for the button of his jeans, and soon they were both naked in the night, their bodies touching, caressing, embracing in the moonglow. A light dusting of perspiration created a smooth film over them, and when Jefferson moved over her, Andrea was breathless in anticipation. She felt the gentle nudge of his knee parting her legs, and sighed in relief as he settled himself against her.

Slowly, gently, forcing himself to be in control, Jefferson entered her. She gasped at the twinge of pain, but his steady rhythm eased her through the first uncomfortable spasm and pushed her into warm, liquid union. His mouth never left hers, and his hands continued their uncompromising kneading of her body. She found herself blending with him, encouraging him with her hands. His hot body over hers and the cool sand beneath her touched her skin. She felt hot licks of flame bursting within her while her breath came in short, quick gasps, and as his motion quickened, so did her response. The ache grew and consumed her until at last Jefferson pushed her over the brink of yearning to satisfaction and she moaned quietly beneath him.

The sounds of the night seemed to be amplified to her as afterglow settled upon her. The waves below them, her hammering heart, Jefferson's erratic breathing, all seemed to weigh against her.

"Do you have any idea how beautiful you are?" Jefferson asked, stroking a strand of black hair out of her eyes.

"Tell me."

"It would be very easy to fall in love with you," he admitted. "Too damned easy."

Andrea sighed contentedly and pressed her body more closely to his. Everything seemed right with the world.

That was how it had all started, Andrea mused idly as she regarded her empty glass. It had been nearly ten years ago, and she could still visualize those warm, seductive summer nights filled with lovemaking and the brilliantly hot, cloudless days of walking on the beach. She remembered laughing into each other's eyes, running from an occasional rain shower, sleeping soundly in the cradle of Jefferson's strong arms. Was it as romantic as it seemed? Or had her memory been colored with the passage of ten long, lonely years? Had it been a special, magical time, or was she the victim of her passion?

The sound of Jefferson's footsteps broke through her pensive thoughts, and she pulled her eyes from the empty glass toward the door. His anger seemed to have disappeared for the moment, and his eyes, though wary, held hers in a commanding but friendly embrace.

His dark hair was still wet, evidence of a quick shower,

and, for a moment, Andrea was mesmerized by his bold features. In one hand he carried a tray of food—cheese, bread, pieces of ham—and in his other hand he held a pair of slippers that had to be at least four sizes too large for Andrea's small feet.

"This is the best I could do. I'm not really prepared for visitors here," Jefferson stated half-apologetically as he set the tray of food on a nearby table and handed Andrea the worn, scruffy slippers.

"Everything looks fine to me."

"Are you hungry?"

"Not really," she admitted with a weary sigh.

"Tired? Or just too nervous to eat?" he guessed, as he cut a thick slice of ham, and offered her a makeshift sandwich.

Her eyes raised to his. "You have to admit, this isn't exactly a normal situation."

He smiled in spite of himself. "I guess you're right. I knew that Bryce Cawthorne, cuss that he is, would find some way to get at me. He doesn't exactly lie down and die when you give him no for an answer. But I never, not in a thousand years, would have guessed that it would be you he'd send to track me down. Especially on a night like this."

"Then you did expect someone?"

His smile pulled into a frown. "I knew that Cawthorne would find a way to try again."

Andrea took a bite of her sandwich. "So, you think that he's persistent?"

"At the very least! What I didn't realize was that he would be able to get *you* to go along with him. For one thing, I thought you knew me better than that. Why would I consent to an interview . . . especially now?" He grimaced at the thought, and his eyes narrowed suspiciously. "I should have expected something like this from Cawthorne . . . but then, I didn't know that you worked for him." His eyes impaled her. "I didn't have a chance to keep up on your whereabouts." He set the remainder of his sandwich aside. "Did I?"

"That was the way you wanted it," she reminded him.

"I don't think so." He sat on the floor and leaned against the chair where she sat, curled in his warm robe. He stared into the fire.

"Don't you remember?" she asked hesitantly. The light mood in the room had changed. She could sense that Jefferson was baiting her, deliberately leading her into the past, and she knew that it was dangerous emotional territory he intended to dissect.

"Why don't you give me your version of the story," he suggested in a rough, deep voice.

"The story?" she repeated innocently.

"Don't play games with me, Andrea. You're a big girl, now . . . sophisticated. Don't pretend to be the naive innocent you once were. I wouldn't believe it! You know what I'm talking about." His narrowed eyes seemed to study the flames that shadowed his face. "I want to know exactly how you interpret our final days together, and just what happened between you and me."

"You know very well," she replied, her throat constricting and her words raspy. He reached for his drink and as he swirled the amber colored liquor he looked listlessly into the small whirlpool he had created.

"Do I?" he prodded. "Why don't you explain it to me?"

At that precise moment Andrea knew the feeling of fear that must have come over each witness who had been called to the stand for cross-examination and interrogation by Jefferson Harmon, the lawyer. Although he seemed dispassionate and lost in thought, Andrea knew instinctively that he was coiled, patiently waiting to trap her. He would encourage her to say just the wrong thing, and then he would pounce mercilessly upon her.

Her silence encouraged him to speak quietly to her, and the seductive ring of his voice against the low howling of the wind made her stomach knot in dread and her breathing become labored.

"Come on, Andrea, you remember, don't you? It was late in the fall, you had already gone back to school, and the election was just over, isn't that right?" He didn't wait for her to respond. He could feel her strained composure electrifying the air. "Wasn't that about the time that Martin found out about us?"

She closed her eyes, vainly trying not to recall the angry, embarrassing scene with Martin and her parents. It seemed so far away. "I guess so," she stammered breathlessly.

"You know so!" Jefferson blasted, and then, in a softer voice, "Would you like another drink?" The question was sudden, jarring Andrea from her uncomfortable reverie, and the pain of those half-forgotten memories came crashing around her.

"Yes . . . thank you," she murmured politely, wondering how she could change the course of the intimate conversation. She didn't want to remember the humiliation, the rage, the agony again. Only the bitterness that had forced her away from Jefferson would resurface.

Jefferson strode over to the bar, and just as he was pulling out a bottle with an expensive label, he paused dramatically. "That's right!" he said, almost to himself, as if a sudden thought had struck him.

Andrea rose to the bait. "What?"

"I remember now, it *was* in November, about this time of year. The election was over, I was a senator, or would be in January, and your brother, Martin, was visiting you at U.C.L.A. He'd just completed basic training at the time!"

Andrea swallowed with difficulty. "Jefferson . . . don't," she pleaded, watching his disciplined theatrics with increasing horror. Dear God, he's enjoying this, she thought desperately to herself, he's actually enjoying dredging all of this up again!

"Don't what?" he shot back at her, pouring a stiff drink and walking back to hand it to her. "Don't talk about the past?" he asked levelly, watching her blanched face. "Don't bring up the subject of that pitiful excuse you call a brother?" he demanded. Her eyes darkened in rage and began to fill with tears. "Or don't remind you of the fact that you left me high and dry, all alone, to face your family, the other members of the senate . . . and the press?" His mouth had hardened into a tight, drawn line as he remembered the loneliness and shock he had felt when his affair "with a left-wing radical war objector" had splashed across the headlines coast to coast.

Jefferson ignored Andrea's outstretched hand and set the drink on the nearby table with such a force that some of the liquid sloshed onto the table, blurring the print of an open newspaper and smearing an image of Lara's face. Jefferson's grimace hardened.

"I didn't mean to hurt you—or anyone," Andrea attempted to explain, closing her eyes as if to shut out the pain.

"Then, why, Andrea? Why did you lie, and for God's sake, why did you run away from me? If only I could have talked to you!"

The torment in his voice pushed her deeper into her despair. "I, I couldn't face you. I couldn't face anyone. Can't you understand that? I was only twenty years old!" Andrea cried. "Dear God, Jefferson, how could I face you?" she asked, the tears beginning to stain her cheeks. She let them run, unashamed of the emotions they so poignantly displayed.

"Then why did you lie to Martin?" he persisted, forcing himself to look away from her anguished, tear-stained face. He couldn't let her get to him—not again. It would be too damned easy to hold her, to caress her, to kiss back those tears.

"I didn't lie! Not to anyone!"

Jefferson bit at his lower lip and studied her ruefully.

"Then why don't you tell me what happened when Martin got out of basic?" Feeling himself getting caught up in the emotions he had purposefully buried, Jefferson silently cursed himself. Unfortunately Andrea's emotional performance was getting to him, no matter how much he attempted to dissuade himself. He damned himself mentally, knowing that he had always been weak where she was concerned. Why had he even let her into the house tonight? She was destroying all of the walls of bitterness that he had built to surround himself for the past ten years of his life, and he knew instinctively that with the collapse of those walls would go all his self-control and restraint. He reminded himself that no matter what, he couldn't trust her . . . not again . . . not ever!

"It . . . it was a difficult period," she began, her dry throat burning with raw feelings that threatened to strangle the words of explanation that she had begun to whisper. Jefferson's cool hazel eyes never left her face. "Martin came to see me . . . of course he hated the army. He had orders to Vietnam." She sighed wearily. "He was frightened, and appalled that my father wouldn't condone his desertion. Martin wanted to come up here to Canada and apply for citizenship, but my parents had both suffered through World War II, and they thought that he was being disrespectful to his country—a traitor."

"So what did that have to do with us?"

"You have to remember that Martin blamed the country, or, more specifically, the politicians for the war." Andrea's shoulders sagged at the memory, and a painful shadow crossed her pale green eyes. To Jefferson she was incredibly alluring, and he felt his heart twist for her. Was she really suffering or was it a well-practiced act, he wondered silently.

Andrea's voice was barely a whisper as she continued. "He found out that I had been seeing you, and, although I never admitted it, he surmised that we had been sleeping together." Andrea's memory flashed, and she saw once again the look of shock and disgust on Martin's face when he realized that his accusations were true. And something else had registered in his eyes—was it satisfaction?

"He thought that we'd slept together? Did you try to deny it?"

"No."

"So what happened?"

"First he told my parents." She sighed, remembering the tears of her mother and the stern, ashen face of her disapproving father.

"Martin told your parents?" Jefferson repeated. "Nice guy, wasn't he?"

Andrea's eyes plunged into Jefferson's derisive gaze. Her chin tilted defiantly, and she seemed to collect herself and become cold.

"Is that why your parents called me?" he asked, aware of the stiffening of her spine and the proud toss of her hair as she shook it out of her face.

"I . . . I guess so."

"But that's not all of it."

"No. He had a friend, an editor for a left-wing campus paper, and Martin told him about our affair."

A rage, deep and primeval, started to flame within Jefferson. His lips compressed into a thin white line as he continued to question Andrea. "What else did Martin tell his *friend?*" he asked slowly, his hoarse voice threatening to explode.

"You know the answer to that!"

"I want to hear it from you!"

Andrea drew in a shaky breath and closed her eyes, as if she wanted to hide from the truth. "He told his friend at the paper that—that I had been pregnant."

"Go on."

"And—and that I had been forced to have an abortion . . ." she admitted as a sob ripped through her words.

"And that I forced you?"

"Yes . . . yes, because of your career and my . . . no, my brother's political leanings!"

Jefferson came over to the chair in which she was nestled. He put each of his hands on an armrest, imprisoning her within the aged leather as if he expected her to attempt to escape. His angry eyes roved restlessly over her face, calculating her emotions, before resting in the depths of her green gaze.

"But you weren't pregnant, were you?" he asked slowly, trying not to shout out the question that had stolen so many nights of his sleep.

She shook her head negatively, allowing the sweep of her ebony curls to brush against the pale whiteness of her skin. "How did you know?" she whispered.

"I thought I knew you well enough, and I hoped that if you had been carrying my child, you would have had the decency to tell me about it. What I didn't expect was that you would leave me hanging, avoiding me, letting the press conjure up anything they so pleased about us!" He rose from the chair, trying to assuage the intimacy he felt every time he was near to her. He attempted not to see the soft invitation of her eyes or the dusky hollow between her breasts, partially exposed by the overlapping lapels of the robe.

Andrea was expecting the next question, but when it came with such unmasked vengeance she felt her confidence ebb from her. "Why did Martin lie, Andrea?"

"I don't know."

"But surely you have an opinion. You can guess."

Again she shook her head, trying to dispel the agonizing image of her brother as he had been then: young, loud and full of hate. And she tried not to dwell on his image today or the jagged, white scar that cleaved his once-handsome face. "Who can tell?" she asked rhetorically. "It's been ten years, Jefferson. I don't know what he thought or what he was feeling. Maybe he thought that somehow you could help his cause, keep him out of the war. Perhaps he thought that you could use your influence to help him."

"He knew how I felt. I had answered his letters. There was nothing I could do!"

"Well, then, I don't know. Perhaps he thought that if he drew attention to your situation, something would prevent him from going to Vietnam."

"That's crazy!"

"He was scared, damn it!"

Jefferson halted his scathing reply and took a swallow of his drink. He looked once to the floor and then at Andrea's downcast head. His voice, full of suspicion, was flat and emotionless. "Did you put him up to it?"

Andrea's lowered eyes flew to Jefferson's face. "Of course not! I didn't want anything to do with it—with any of it. I couldn't believe what he'd done!"

"And yet you stand up for him now?" Jefferson's lips curled in disgust. "After he used you—used us!"

"He's my brother!"

"He's a jerk!"

"Oh, Jefferson, don't—"

"Why not? It's the truth! That bastard of a brother of yours told lies, vicious lies about you, went A.W.O.L. to disgrace your family and nearly ruined my reputation as a member of the senate. What else could you call him? I don't doubt that he was scared, Andrea, but a lot of us get scared, and we don't lash out at everyone or everything. He had no right to try and destroy any of us!" Jefferson threw out, vehemently. His gaze knifed through her. "And what about you; why did you run away?"

Andrea's oval face drained of color. "I couldn't face you. I couldn't face another argument, another confrontation about Martin," she whispered.

"So you hid!"

Andrea remembered the reverberation of her father's

voice, the look of utter humiliation in her mother's blue eyes, the shaming knowledge that she had wounded them both irreparably. "My parents enrolled me in a private school in Oregon," she sighed. "They wanted to shelter me from the press, to avoid any further scandal."

"I don't doubt that. The article in that left-wing, radical college paper somehow made it to the national press, and I can bet who was responsible for that. Oh, yes, your brother did quite a job on us, didn't he?" he suggested as his eyes darkened with a boiling wrath. Andrea found it hard to meet his demanding stare as he continued to speak.

"And why didn't you call me?" Jefferson asked suddenly.

"My parents . . . didn't want me to see you again."

"And you agreed?" he asked, incredulous.

"I had no choice!"

"You hid, Andrea! You hid behind the lies that your brother contrived!"

"No, no, you don't understand!"

"You bet I don't!" His large fist crashed against the gray stone of the fireplace. "How can you possibly sit there and try to defend your brother after all of the cruel lies that he told about you and me? Don't you remember the public embarrassment that you suffered . . . that I suffered?" Jefferson asked, accusingly, his voice harsh and his dark eyes knowing.

Andrea's defiance tightened her face. "That's what this interrogation is all about, isn't it?" she charged. "Your main concern at the time, as well as now, was your reputation, your public standing. Martin was scared, worried for his life, and all you could see was that he was tarnishing your image as a public figure! This entire argument is about your career, isn't it?"

His voice was low, deathly quiet, as he tried to hold on to the remnants of his patience. "It has nothing to do with my career," he growled, the intensity of his words slicing through the air. "If I had cared so much about my career, would I have ever resigned as governor?"

"That was different!"

"How?" The question thundered from his voice and echoed in the rafters.

"Because of your *wife.*" Andrea stammered, feeling her pulse jumping and her nerves beginning to stretch to the breaking point.

"My *wife?*" he whispered callously, and his gaze moved involuntarily to the sodden picture on the end table. He shook his dark head sadly, for a moment lost in thought. "My wife wasn't the cause of my decision to withdraw from public office!" Contempt distorted his arrogant features as the firelight shadowed his intense gaze. His deep voice lowered an octave. "I thought you knew me better than that," he whispered, leaning against the broad mantel of the fireplace. "But then, I've been wrong about you before."

"What's that supposed to mean?" she breathed.

"It means that I thought you were stronger than you actually proved to be. It means that I expected you to stand by me, to publicly refute the lies that your brother propagated. But, no. You couldn't handle anything that tough, could you? You left me to stand alone. The fact that you ran away only added fuel to the fires of gossip!"

"I was only twenty years old!"

"You weren't a kid, Andrea. You were a mature *woman!*"

Andrea felt the truth of his words pierce her, and all of the excuses that she had made for herself seemed feeble and weak. "My parents . . . they wouldn't let me see you," she repeated. "They wanted to protect me from you. They were afraid of the press."

"This has nothing to do with your parents!" Jefferson interrupted, his hot words knifing through the air. "This only involves you and me!"

"Then why do you insist on bringing up Martin?" she shouted back at him, her raw emotions reflected in the raspy, desperate tone of her voice. "Why do you continue to badger me about him?"

"Because I have to know!"

"What? What is it that you want from me?"

His voice was dangerous when he responded. "I want to know how on earth you can still call him your brother after what he did to us?" Jefferson's fingers curled tightly over the drink, and he refused to take his gaze off her face as he finished the warm liquid in one swallow.

Andrea closed her eyes, avoiding his scrutiny. She realized that her shoulders were shaking, but she tried to keep a fragment of her poise. The headache that had been building ever since Jefferson's intense questioning began was throbbing mercilessly at her temples, and Jefferson's dark, unguarded stare pierced her to the heart. Her voice quaked when she spoke. "It's been hard," she admitted, biting the tip of her thumbnail and feeling her breath pass raggedly out of her lungs. "But I've had to forgive Martin."

"Why?"

"So that he could forgive *me!*" she breathed, letting out the incriminating truth.

"I don't understand."

Andrea's eyes studied her glass, looking into the clear liquid as if seeking the answers to his questions. "Too much time has passed. We—he and I—we had to bury the past." She pressed the cool glass to her lips before finally taking a steadying swallow. She didn't want to think about Martin or his buddies or the anguish and physical pain that he had found during the war. She didn't want to remember how much he had suffered, nor did she want to confess her own sins.

"Because you're older . . . he's older? That makes what he did right?" Jefferson challenged, sensing deep, heart-wrenching emotions savagely tearing at her.

"It will never be right," Andrea whispered, as if no one was with her in the room. "But then, Martin will never be the same again . . . not ever."

Jefferson hesitated, seeing the blanched and pained expression that crossed the beauty of Andrea's face. Though she tried to hide her agony, Jefferson's probing gaze sought it out. His dark brows drew together pensively, and he waited for her to explain her enigmatic statement.

"Because of Dad's insistence, Martin eventually went back to the army. Within several months he was sent to Vietnam, to the front lines of the war."

"And?" Why did Jefferson have the feeling that he really didn't want to know the outcome? All the muscles in his body tensed, became wary, as if waiting for some unknown attack on his senses.

"This time Martin followed orders," Andrea stated grimly. "At first he seemed to adjust, at least that's what my folks said. His letters home appeared to be normal." Another sip of brandy interrupted her story. "But then we got a . . . military cable. Martin had been injured." Andrea felt tears well within her at the memory. "My parents were frantic. It took nearly a week to get any further information about him. No one seemed to know if he was dead or alive." Andrea paused, and Jefferson felt a weakening sense of dread skitter up his rigid spine. "It was a land mine. According to the army, Martin was lucky—he survived. Several of his buddies weren't so fortunate," Andrea choked out through the streaming tears that fell over her cheeks. She didn't endeavor to hide the wet stains that reflected the glow of the fire. Nor did she try to disguise the guilt that had weighed so heavily on her fragile shoulders.

"His injury was serious?" Jefferson surmised.

Andrea's eyes, shining with pooled tears, probed deeply into his. Slowly she nodded, the words strangling in her throat. When she did speak, her voice was barely audible over the storm. "It's been a nightmare," she confided. "The shrapnel caught him and embedded itself in his right side. Fortunately, the pieces that hit his abdomen and chest didn't penetrate any of his internal organs. He has scars, of course, and his right hand has lost most of its mobility—it's nearly useless, despite several operations. But, but . . ."

"What?"

Andrea bit at her lower lip. "Oh, God, Jefferson. Martin's *blind!*"

Jefferson stiffened, and Andrea's voice cracked with ravaged emotion.

The strain of the night caught hold of Andrea, and she leaned heavily in the chair. She rested her forehead in her palm, closing her eyes to the black, tormented thoughts that gripped her. Finally, with a self-deprecating smile twisting her pale lips, she continued. "And do you know what the worst part of it all is?"

He waited, not wanting to hear. Something angry in her voice made his dread mount.

"All the while that Martin was over there, in Vietnam, fighting for his country, *my* country, I refused to write to him. Not one lousy letter. Because," she sobbed, tears stinging her throat, "because of the lies and the gossip that he had spread about you and me! I couldn't find the compassion in my heart to even write him one damned postcard!"

"It's not your fault," Jefferson asserted. "You can't blame yourself." He tried to find adequate words to console her, hoping to find a way to lessen the guilt that she had borne on her slim shoulders.

"If only I could believe that," she sighed. "But, I never will. Martin was in a foreign country, fighting a war that no one cared for, and all *I* could think about was my damned reputation!"

Jefferson couldn't take any more. He was beside the chair, and his large, strong hands took both of hers in their tender grasp. "Don't torture yourself," he pleaded, forcing her eyes to meet the kindness and understanding in his.

"I'll never forgive myself."

"You were young. You said so yourself."

"And you pointed out that I was a woman, capable of making my own decisions, my own mistakes."

"We all make mistakes."

Coaxingly he pulled her out of the chair to sit next to him on the floor before the fire. He cradled her gently in the strength of his arms and rocked her softly. "It's all right," he murmured into the thickness of her shining black hair. "It's all right now. You're with me. . . ."

Chapter 5

IT WAS WELL AFTER MIDNIGHT BY THE TIME JEFFERSON FOUND himself in his bedroom, alone. It had taken him over an hour to calm Andrea and convince her to try and relax. He hoped that she would forget about her brother—at least for a while.

Thoughts, like demons, continued to play in his tired mind. He made a contemptuous sound, directed at himself, as he pulled on his pajama pants and played back all of the words of comfort he had whispered to Andrea in the cozy solitude of the den. The warm, seductive mood cast by the dying embers and the vulnerability of the woman in his arms had brought out tender, caring words of love that he couldn't possibly have meant. Somehow he had been able to calm Andrea, but now he could feel in his body all of the tension and guilt that had been lying dormant in hers. *God help me,* Jefferson thought as he flopped down on the large, oak bed and gazed, unseeing, out the window and into the windy, dark night. The rain had stopped beating against the roof, but still the gusty wind whistled against the interior of the island.

She was still in the shower. Jefferson could hear the hot water gushing through the ancient pipes of the house, and he could imagine the warm, clear rivulets of steamy water as they cascaded over her thick, raven hair to slide caressingly down the naked length of her creamy skin. The wayward thought issued restless stirrings in his body, and the same aching need that had bothered him since he had first seen her standing drenched on his doorstep, assailed him.

Angrily he rolled off the worn patchwork quilt, not caring that the bedclothes were rumpled or that his bare feet encountered the icy chill of the hardwood floor. He paced restlessly, rubbing the back of his neck, before finally resting at the foot of his bed to gaze thoughtfully out of the window at the ghostly clouds crossing the pearllike moon. The dark clouds, tangled as thickly as Jefferson's conflicting emotions, partially hid the moon and shadowed the island in the murky night. The sandy strip of beach, usually visible even in evening, was imperceptible to the naked eye.

All of the promises that Jefferson had uttered passionately to Andrea while she was lying vulnerably in front of the scarlet embers of the fire came back to haunt him. All of the whispered words of care and affection rang incessantly in his ears. Did he mean them? Could he possibly? After all of the years of doubts and mistrust? How could he fall victim to her so easily all over again? Why couldn't he just forget that she was sleeping in the next room?

A low moan from the pipes made Jefferson acutely aware of the moment when Andrea turned off the water in the bathroom. In his mind, brilliant, vivid flashes of imagination convinced him that she was stepping out of the tiled shower and buffing her body with the thick pile of the cherry-colored towel.

"Stop it!" he muttered aloud to himself, slamming a palm onto the oaken frame of the bed. He was being a damned fool! She had betrayed him once, and she would do it again. Why else would she wait ten years to show up?

In frustration, he threw himself back on the bed, forcefully attempting to drive all haunting thoughts of Andrea from his mind. It had been a long night, full of false promises and soul-searching. First the phone call from Lara, reinforcing Jefferson's concerns over the welfare of his child, and then Andrea, out of the past, out of the night, into his home . . . like a sea witch.

Andrea pulled on the T-shirt that Jefferson had given her as a substitute for a nightgown. She tried to ignore the smell of it. It seemed to exude that special, clean, virile scent that was uniquely Jefferson's. Andrea closed her eyes for a moment, breathing in the lingering scent, and found herself thinking about Jefferson's warm embrace and the soft commanding pressure of his fingertips against her body.

With a jerk she opened her eyes, discovering that she was blushing at her own image in the steamy mirror. Don't do this to yourself, she cautioned, knowing full well that all of the loving words that Jefferson had whispered to her in the den had only been to calm her. When she had quit sobbing against his shoulder, the gentle words had silenced, and the consoling motion of his hands against her shoulders had slowed. She had sensed that if she would have given him the slightest invitation, the gestures of solace could have heated into passion, and that Jefferson would have made love to her before the fire.

As it was, she hadn't encouraged him, afraid of the outcome, knowing that he would be able to see with his probing eyes what must be so utterly transparent: that she loved him with the same ardor of ten years before. She loved him.

After quickly drying her hair with the towel, she left the creamy-white tiled bathroom and padded, barefoot, into the bedroom that Jefferson had assigned to her. It was large, and the ceiling was comprised of open beams and aged, wooden planks. The walls were rough plaster, colored only with splashy seascapes. The bed, sitting regally in the center of the room, was a massive four-poster, complete with down-filled ticks that seemed to caress Andrea's skin in their light-weight fluffy thickness. This was the first night that Andrea had slept alone in the

immense Tudor home, and involuntarily her thoughts
rambled to Jefferson's room and the nights of unleashed
passion that they had shared together beneath the soft
folds of a hand-crafted patchwork quilt. Andrea couldn't
help but wonder how often he had shared his bed, *that*
bed, with his wife.

Don't think about it, she warned herself as she closed
her eyes against the soft comfort of the downy pillow.
After a few restless moments she drifted off to a fitful,
dream-filled sleep in which erotic images of Jefferson
sifted through her subconscious.

Jefferson found sleep elusive. His mind, reeling with
conflicting thoughts of Andrea and her brother, seemed to
throb with contempt for his ex-wife and worry he felt for
his daughter, Megan. The crowded images, along with the
disturbing knowledge that Andrea was only an unlocked
door away, made sleep impossible.

After three hours of frustration, he could stand the
charade no longer. The wind had died in the darkness, and
the silence in the large house seemed deafening. With
anger and hostility aimed primarily at himself, Jefferson
threw back the rumpled sheets and quilt and determinedly
strode across the room to the doorway. He hesitated only
slightly, and then, with his jaw set squarely in determination, he walked down the corridor, his footsteps echoing
against the wood. He didn't attempt to quiet his tread; it
would have been a foolhardy, useless gesture in his own
home. Andrea would soon find out that he was coming
anyway.

He opened the door to her room with a jerk, but the old
hinges creaked only slightly, and Andrea seemed undis-
turbed. Jefferson's heart began to thud recklessly against
his chest as his eyes became accustomed to the half-light
and he could see her face serenely resting upon the pillow.
The storm had quieted, and the moon cast a thin stream of
silver light through the window. In the dim ethereal glow
Andrea rested peacefully, her oval-shaped face surround-

ed by tousled black hair, a stark contrast to the milky-white pillowcase.

Jefferson reached out and grabbed the doorjamb to steady himself against the wave of emotions that washed over him as he looked down upon her. Resolutely he fought the growing urge to walk over to the bed, throw back the covers and crush her pliant body to his. Why, in heaven's name, after all of the torment that he had suffered at her hand, did he still feel the urgent, pressing need to make love to her? Why did he ache to feel her warm, supple body pressed rapturously beneath his until they were both spent in silkily perspiring afterglow? Earlier in the evening she had been so willing, so yielding against him. He felt the traitorous heat in his loins begin to swell at the vivid memory.

Andrea's dream gave way to wakefulness, and her eyes fluttered open against the darkness. For a moment she was disoriented. The large, unfamiliar bed with its cozy down coverlet was strange. The moon, silver and pale through the lead glass window, and the dull, constant thudding of distant waves crashing relentlessly against the shore was foreign to her. Where was she? Cold air in the room touched the light T-shirt that she was wearing, and she felt her nipples respond and tighten. Involuntarily she hiked the warm, feathery comforter more tightly around her neck, and she moved her head into a more comfortable position against the pillowcase. Still groggy, she blinked and realized that she wasn't alone. Her eyes locked with that of a man standing near the door.

The scream in her throat died before it reached her lips, as conscious, rational thought overcame her and she recognized Jefferson, the elusive lover of her dreams. Her cloudy mind, still drugged with sleep, instantly cleared. Jefferson's hazel eyes, shadowed in the dark room, reached out to her, begged for her understanding. Without breaking his gaze, she read his mind, and she rolled over slightly before pulling the coverlet open and boldly inviting him into her bed. The honesty and promise in her misty eyes assaulted him, but after a moment's hesitation and a great deal of self-deprivation and grit, he slowly inched backward out of the room. His eyes did not leave hers until he shut the door and she was alone again.

Andrea watched his retreating figure silently, and bore his rejection painfully. He was clad only in pajama bottoms, and the stark nakedness of his bare chest, strident with lean, supple muscles, stood out in the semi-darkness of the room. When he slammed the door of her room, effectively closing her away from him, Andrea cringed. She was sure that she could hear the clap of the door along with his anger echoing down the long corridors of the ancient house and reverberating in the night.

Jefferson spent the remaining few hours until the light of dawn in restless frustration, torturing himself with thoughts of Andrea. Conflicting emotions ripped him, and one moment he would decide that he could trust the raven-haired beauty, only in the next moment to discard the idea. Although his simmering passion for her refused to subside, he denied himself the pleasure of her bed, and waited impatiently for the long, dark hours of the night to slide toward morning. When the first dim rays of dawn pierced the darkness of his bedroom, he was still without a solution to his aching need for her.

His mind kept reminding him that Andrea was once again obviously setting Jefferson Harmon up for a fall. Why else would she appear on his doorstep so soon after the finality of his divorce, begging to see him? Angrily he remembered that Andrea had left him torn and naked to the world once before . . . ten years past. At the time she didn't seem to give a damn that he alone had to battle the scandal, including the pressures from both the public and the press. She had never once had the compassion within her to let him know that she was alive . . . that she was safe.

All of Jefferson's attempts to pursue her had been

thwarted, largely by her protective family. Her parents, shocked and shaken at the scandal, had effectively cut off all means of communication between their daughter and her lover-politician. Clay and Sylvia Monroe had been adamant, refusing him entrance into their home, denying his requests to see Andrea again. Although at the time Jefferson wanted desperately to bridge the abyss of misunderstanding that Martin's lies had hewn, it had been impossible. Andrea's parents made it clear that they never wanted their eldest daughter to see Jefferson Harmon again. In their opinion Jefferson was merely a scheming, egocentric politician bent on using and abusing their daughter.

Eventually Jefferson had given up his quest of Andrea, vowing to himself that he would never let another woman touch him or control his emotions with the same intensity as he had allowed Andrea to do. Until last evening Jefferson had been able to keep his promise to himself, but the sight of Andrea again had shaken all of ten years of bitter resolve.

After Andrea had left him, and he had no means by which to find her, Jefferson had decided that he would banish her from his memory forever, or at least until she decided to seek him out. And it had worked, until last night.

So here she was, planted as firmly back in his life as if she had never left him—despite all of his efforts to the contrary. The thought that bothered him more than anything else was the knowledge that he *wanted* her back in his life. But how could he trust her?

The flimsy excuse that her boss had supplied Andrea with didn't wash with Jefferson. There was no doubt that Andrea was sent with a message from Bryce Cawthorne, but there had to be more, much more, to the story. Jefferson had dealt with Cawthorne in the past, and Jefferson knew that the ex-actor, despite his flamboyant Hollywood life-style, was not necessarily a gambler. Bryce

Cawthorne expected more from Andrea's visit to Harmon island than one lousy phone call from Jefferson. It was obvious that Cawthorne wanted this interview, and badly. Cawthorne, with or without Andrea's knowledge, was banking on the intimacies of the past affair to aid his cause. Jefferson knew that Andrea's employer assumed that she would be able to persuade Jefferson, by any means possible, to do the interview.

Jefferson's reasoning explained only too well Andrea's willingness to surrender before the dying fire and in the morning darkness of her bedroom. She gave in much too easily. It wasn't that Jefferson doubted the flames of desire that blazed in Andrea's intelligent green eyes. Nor did he discount the fluttering beat of her naked pulse. It was her motives that bothered him and interrupted his sleep.

Although the thought tasted bitter to his mind, Jefferson realized that he no longer knew Andrea Monroe. In the last ten years she had matured and grown up. What kind of woman had she become? Was it possible that she would stoop to anything, including sleeping with a man she didn't care for, just to further her career?

Jefferson closed his eyes and gritted his teeth together in disgust at the incriminating thought. He didn't want to imagine Andrea as a callous businesswoman to whom hopping into bed with a man was all part of a "business deal." And yet, he no longer knew her. . . .

Pushing the bedclothes aside, Jefferson rolled over to sit on the edge of the bed, lost in thought. How desperate was Andrea? How far in debt were Bryce Cawthorne and Coral Productions? Were they really on the verge of bankruptcy, as Andrea had hinted, or did Bryce Cawthorne just smell the opportunity to sell expensive advertising minutes by splashing Jefferson Harmon's life before the American public? Jefferson's eyes narrowed suspiciously as he pulled on his jeans. Moving with swift decisiveness, Jefferson pulled on a work shirt and rolled up the sleeves. He had a lot to accomplish this morning. He had to find a way to probe more deeply into Andrea's mind in order to read her soul. If she really did care for him, that was one thing, but if she was indeed the fraud that he suspected, Jefferson intended to find out about it and expose her for the liar she was. Two could play this game of deception.

Andrea slowly opened a sleepy eye to the invasion of sunshine that was saturating the room with its golden rays. Groggy, she lifted her head and then remembered where she was . . . and with whom. The morning air was frigid, and the sheets, when Andrea moved against them, felt like ice. Quickly she slid out of the bed, tugged on the over-sized robe and slippers, and hurried over to the window to survey the damage of the storm.

From her vantage point on the wooden windowseat, Andrea watched the cold gray Pacific, calm after the zeal of the night's tempest. Pieces of debris from the sea had been deposited by the wild tide and were scattered along the sandy strip of beach below the cliff. Closer to the manor, above the rage of the water, fir branches that had broken loose from the trees near the stables littered the grounds, along with small dark shingles that had been torn from the roof of the house by the storm in its fury.

The turbulence of the Pacific Ocean had always fascinated Andrea, and now, as she watched the calm waves belie its wrath, she was once again in awe of its power. The changing face of the sea served to remind Andrea of the varying moods of the volatile yet kind man who resided in the house, the only man that she had ever truly loved.

A disturbance on the beach caught her eye, but only proved to be a slight altercation between two vying sea gulls. Shifting her gaze to the left, Andrea found that she was unable, from her window, to see the dock, as it was hidden by a protruding edge of the cliff. She opened the window and craned her neck, but still she was unable to spy the aged wooden pilings or assure herself that the motor-launch and the sailor were still docked and waiting for her. Cold sea air, freshened by the scent of recent rainwater, filtered into the room and felt invigorating against her skin.

She squinted against the morning sun as she remembered, hazily, that Jefferson had entered her room sometime late in the night. Her brow furrowed as she wondered if she had misread his intentions. It had seemed evident at the time that he had come into the room intent on making love to her, but something had stopped him. Perhaps in her slumbered state she had been too willing to comply. Perhaps it was too soon after his divorce, but for some unknown reason, Jefferson had rejected her once again. The sting of that refusal still burned hotly in her memory and against her cheeks. A feeling of deep humiliation and embarrassment welled within her as she realized that she and Jefferson had drifted too far apart on the seas of mistrust to ever be able to accept each other again.

Andrea pinched her lower lip against her teeth. It was obvious that she should have listened to the more sensible side of her nature and never have come to the island in the first place. Neither Bryce's requests, nor her own girlish fascination with Jefferson, should have colored her judgment. But they had. And she had succeeded in accomplishing nothing other than baring the disturbing emotions that she had kept safely locked within her for nearly ten long years.

Suddenly Andrea understood that it would have been better for her to have left the island last night, while she had the chance. The stormy sea would have been preferable and much less heart-wrenching than the storm of emotions that had battled within her ever since she had looked once again into Jefferson's enigmatic gaze.

Impatiently she closed the window and smoothed the wrinkled bed. Fortunately, she decided, she was leaving the island today, within the hour, and she would be able to put some much-needed distance between Jefferson's compelling magnetism and the traitorous desires of her body. Why was it that her body seemed always to overshadow her mind when she was close to him?

She plumped up a pillow, pulled the tick over it, and mentally forced the feeling of disappointment welling within her because she was leaving the island back to a far corner of her mind. Rather than dwell on the unsettling predicament and intense emotions that existed between Jefferson and herself, Andrea cinched the belt of the over-size robe more tightly around her waist and hurried downstairs. For a brief moment she thought of awakening Jefferson, but decided against it. What more was there to say?

Her clothes were still in the den, draped over the fireplace screen, and although they were probably wrinkled, they certainly would be dry and warm. She imagined herself running into the den, tugging on the skirt and sweater and sneaking out of the house before Jefferson's eyes met the morning light. She felt a twinge of guilt at the thought—the least she could do was say good-bye—but she dismissed it. Better to be gone when he awoke rather than face him when the wound of his rejection was still so open and fresh.

Andrea hurried quietly down the hall, past the closed door of Jefferson's room, to the head of the stairs. Hiking the long robe over her ankles, she began to descend the polished rosewood steps. The arguments of the night before pounded relentlessly against her head, and the comforting words of passion and love that Jefferson had murmured into her hair while they lay in embrace before the fire seemed to haunt her. Andrea knew that she had to avoid Jefferson. All of the caring words, the whispered promises, the loving endearments, were said only to placate her in the darkness, and wouldn't stand the bright light of the new day. She didn't want to bring up every-

thing that he had promised—not now. She couldn't bear to
have him feel obligated to her because of some thoughtless
promise in the night, and she knew that she couldn't stand
the punishment of his denials. She knew that he had
uttered words he couldn't possibly have meant, and he
knew the same, but she just couldn't stand the thought of
hearing it spoken aloud—from the same lips that had been
so compassionate and forgiving in the night.

She was almost at the bottom of the staircase, her hand
poised against the carved banister, when his voice called
out to her. At the sound of her name, uttered by the man
who meant so much to her, she froze, but after that first
arresting, heart-stopping second, she collected her poise
and rotated to face him.

Jefferson was standing on the landing above her, casually leaning over the railing, and regarding her with tired but
intense eyes. He seemed weary, though he attempted to
smile, and she surmised that he had slept no better than
she. The flash of his familiar half-smile, shadowed in the
darkness of an overnight's growth of beard, seemed to
welcome her, touch her.

"What are you doing up so early?" he drawled. His
hastily donned plaid shirt was rolled up at the sleeves and
gaped open, exposing an expanse of muscular, tanned
chest and a mat of thick, curling black hair. Andrea moved
her gaze from his bare skin upward to meet his direct and
inquiring gaze as he continued to speak. "I know," he said
with a wink. "You got up early because you wanted to
surprise me with breakfast in bed!"

"Dreamer," she laughed back at him. His lighthearted
tone was somehow infectious and chased away all of her
restless doubts. "You can't be serious."

"Oh, but I am. I always awaken ravenous . . . or don't
you remember?"

Her voice seemed to catch. "It's been a long time," she
murmured.

"Too long," he agreed, never letting his eyes move from

the feminine contours of her face. Andrea felt the house beginning to close in on her with his shadowed gaze.

"I think that I had better get ready to go."

"Why?" Slowly he began to descend the stairs. She waited, feeling her breath begin to constrict in her throat. "The least that you could do is have breakfast with me." He was standing one step above her, leaning against the banister, whisperingly close to her.

"Oh, Jefferson," she sighed, trying to get hold of her composure. "What's the point?"

"I think we have a lot to talk about."

"We tried that last night!"

"And you don't think we accomplished much?"

"Do you?" Her dark brows lifted as she turned to face him.

"You can't expect to solve ten years' worth of problems in one evening," he countered, rubbing his chin.

"I don't *expect* anything."

"Then why did you come here?" His voice was low and commanding, and his fingers found the soft flesh of her upper arm. She felt a warmth ooze from her at his touch.

"We went through this last night. I came here as a favor to my boss."

"Cawthorne?" Jefferson asked, his fingers tightening on her arm and a dark, guarded look deepening his gaze. "Do you grant him many?"

His abruptly savage tone startled her. "What?" she asked, hoping that she was misreading him.

"*Favors.* I asked you if you grant many to Bryce Cawthorne."

Her eyes narrowed as she caught the meaning of his words. "What are you suggesting . . . that I sleep with my boss? Dear God, Jefferson, is that what you think of me?" Angrily she pulled her arm out of his imprisoning hold.

"I don't know you . . . not anymore."

"So you just automatically think that I sleep with Bryce?" She was incredulous, indignant and incensed.

"Let's just say that it seems more than a little peculiar that you would wait for ten years in absolute silence, not once trying to contact me, and then, the minute your boss asks you to call on me, you jump at the chance." Jefferson leaned back against the railing, crossed his arms over his chest and cocked his head to one side, waiting for her response.

Her lips had thinned with her anger. "That's not exactly how it went."

"No?" His eyebrows raised as if to say, "enlighten me."

"You were married, remember?"

A dark cloud passed over Jefferson's face and wiped away his self-assured smile. "How could I ever forget?"

"I don't think that your wife would have appreciated my calling to chat with you about old times. Do you?"

"Lara has nothing to do with us," he maintained, his face muscles tight with strain. "And besides, what about the two years before I married Lara. Where were you then?"

Andrea shifted uncomfortably on the stairs, and some of her rage seemed to quiet. "I told you. Those two years were difficult for me, for my whole family, because of Martin."

"So you did," was the brief, succinct reply.

"Look, Jefferson," she began, her palms rotating expressively skyward. "I'm not trying to say that I handled the situation very well, but I'm not apologizing for my actions, either. I was too young, and it was a long time ago. Too many things have happened to you and me since then. I'm sorry I came here last night. It was a mistake."

"Do you honestly believe that?" he asked more gently.

The honesty in her light eyes challenged him. "I don't know what to believe."

Jefferson's lips pressed together thoughtfully, and his hand against the railing tapped nervously while he stared at her in ponderous silence.

"Perhaps we should start over."

Her heart stopped. "What?"

"Let's just start getting to know each other again. Today. What do you say?"

The change in his mood surprised her, but there was a wariness in his gaze that stopped the ecstatic surges that had begun to run through her blood. "I'm—I'm leaving soon."

He shrugged dismissively. "Not without eating. How about breakfast?"

The lightheartedness of his banter infected her and reminded her of a happier, more carefree time in her life. "All right," she agreed after only a moment's hesitation. "If you're doing the cooking."

"So much for my romantic fantasy of having breakfast in bed, served by a dark-haired sea witch," he said mysteriously as he took her hand and led her into the kitchen.

"You're living in the wrong century," she chided. "Don't you realize this is the nineteen eighties? You should be the one serving me breakfast in bed."

"Gladly," he replied fervently, and his face sobered.

"I don't think so," she quipped with a laugh that sounded as false as she felt. The burning sting of his rejection in the moonlight was too painful to be so easily forgotten. She wouldn't give in to temptation again.

The atmosphere in the cheery kitchen seemed to thicken with his probing, watchful stare. She knew that he was reading her thoughts. "I'm sorry about last night," he admitted, noticing the flaming blush on her cheeks.

"It's all right."

"No, I should never have come to your room."

Andrea lifted her chin slightly. "Why did you?" she asked as a trace of indignation lighted her pale eyes.

"I wanted to see that you were all right."

"No, Jefferson, that's not the reason that you were there, and we both know it. I don't expect much from you, but I do think that you owe me honesty. It was something we shared together in the past, and no matter what has come between us, I hope that now, today, we can be open with each other.

"The reason that you came into my room last night was because you wanted to make love to me. Don't try to deny it. A woman can read the passion in a man's eyes. But for some reason the minute that I awoke and offered to love you, you changed your mind." Andrea's short speech had rolled off of her tongue before she could really consider it. Jefferson had listened, not interrupting her. For a moment the silence was intense and oppressive as Andrea waited for his response.

"It's not a step to be taken lightly."

"I agree."

Again tense silence filled the room while they stood staring at each other. It was Andrea who managed to find her voice and drag her eyes away from the magnetic, enigmatic gaze of the man who still intrigued her beyond the limits of rationality.

"I thought you wanted breakfast."

"I do."

"Then just point me in the right direction, and I'll get started," Andrea suggested.

"I thought you expected me to cook."

Andrea's lips quirked into a smile. "Some other time. For now, why don't you go and get cleaned up, and I'll see if I can fix us some kind of a meal."

"You won't try to run out on me?" he asked pointedly as his fingers scraped against the thick hairs of his chin.

"Promise."

"Good."

In a moment, he was gone and she heard his feet treading overhead. Rather than allow herself to think or puzzle over him and his erratic behavior the night before, she busied herself in the kitchen. It was an immense room, equipped to handle even the most sophisticated of banquets. The countertops were made of cool dove-gray marble, and copper pots swung overhead from exposed beams in the ceiling. A cooking island graced the middle of the room and had the luxury of a small sink inlaid against rust-colored tile. The floor was of polished oak, with only one spot of wear beginning to mar the shiny patina near the sink. Andrea thought that the kitchen, though old, was every cook's dream, and she considered it a pity that it was no longer used to prepare lavish feasts.

While Jefferson was upstairs she put together a decent, if somewhat meager, meal from the leftovers she found in the pantry and refrigerator.

"Efficient, aren't you?" Jefferson noted as he walked into the kitchen and took in the domestic sight of Andrea frying slices of ham.

"Years of practice," she called over her shoulder as she pulled a hot tin of biscuits from the oven.

"You cook like this for yourself?"

"Hardly," was the dry reply. "I barely have time for toast and coffee before I head for the office. It's a forty-minute drive."

They sat opposite each other at the small café table near a bay window. After Jefferson ate heartily, he sipped the strong black coffee and regarded Andrea over the rim of his cup. Even after what must have been a mostly sleepless night, she carried herself with a serene pride that enhanced her natural beauty.

"Do you live alone?" he asked, setting his cup on the table.

"Yes. I had a roommate once, but it didn't work out."

A muscle twitched in Jefferson's jaw. "Why not?"

Andrea shrugged. "Different life-styles."

"Were you good friends?"

"Not particularly. Why?"

Jefferson frowned into his cup. "Just curious."

"Sally liked to hang out at the singles bars. I didn't. It became a problem, and I moved out." Andrea smiled in spite of herself, noticing the relief evident on Jefferson's face. Once again his eyes were searching her face, studying her intently.

After the dishes were done, Andrea became adamant about leaving the island.

"I've got to go," she stated, heading for the den to pick up her raincoat.

"No, you don't."

"I can't expect the sailor to wait for me all day long, can I?" she asked, pulling the thick curtain of her hair from beneath the collar of the pewter colored coat.

"You don't have to worry about him," Jefferson replied with an indifferent shrug.

"Why not? Do you think he's too hungover to get me back to Victoria in one piece?"

"No."

"Then?" Her question was tossed over her shoulder as she shrugged more comfortably into her coat and hiked the collar closely to her neck. Though the day was filled with shafts of November sunlight, it was still chilly, and Andrea had no doubt that the ride over the water toward Vancouver Island would be a cold one.

Jefferson's arm reached out and found hers before she opened the door. "I sent the seaman home, Andrea."

She whirled on him. "You did *what? Why?*"

"I wanted more time alone with you," he admitted, hating himself for his deception and duplicity. Why was he suspicious, and why did he want her so?

"Don't you think you should have asked me first?"

"I didn't want to disturb you."

"Right. Just like you didn't want to disturb me last night?" she accused sarcastically.

His jaw hardened. "I'm sorry about that."

She glared at him for only a minute before jerking free

from him, opening the door and running down the sandy path that led from the front of the estate toward the edge of the cliff. Once in sight of the sandy strip of beach she stopped and surveyed the gray tide frothing against the aged wooden moorings. The boat was gone.

She knew that Jefferson was beside her—she could feel his eyes boring into her—but she was angry and afraid. Angry that he had manipulated her, and afraid that being manipulated was exactly what she had wanted and expected of him.

"You should have asked me before you let my transportation leave."

"You're right, but you were sleeping, and the man was in a hurry to be on his way." The lie slid over his tongue easily. Too easily, he thought. But how could he explain to Andrea that he had sent the seaman packing just so that he could gain more time alone with her, to try and understand her, to try and trip her up in her own set of lies?

"But I owed him money."

"I took care of it."

Bewildered, she stared at the dark sea. "And how am I going to get back to Victoria?"

"I'll take you there."

"When?" She found herself wishing that he would say never, but she knew that the sooner she left Jefferson, the better it would be for her.

"I'm leaving myself this evening. I'll take you back then. Is that all right with you?"

"You haven't left me much choice, have you?" she countered.

"Did you really want one?"

"I like making my own decisions."

"Come on," he suggested, ignoring the rebellion in her eyes, "let's take a walk on the beach."

"Now?"

"It's a beautiful morning for it. Why not?"

He touched her lightly on the neck and she felt the anger and indignation of a few moments before begin to flow from her body. He was standing behind her, and his arms closed around her waist. "Come on," he prodded gently, lightly kissing her cheek. "Let's get to know each other again."

Chapter 6

AN UNSEASONABLY WARM BREEZE PUSHED ANDREA'S HAIR away from her face and pressed her rough skirt against her legs as she walked with Jefferson down the desolate ribbon of sand that served as a weak barrier between the jagged, rocky cliff and the blue ocean. Although she and Jefferson were alone, they walked slightly apart from each other in solitary concentration.

They were nearly to the far end of the beach before Jefferson reached down and picked up a rotten slat of wood on the sand and hurled it back to the sea from which it had drifted. Andrea couldn't help but notice the athletic slant of his body as he tossed the driftwood, nor could she ignore the passionate play of feelings that was evident in the tense, angular planes of his face. Jefferson stopped walking on the wet sand and watched the driftwood float in the foam of the tide before scratching the back of his head. He began to speak softly over the noise of the waves.

"Why haven't you asked me about Lara?" was his surprising question.

Andrea felt her own footsteps falter at the name of Jefferson's beautiful ex-wife. She bit her lip and shrugged her shoulders in feigned indifference. "I don't know. I guess I didn't want to pry."

"Even after the interrogation I gave you last night?" A rueful smile that didn't light his eyes flickered over his grim lips.

"Some things are better left unsaid, I suppose."

"Meaning that you're not interested?" Jefferson asked, thinking once again of the importance of the interview and Bryce Cawthorne.

"Meaning that I don't want to invade your privacy."

"You, the woman who wants me to do a national interview on television?" he scoffed.

"That's not me. It was Bryce's idea," Andrea maintained, not realizing that she had squared her shoulders automatically at Jefferson's accusations.

"It doesn't matter," he sighed. "I want you to know."

Andrea wondered if there was a way she could escape the intimacy of the conversation. The thought of Jefferson being married to another woman had always caused her pain, and she wasn't sure that she wanted to see more deeply into the secluded and intimate corners of his marriage.

"I'm not sure that you should be telling me any of this," she thought aloud, avoiding his intense gaze.

"Why? Do you intend to run back to Bryce Cawthorne with all of the juicy tidbits of information that I give you?"

"Of course not!"

"Good." There was still a flicker of doubt in his eyes, but he pushed his hands into his back pockets and once again began walking, head bent against the wind. To Andrea he looked older and more strained as he began talking about his wife.

"It was two years since I had seen you," Jefferson began, thoughtfully. "I had given up hope of ever seeing you again. The way I figured it, you didn't want to see me, or you would have made some attempt to contact me."

"I told you my parents put me in a private school."

"Save it, Andrea! You were over a thousand miles away from your father and mother. If you really would have wanted to get in touch with me, you could have called or written, for God's sake."

"I wanted to, really." Andrea sighed.

"Then why didn't you?" he demanded.

"I was afraid. My parents told me that you—"

"That I was just a cheap politician interested in taking advantage of you until another girl caught my interest, right?" His voice hardened, and his face muscles became rigid. "They told you that you would never be able to avoid scandal with the likes of me, isn't that so?"

Andrea's silence incriminated her. Jefferson gave his head a stern shake and muttered under his breath, "I thought so. They probably also told you that all I was interested in was a career."

Andrea closed her eyes against the truth Jefferson spoke, remembering her father's rough, uncompromising words about the evils of men and politics. Jefferson's next question startled her.

"Did they ever tell you that I had come looking for you?"

Andrea's footsteps on the sand suddenly stopped, and she turned her eyes upward to Jefferson's. The shocked expression on her face wasn't lost on him.

"I didn't think so," he snorted, and kicked violently at a rock on the beach. Then he looked beseechingly toward the cerulean sky. "Oh, hell, what does it matter anyway?"

Tentatively her hand reached out to touch his bare forearm. "You came to see me?" she asked quietly.

He jerked his arm roughly away from her sensitive touch. "Of course I did, Andrea. Damn it, I'm not exactly the bastard your parents made me out to be!"

"I always knew that."

Disgust was evident in his condemning look. "You couldn't prove it by me!"

Andrea felt her anger beginning to surface. One moment Jefferson was tender, the next unyielding. She felt as if she were caught in the middle of his conflicting storm of emotions. Her patience, worn thin by the depth of her feelings for such an uncompromising man, snapped. She turned on her heel as if to head back to the house. "Look, Jefferson, all of this bickering isn't getting us anywhere. I understand that you feel I ran out on you ten years ago, and I guess you have that right. But what I don't understand is why you continue to bring me up just to push me down. One minute I think that you want to get along with me, the next minute we're arguing again. I'm tired of it, and I'm going back to the house to wait for you. Or better yet, I'll call for a launch to come and get me. That way I won't be of further inconvenience to you!"

"Don't go."

"I'm not about to stay here to suffer any more of your sarcastic remarks about the past. It's over. . . . Let it go!"

"And what about the future?"

"I haven't really given it much thought," she admitted, "other than to worry about my job."

"Is it that serious at Coral Productions?"

"Would I be here if it weren't?" she murmured.

"Now, that's an interesting question," he mused. "What do you think?"

"I don't honestly know." Her clear green eyes clouded with the question.

Jefferson took Andrea's hand in his and urged her to continue walking with him. At first, she made a feeble attempt at resistance, but finally found herself walking near him, letting her shoulder touch his, letting his fingers control hers.

"I was going to tell you about Lara."

She didn't comment, and an uneasy feeling began to grow in the pit of her stomach. She didn't like the easy way his ex-wife's name rolled off of his tongue.

Jefferson's mouth pulled into a tight frown as his eyes narrowed in memory. "I met Lara a little over a year after the scandal about us had occurred. At first I thought it was going to be the same type of situation, because the minute that the papers got wind of the fact that I was dating one of San Francisco's socialites, they dredged up all of the business concerning you and me, including the alleged pregnancy and abortion." A muscle that had been twitching near the corner of Jefferson's jaw became rigid.

"Lara must have known about you, because while I was dating her, the gossip sheets were covered with speculations as to what had become of you." Andrea nodded at the memory. Even in the small town of Forest Grove, Oregon, she had seen articles in the papers, and several of her close friends had realized who she was and what her relationship had been to California's youngest and most attractive male senator. Andrea pushed the faded memory aside as Jefferson continued to speak.

"It wasn't that Lara was so fascinating, although at the time we got along. It was the timing that was important, I guess," he said with evident disbelief in his own words. "Anyway, at that time in my career, especially after the national coverage of my romance with you, my campaign manager advised me to change my image, to become more of a conformist, avoid rocking the boat politically. One of his ideas, which I discounted at the time, was that I marry and start a family—establish a more stable personal life that would reflect well on my public image."

"No!" The disbelief in Andrea's voice couldn't be disguised. "You married because it was a politically sound move? I—I don't believe it!"

"People get married for many reasons, Andrea."

"What about love, Jefferson? Isn't that the best reason?"

"I couldn't say—not personally."

"But to further your career—"

"It's no worse than knocking on someone's door in the middle of the night, dredging up old, near-forgotten memories . . . for the sake of a career, is it?" Jefferson demanded, his fingers tightening around Andrea's hand.

"But *marriage*, Jefferson. You can't possibly compare

what I've done in the last few hours to what you did—marrying for the sake of your career!"

"I gave up on believing in love when you left me," he asserted.

Andrea was silent and her stomach was churning as she realized how deeply and irretrievably she had scarred the man that she loved. No words could assuage his bitterness. No explanation would suffice. No embrace could ever erase his disdain for love.

"There's more to it than that, anyway," Jefferson began again, interrupting Andrea's dark thoughts.

"What?"

"Lara. She wanted to get married, was anxious, in fact. I guess it was balm to her frail ego that she could snare an up-and-coming politician. From the moment we were married, she was more interested than I in my political aspirations." He shook his head in disgust. "I even think that she fantasized about being the first lady. Ridiculous!"

His eyes grew darker and looked almost deadly. "It was a mistake from the beginning. She didn't care for me any more than I cared for her. I suppose that I was as much to blame as she, because when I realized what a mistake I had made, rather than admit it and seek a divorce, I just engulfed myself deeper in my work, my career. For a while it worked. I kept myself busy with political meetings, and she kept up a lively social schedule. It wasn't much of a marriage, but we both kept out of each other's way, for the most part."

"Then what went wrong?" Andrea asked, clearly puzzled.

"She got pregnant."

Andrea swallowed with difficulty. "You didn't want the baby?" she stammered, remembering the lies that Martin had spread about a false pregnancy.

Jefferson smiled sternly. "No, that wasn't the problem. Although the baby wasn't planned, I was really very happy about it, and I thought that Lara was too. She seemed happy, at first, until she lost her figure to the pregnancy. . . ." Jefferson's dark brows drew together in concentration, as if he were still trying to piece together a puzzle. "I didn't really understand it . . . not at the time.

"When Megan was born, I was ecstatic. It was the first time that I had ever found any real happiness or satisfaction in the marriage. Lara probably understood that, too. But the more hours I spent with Megan, the more I wanted to have with her. She became the single most important thing in my life—even more valuable than my career."

An inner tension, boiling and threatening to explode, was evident on Jefferson's sharp features. He rubbed his chin thoughtfully, as if trying to calm himself, as he squinted into the horizon. Andrea could feel Jefferson's strain flowing into her, through the warmth of his coiled fingers, and she felt as if she were an unwanted intruder into the dark, private corners of his life. A cold feeling of dread settled against her shoulder blades.

"It doesn't take a doctorate in psychology to understand why Lara began drinking," Jefferson whispered, and Andrea felt a wave of shock ripple through her at the mention of Lara's alcoholism—a condition, never proved but often speculated on by the press. "Although it was never my intention, I neglected her," he admitted. "After the baby was born, everything changed. Lara was still very much in the social spotlight, a privilege that she had always held dear, but she wanted more from me than she ever had in the past, and I suppose she really did deserve more attention. I just didn't realize it, not at the time. All of my love and my attention revolved around Megan, and of course, my political aspirations." He closed his eyes as if he wanted to shut out the truth. "You see, other than Megan, the only other importance I saw in my life was becoming California's governor."

Jefferson and Andrea had come to the end of the narrow strip of beach, and he gently led her up a gradual, sloping path. She didn't speak, not wanting to ask him about his life with his ex-wife and daughter. She was afraid to know, and yet she was very intrigued.

"It was a stupid goal."

"No," Andrea shouted without thought, once again remembering Jefferson as she had first seen him, the incredibly perfect aspiring political contender. Jefferson was *meant* to be a leader.

"I had my priorities twisted," Jefferson continued, ignoring her vehement protest. "I should have looked into my life and found what was valuable. I should have realized what I was doing to Lara."

"It wasn't your fault!"

"No? She wasn't an alcoholic when I met her. I have to assume some of the responsibility for her illness. At that time I did nothing to try and discourage her feelings of inadequacy. Without knowing it I was partially to blame."

Jefferson shook his head in disgust, and Andrea knew that his contempt was aimed at himself. "Suddenly my little world began to fall apart, or so I thought. I should have seen it coming, noticed the warning signals, but I didn't. Instead, what had started out as an acceptable, if stagnant and loveless marriage, had smoldered into a living hell. Lara and I began to fight bitterly. We were constantly at each other's throats.

"Somehow we managed to hide most of the battles from Megan and the press. And it was my opinion at the time that, for Megan's sake, it was better for Lara and I to stay married. And Lara knew it. She thought that I would never want to divorce her because it would reflect badly on my career, but the only reason that I stayed married to her was because of Megan.

"It wasn't long before Lara began taking lovers, but I was so angry about the poor mother she had become that I didn't give a damn who she slept with, as long as she was discreet. My only concern was that Megan would find out, or that the press would get wind of it." Jefferson's eyes smoldered in suppressed rage. "I never wanted either of us—me or Lara—to hurt our child!" He looked prayerfully up at the sky. "I was a fool in that respect. How I thought I could hide anything from the press was a mistake." He shook his head and pushed a wayward lock of dark hair out of his eyes.

"It was during the gubernatorial race that I began to suspect that she had a drinking problem. I was too blind to have seen it before, but suddenly it was very apparent. I found hidden bottles . . . she was often unclear in her thinking . . . her speech was thick. Damn!" His palm slapped the worn jeans over his thigh. "If only I hadn't been so wrapped up in my work . . . in *myself!*

"I suggested psychiatry; she ignored me, and told me that I was being ridiculous. Somehow she managed to pull herself together during the election, and despite a flurry of rumors instigated by the opposition, I was narrowly elected as governor. That's when I made another mistake. I had tried to convince myself that after we had moved into the governor's mansion, and she began practicing the role of governor's wife, she would snap out of her depression and put her bottles and her lovers aside. I was wrong."

"So you decided to resign?" Andrea asked, her voice catching.

"Not quite. I suggested counseling again, but of course, it fell on deaf ears. But then, within a year of taking over the responsibilities of governor, I decided that I had to find a way to overcome her alcoholism, no matter what the cost. It didn't matter that I didn't really love her. I had always cared something for her, and she was Megan's mother—my wife."

Andrea felt herself cringe at the intensity of his words. He was speaking as if he were alone, talking to himself. For a moment he was silent, but finally spoke again, this time posing a question.

"Have you read the clippings about my ex-wife lately?" he asked, a tinge of acrimony touching his words as his eyes sought and found Andrea's gaze.

"Some."

"Then you know that I failed. I tried everything money could buy, from expensive drying-out sessions at secluded hospitals in Marin County, to a private nurse in the governor's mansion. But I was stupid!"

"Why?"

"Because I didn't realize that money couldn't buy Lara's willingness to combat the alcohol. And the worst part of the entire mess was that Megan was becoming increasingly aware that, at times, there was something wrong with her mother! Do you know, can you possibly imagine, what it feels like to try and explain to a four-year-old child that her mother is sick because she drinks too much? It wasn't possible to hide the truth, even if I had wanted to. Megan is a bright child and she could see the effect of the booze on her mother. She could *sense* how deep and traumatic Lara's problem was!" Anger and suppressed rage surfaced on his face, darkening his eyes. "How long could I protect my daughter with feeble excuses and vague answers to her questions?" Jefferson's stony gaze impaled Andrea.

"I don't know . . ."

"Neither did I! There seemed no way to battle the problem effectively and it was beginning to have adverse effects on Megan. What little family life we had shared together was being destroyed, day to day. The harder I tried to persuade Lara to get help, the more determined she was to fight me, and the more bitter she became." He paused, thoughtfully. "I suppose, in retrospect, that I was a catalyst for Lara's rebellion. For the first time since we were married, Lara was commanding most of my attention. I was paying more attention to her than I was to my career . . . or even Megan."

"When I realized that everything else I had attempted to do for Lara had failed, in a final effort to save the marriage, I decided to resign the governorship. It seemed to be the right thing, the only thing I could do to protect my family . . . my child. My turbulent personal life was making a mockery of my responsibilities as governor, and I felt that it was in the best interests of both the state of California and my family to resign and end the speculation and gossip about my family. I had hoped that a more quiet, peaceful life would bring Lara out of her moody depressions and, perhaps, give a more normal, stable existence to Megan. I was foolish enough to believe that it just might work. We certainly had enough money, and I knew that I could always go back to practicing law."

"But the resignation didn't go as planned," Andrea guessed, feeling icy wisps of dread tease her spine.

Jefferson shook his head as if trying to dislodge an unpleasant memory. "It backfired! When I told Lara about my intent to resign, she lost what tenuous control on herself she had maintained. She was livid, appalled that I would even consider such drastic, socially unacceptable action, and she tried her best to talk me out of it. I don't really think that she took me seriously. Not at the time. She wasn't convinced until she saw the actual resignation on television. To Lara, it was the ultimate humiliation, a public admittance of *my failure*—a social embarrassment!"

"Oh, dear God," Andrea murmured fervently, seeing all too well in her mind's eye the pain and humility that Jefferson had suffered. For a while she and Jefferson walked in silence, picking their way up the overgrown path. Jefferson seemed lost in his own dark thoughts of the past, and Andrea sensed the simmering tension that had taken hold of him with his reminiscence. So intent had she been on his story that she hadn't realized their eventual destination. Now, as she stepped over the final small crest in the hill, she stopped dead in her tracks. Jefferson was leading her to the same fateful ledge where they had first sealed their love, ten years ago. She felt as if all of the air had been driven out of her lungs as her eyes looked over the calm expanse of ocean, just as she had when she was barely twenty. She wetted her lips, hoping somehow to alleviate the parched feeling in her throat.

"You remember?" she asked, in a raw, emotion-filled voice. She lifted her eyes to witness his reaction. Why was he bringing her here, back to the place where all of the love and pain had begun?

The severe smile that curved over his lips didn't reach the hazel depths of his eyes. "Yes," he whispered, pulling her nearer to him, "I remember." For a moment he drew his eyes away from her captivating gaze and looked skyward in supplication as he shook his head. "I've tried to forget," he admitted. "But I couldn't. You don't know how many times I wished I could forget you—hoped that I could erase you from my mind." His whisper was filled with self-deprecation. "You couldn't begin to guess how much I wanted to forget you." At the thought his entire body tensed, and Andrea was pressed forcefully against his long, hard frame. His strong arms wrapped more urgently around her, crushing her against him. "I wanted to forget you," he moaned. "Dear God, how I tried."

Andrea felt as if he were about to say more, to explain his feelings for her, but if so, he quickly changed his mind. His palms spread across the small of her back, pushing every inch of her body against his. They stood on the ledge together, her legs braced by his, her breasts crushed against his chest, his chin resting against her forehead. Andrea could feel his tense muscles against her, warming her in spite of the cool November breeze that ruffled his hair and lifted her skirt.

Andrea floated backward in time on distant memories. The salty air, cool and fragrant, touched her face, just as it had in the past. Jefferson held her impatiently, rigidly against him, the way he had in her dreams. The surf roared in the distance, just as it had when this man had first taken her.

Slowly, as if his thoughts had taken the same path as hers, his grip on her slackened, and his hands came upward to cup her chin. His head lowered, and his lips, cool when they touched hers, quickly heated with smoky desire.

"I want you, Andrea, just as much as I did the night that we first made love." Andrea felt her knees weaken as his lips brushed slowly, seductively over hers in unhurried, lazy strokes. Involuntarily she let her head fall backward, grateful for the feel of his kisses against her face and throat. She sighed into the wind and slowly clasped her hands behind his neck.

His kisses, soft and insistent, moistened a trail down the soft column of her throat to rest where the neck of her sweater barred further exploration. He pinched the sweater between his teeth and pulled it away from her neck, allowing a cool whisp of air to float downward against her shoulders. She shuddered and he released the sweater, only to bury his head between her breasts. His words, torn from his throat to burn against her skin, were muted. "Let me love you again," he pleaded. "Let me make love to you, here, as we did in the past, until we can forget everything else."

It was a plea, and Andrea wanted desperately to give in to him, to recapture all of the beauty and love of the past, if only it were possible. She felt her resistance weaken and her muscles begin to relax in his embrace. He must have sensed her invitation because she felt his breath, hot and damp, against her sweater.

Andrea sighed as Jefferson lifted his head to capture her mouth with his. Their lips met and molded together in a wet, sweet embrace. Andrea hardly noticed the sensation of falling backward. She was only vaguely aware of the feel of cool sand through her clothing; so intent was she on the feel of the man bending over her, the man pressing her against the ground, the man she had never stopped loving.

A passion she had once suspected of having died began to live in her again. Familiar yearnings, buried for ten years, spread throughout her body, warming her against the early November morning. His lips, erotically familiar, kissed a path of forgotten promises across her cheeks and neck. She felt a new, pulsing warmth in her veins curl upward through her body until a soft, rosy blush colored her skin. Willingly her mouth parted in silent invitation to his insistent tongue, and she felt a shudder of anticipation quake through her as he explored the most intimate regions of her mouth. Her tongue met the passion in his and rose to intimately entangle with it. He groaned as he felt her submission.

"Let me love you," he whispered against her ear, repeating his pleading demand, as he slid the coat, which had been unbuttoned, off her shoulders.

"Jefferson . . . I . . ."

"Shhh, don't think, just love me," he persisted as he continued to kiss her.

I do, she thought to herself. I always have. Oh, God, Jefferson, if only you could guess how fervently I love you! Her response never got past her lips, because she knew that it didn't matter. It hadn't mattered in the past, it couldn't possibly now. They had no future together. And yet they had today, this morning, right now, beneath the warm Pacific sun.

His lips were persistent as they seemed to melt against her throat. They moved slowly, insistently against her chin. Despite the cowl neck of the sweater, he plunged onward, pulling the warm fabric away from her neck to allow his enticing lips to seek and find the pulse that fluttered deep in the hollow of her throat. His tongue rimmed the delicate circle of bones at the base of Andrea's throat and moved restlessly against the confinement of her sweater.

An aching need began to bloom within Andrea's body. Warm bursts of liquid fire raced through her veins and flooded her senses. The gentle persuasion of Jefferson's hands moving in circular patterns against the small of her back and his hot lips rubbing insistently against the barrier of her sweater began to arouse a yearning that Andrea couldn't deny. Involuntarily she arched against him.

Jefferson pulled his head away from her neck to gaze into the passion-clouded green depths of her eyes. A smile of satisfaction softened the planes of his face. "It hasn't changed for you, either," he murmured. "You want me as much as I want you."

"I've always wanted you," she admitted, saying what she had attempted to deny for ten years.

"You are a witch, aren't you?" His eyes never left her face as he tugged the cashmere sweater from the waistband of her skirt. Slowly his fingers wedged between the soft fabric and her warm flesh. She closed her eyes against the sweet, passionate desire that was growing within her at his persuasive, gentle touch. She sighed contentedly as Jefferson lifted her torso from the ground and pulled the sweater over her head. For a moment their gazes locked, and then he let his eyes move over her partially nude body. He gasped at the sight of her breasts, two softly rounded mounds, pushed together by the filmy white fabric of her bra. He groaned and let his face fall between them, softly kissing the top of one and then the other. His hands pushed the soft flesh more closely to his cheeks as he sighed against her.

Andrea let out her breath, and she cradled Jefferson's head against her as if she never wanted to let go. Her fingers entwined in the thick curls of his hair as she kissed the top of his head and murmured his name over and over.

With agonizing languor his thumbs moved against the lacy fabric of her bra, enticing her nipples to strain against the silky garment. The intimate circles his thumbs created started a whirlpool deep within Andrea, and she felt as if the center of her being was being slowly drawn from her.

Jefferson lowered his head and took the clasp of her bra in one hand. His lips grazed and teased her skin as, slowly and surely, he unhinged the wispy material and the bra parted, letting Andrea's breasts free to feel the cool Pacific air and the heat of Jefferson's torrid breath. He took one soft globe in his hand and kissed it as he kneaded the soft flesh. Torrents of lava singed her blood as he softly took a nipple in his mouth. His tongue caressed it, sliding wetly against the taut, ripe skin.

With his free hand he reached behind her and pushed against her back, pressing the firm muscles forward, thereby thrusting more of her breast into his expectant mouth. It was as if he couldn't get enough of her—as if he wanted to devour every inch of her. His tongue stroked and teased at her breast, nudging her higher and higher in the euphoric satisfaction that he wanted her, needed her—perhaps loved her.

He found the other breast, and as if to apologize for ignoring it, he took it hungrily in his mouth to suckle and nip at with renewed fervor.

The ache that was growing in Andrea spread upward and a sleek film of sweat converged in dewy droplets over her skin. Her fingers reached up and began to unfasten the buttons of Jefferson's shirt expertly, as if it had been only yesterday when she had last undressed him. The shirt parted and slid unnoticed to the ground.

Andrea opened her eyes to gaze at him. His physique was as muscular and athletic as she remembered; tanned to a deep bronze that was darkened by the thick, near-black hairs on his chest. Her fingers caressed his flesh, and electric currents seemed to pass from him as she touched his darkened male nipples. He lifted his head and boldly she pulled him down on her, letting her lips taste the salty maleness of his chest as she kissed the flattened muscles. He groaned when she took a male nipple in her mouth and gave him the same pleasure he had sparked in her.

"Dear God, Andrea," he sighed, "what are you doing to me?" He closed his eyes and fell victim to the pleasure that she was creating. His voice was rough with denied passion. "What have you always done to me?"

He rolled backward on the sand and pulled her over

him. His hands dipped below the waistband of her skirt to brush against the hill of her buttocks, only to retreat for an instant. And then, in a moment of total abandon, Jefferson jerked the skirt off of her and pushed her legs free of her boots. Savagely he ripped off her panties and held her against him, naked in the sun.

"Undress me, Andrea," he whispered into her ear. "Take off my clothes and let me lie with you naked to the world."

A thousand tingling sensations coursed through Andrea's body as she slowly undid his belt and lowered his jeans from his body. Thrills of excitement awakened within her as she touched his skin and slid the pants off him. Her eyes roved boldly over his body, noting the way his muscles tensed at her light touch and the glowing film of perspiration that glistened against his tanned skin. She saw all of him and realized just how anxious he was for her. But he waited, slowing the pace of their lovemaking, expanding the sensual experience.

"Come here," he whispered as she finished undressing him. He was still lying on the ground, propped by only one elbow. She lifted her gaze, and as her eyes locked with the stormy intensity of his, Andrea reached up and touched one lean, firmly muscled shoulder. His muscles tensed expectantly, displaying the flat contours of his chest and stomach.

As Andrea watched him Jefferson swallowed with difficulty but held her gaze steady. He held his lower lip in his teeth as if attempting to restrain himself. With one finger he touched her cheek and brushed away an errant strand of wayward black hair that had been caught in the brisk morning wind.

"This is the time to stop," he told her, giving her one last avenue of escape.

"Do you want to?" she asked, suddenly chilled.

Again the muscles in his arms flexed, and he expelled a gust of wind from his lungs. For a moment he seemed

suspended in time, but just as quickly he came to life. His
smile was almost boyish in its charm. "Do I want to stop
making love to you?" he echoed as he grabbed a fistful of
sand and let the minute crystals slide through his fingers.
"I don't think I could."

"Then don't—not ever," Andrea whispered, letting her
palm caress his cheek.

He took her hand in his and pressed a wet, passionate
kiss to her hand before gently pulling her to him. "I
won't," he promised as he rolled her onto her back and
she felt the cool, damp sand press against her. Her hair
splayed out in shiny black ringlets on the ground, and
Jefferson paused for a moment to gaze upon her. He
looked down past her wide, smoky-green eyes, past the
alluring tilt of her chin, past her rosy-tipped breasts, taut
in the autumn air, to rest on her soft, warm flesh. Then
slowly his eyes took in the rest of her, including the
seductive curve of her hips and the tight, firm muscles of
her calves. Lying naked in the morning sun, embracing
him as she had in the past, Andrea appeared more alluring
and inviting than Jefferson could ever have imagined. He
silently damned himself for his impetuous need of her. She
was beginning to capture him, body and soul, just as she
had in the past. Was it possible to ever get enough of her,
he wondered to himself as his passionate gaze swept over
her supine form. Could he use her, make love to her, until
he was satiated, and somehow drive her out of his mind
forever? She seemed so willing. Wouldn't it be wiser to
keep her on the island and make love to her until he was
exhausted and she was expunged from his blood?

Another look into her deep, unguarded stare, and
Jefferson cast all of his conflicting emotions and lingering
doubts to the cool Pacific wind. There was something
about Andrea Monroe that set her apart from any woman
he had ever met, and Jefferson knew instinctively that it
would be impossible for him to ever get enough of her
despite whatever seemingly insurmountable barriers had

grown between them. As man and woman they were physically attracted to each other—mutually entwined. He hadn't been able to get her out of his mind for the last ten years, and he knew that the next ten would be no different. She was part of his blood.

Slowly Jefferson lowered his body over Andrea's form. His fingers started well down the length of her leg, lightly stroking the curve of her calf and the outside of her thighs. Her reaction was to suck in her breath and close her eyes, thinking only of his fingers and the hot path that was being traced over her rib cage to linger at her throat. He kissed her neck, the hollow between her breasts and the soft skin of her abdomen.

When she moaned with pleasure, his hands traveled up the inner sides of her thighs, gently touching the muscles in warm, sure strokes. Andrea shifted her hips upward, feeling the coiling heat in her body begging for release. Jefferson's hands took hold of her hips and he kissed the skin near her navel before gently pushing her legs apart with his knee. Still he didn't take her. This time, after waiting for ten long, agonizing years, he was going to make her want him with the same urgency that controlled him.

"Please . . ." Andrea murmured, knowing that he could soothe the ache that was burning within her. "Jefferson, please . . ."

His eyes fell from the passion of her gaze to embrace the white soft fullness of her breasts. The cool autumn nip of the sea air and the persuasive touch of his hands made her sigh in yearning. Expertly he toyed with her, letting his inflamed eyes and gentle fingers tease her until she thought she would go insane with her desire for him. His lips dipped and brushed her sensitive skin until at last, just as she thought she would cry out with desire, his mouth descended over hers and he settled comfortably between her parted thighs.

She moaned against him, holding his head firmly in her

hands and entwining her fingers in his thick, rich, near-black hair. She pressed him more tightly to her, as if she would never let go. Her body arched against him as the burning passion in her veins melted to the deepest core of her. Her breath became shallow, and her heart thundered in her chest.

When Jefferson realized her need, the teasing and game playing were finished. It was as if the moment that she felt herself lost to him, he sensed her complete surrender and could deny himself no further. She felt him press close to her, sealing her to him. There was only one weighty pause in the lovemaking, and Andrea opened her eyes to see a flicker of hesitation cross his hazel gaze, but in a minute it was gone, and once again Jefferson's impassioned lips found hers in a bruising, insistent kiss. The kisses that plundered her lips were urgent demands that fired her pulse and fueled her need.

His hands and fingers stroked and caressed her as she felt the weight of his body settle upon her. In one breathless instant he broke the fragile barrier that he alone had crossed in the past. He came to her, pushing himself against her, filling her need in deep, swift strokes that drove her further and further into a dizzying, sensual pleasure that took her breath away. She felt the air constrict in her throat as he gently lifted her into a reeling, pleasure-filled world that warmed her from the inside out.

His breathing became labored as the tempo of his sweet rhythm increased into a throbbing, burning, unyielding demand that enticed a warm, moist response from her most feminine core.

"Oh, Andrea," Jefferson groaned, his voice raw in his despair, "I've wanted you for so long . . . so long." His voice trailed off and was lost against the sound of the crashing waves and Andrea's own labored breathing. The intensity of his desire increased until she felt herself begin to melt and Jefferson's answering explosion of surrender.

"Oh, God," she sighed nearly inaudibly as she lay spent

in his arms. Was it happiness or fear that forced a lump into her throat? Tears filled her eyes.

It was in the long, silent moments afterward, when her rapid breathing had slowed, and the serenity of afterglow had begun to fade that Andrea came floating back to the present and the realization that she, once again, had willingly been captured in the same alluring trap that had ensnared her so completely in the past.

Chapter 7

"It's time for us to leave." Jefferson voiced the dread that had been welling in Andrea the entire afternoon. After their lovemaking above the calm Pacific Ocean, Andrea had found it difficult to think of anything other than spending time with Jefferson, and all too quickly the peaceful day was gone.

Dusk was brewing as Jefferson loaded his suitcases into the motor launch that was moored in a sheltered cove not far from the dock. He helped her into the small craft and then manuevered the boat away from Harmon Island and toward the distant lights of Victoria. Even through the purple-colored dusk, the lanterns of the city were visible, and soon the small vessel had crossed the gray stretch of salt water that separated Jefferson's Canadian retreat from the larger land mass of Vancouver Island.

As Jefferson docked the boat in the marina he took Andrea's hand and helped her out of the craft. "I'll take you to dinner," he suggested. His face was cold, as if he dismissed the afternoon as something in the past.

"It's not necessary," Andrea murmured, beginning to feel a twinge of the loneliness that was bound to assail her when Jefferson was gone. Hurriedly he hailed a passing cab.

"Of course it is," he refuted. His smile, though distant,

was sincere, and Andrea was forced to answer with one of her own.

"If you insist."

The drive to the town house was quick and silent. While Jefferson waited downstairs, Andrea hurried up the polished staircase to shower and change. It felt wonderful to wash the salt and sand from her long black hair and skin.

The emerald green jersey dress was perfect for the evening—sophisticated yet sexy. Its soft folds molded to Andrea's curves, displaying just the right hint of femininity. The wide boat neck showed off her collarbone and a little shoulder, and the slit of the skirt flirted at Andrea's knees, exposing a touch of her leg.

Jefferson's appreciative glance as she hurried down the stairs gave Andrea some of the confidence that had been ebbing from her since twilight had descended upon the city. Somehow it had seemed that once in the charming city of Victoria, Jefferson had become withdrawn and brooding again. Andrea could feel the barriers that they had broken during the day begin to build between them.

"What are you trying to do to me?" he asked as she reached for her coat.

"What do you mean?"

"Oh, Andrea," he sighed, taking the coat from her hands and tossing it over the arm of a velvet sidechair. Passionately he pulled her against him, holding her so tight that she found it difficult to breathe. His kiss, burning with renewed desire, took the wind from her with its fire. She felt drawn into the circle of his intense need.

When the kiss ended, it was Andrea who backed away from his embrace, forcing herself to get a grip on her emotions. With only a touch of Jefferson's hand, or a lingering kiss from his lips, she fell victim to him.

He felt her restraint, and as he helped her with her coat, his voice whispered into her ear. "Regrets?"

"About today?"

A curt nod was his only response as he opened the door and they stepped into the ghostly glow of the lanterns.

"No. I have no regrets," she replied.

He cocked a dark, questioning black brow over his stormy hazel eyes.

"Really," she explained, hurriedly.

"But . . . ?" he prodded, sensing her hesitation.

"But it reminds me of the past, and I'm not sure that either one of us should think about it."

"We can't escape it."

"But we don't have to *relive* it."

"Then you do have regrets," he stated with finality.

Only that things hadn't turned out differently for us, she thought to herself. Andrea hiked the collar of her coat more closely to her neck to ward off the chill of the night. Without a thick bank of fog the temperature of the town had dropped considerably since nightfall.

Jefferson noticed Andrea's gesture to ward off the cold, and though his lips were set in a thin, grim line of determination, he placed a comforting arm over her slim shoulders and rubbed his hand up and down her upper arm, as if to give her warmth. Rather than take a cab, he insisted that they tour the waterfront on a double-decker bus, and before long Andrea felt the tension and strain begin to leave her body. Both she and Jefferson became swept up in the charm of the London-like city with its illuminated, ivy-covered brick buildings, horse-drawn carriages and incredible view of the ocean. They stopped to eat at a local fish-and-chips house on the waterfront and spent a relaxing evening drinking imported beer and eating the specialty of the house. The small restaurant, with its weathered pine interior, checkered tablecloths and candles lighting the tables, seemed homey and charming. A cheery fire near the bar added warmth and character to the old establishment.

Andrea secretly wished that the evening would never end. She was swept up in the romance of the tidy little pub, the smiling man seated opposite from her, and the dark promise of the night. From their table she was able to look across the black water into the night, or see the reflection of the fire in the paned windows.

Jefferson glanced at his watch and tossed his napkin onto the table. "I've got to go soon," he whispered.

"Can't you stay?" she asked impetuously.

His smile was harsh as he took her hand in his. "No. I have an important matter to clear up."

"Megan," Andrea guessed, her eyes meeting his.

"Yes. Megan." He drew his hand away from hers and rubbed his chin savagely as he looked out over the black water. "I have to get her away from Lara before something happens."

"You're afraid for her."

"Yes. Wouldn't you be?"

Andrea didn't know what to say. "I don't think that Lara would hurt her."

Jefferson's eyes sparked. "Of course she wouldn't! Not intentionally! But haven't you been reading the papers? Lara was in another car accident just two nights ago. It was her fault, because she was drunk again. How long do you think it will be before Megan is injured?" he threw out vehemently.

Andrea blanched. "I . . . I don't know."

"Damn right, you don't. No one does. But I can't take any chances. Not anymore. I was telling you about my marriage earlier today, but I didn't finish, did I?"

"You don't have to explain."

"But I think you should know! You were the one who needed an interview, remember?"

"But I don't want to intrude."

"Don't you?"

"Look, I think that it's time we left."

Andrea began to rise, but Jefferson's hand reached out and pulled her back into her seat. "Stay. I want you to know how it all ended."

Noticing that other patrons in the tiny restaurant were beginning to cast interested glances in their direction, Andrea decided to sit back in her chair to avoid causing a scene. The last thing that she needed was the press to get wind of the fact that she was seeing Jefferson again.

"I think I was beginning to explain about my resignation."

Andrea nodded, avoiding Jefferson's piercing stare.

"That night," Jefferson began, in a voice devoid of emotion, "after I had officially resigned, I got home quite late because I had decided to clear my personal things out of the governor's office right away. Megan was in bed, and Lara was waiting for me. She had been waiting for some time and had been drinking for hours." He paused, and all of the muscles in his face became rigid with the memory.

"We quarreled bitterly. Lara was as drunk as I had ever seen her, and she was loud. She shouted accusations at me, and insults and taunts. I tried to talk her into going to bed, but she was too interested in venting her wounded pride and belittling me. The argument became heated, and I didn't realize it, but Megan had awakened. She had come down the stairs and was standing on the landing, just staring at us, watching us verbally tear each other's throats out." Jefferson's face clouded with self-disgust and pity for his child. "The look on Megan's face made me realize that I had to get her away from Lara and her drinking problem.

"For some time, Lara was remorseful about the fact that Megan had witnessed her in such an intoxicated state. Lara even allowed herself to be committed to a private hospital to combat her alcoholism. But in the end, when she came home, she couldn't control herself."

Andrea felt as if someone were twisting a knife in her stomach as she watched the play of emotions contort Jefferson's angled face.

"Her behavior became so intolerable that I demanded a divorce—and custody of Megan. I was afraid for Megan's safety when she was alone with Lara. I had finally realized that I would never be able to help Lara, and that the marriage couldn't be saved. Divorce was the only way to save myself and my child from being destroyed by Lara and her alcoholism."

Andrea listened to Jefferson's story with difficulty. She tried to hide the tears in her eyes, but failed. All of the years that she had silently wished that she could exchange places with Lara Whitney Harmon came hauntingly back to her, and she felt enormous guilt for those emotions. Suddenly she felt pity for the woman who had become Jefferson's wife.

Jefferson's arm stretched across the table and he touched her wet cheek. "Tears? For whom?"

"You . . . your child . . . your wife . . . I don't know," she breathed, and dabbed at the corner of her eyes with her napkin.

"There's no reason to cry."

"I know."

"Remember, you're a reporter after a story," he reminded her sharply.

"I'm not!"

"No?"

"I would never use you," she hissed, her eyes narrowing at his insinuations.

"You have in the past."

"Not I."

"Okay, your brother did."

"And you'll never trust me again," she whispered, suddenly realizing how deep the rift between them had become. Her eyes, wide with understanding and horror, stared at him accusingly.

At that moment the waiter came with the check. Jefferson paid the bill, helped Andrea with her coat and guided her toward the door of the small restaurant. The chill of the night couldn't match the cold feeling deep in Andrea's heart. All of the time that she had spent with Jefferson alone on the island had meant nothing to him.

He was suspicious of her. He didn't trust her, and yet he
had made love to her as if he meant every loving motion.
And she had been stupid enough to fall for him all over
again. In fact, he obviously thought that she had seduced
him for her own interests: the interview.

Somehow they made it back to the town house. The cab
ride was silent, with only a half-smile or a quick response
to the cabby's questions breaking the thick, suffocating
stillness in the back seat of the cab.

At the doorstep she paused, only because of the pressure Jefferson placed on her upper arm.

"I didn't mean for everything to turn out this way," he
offered.

"I know."

"Then you understand that—"

"No, Jefferson, I don't understand you at all. I thought I
did once, and I foolishly hoped that I could again, but I
was wrong."

"I'm sorry."

"Not half as sorry as I am," she whispered, feeling tears
again burning the back of her eyes.

"You understand that I can't do the interview."

"I never expected that you would."

She turned to place the key in the lock and found that
her fingers were trembling with the feelings that were
twisting her insides.

"Andrea."

She couldn't look at him, but held her palm out in
protest. "Don't talk to me about anything. I don't want to
think about it anymore."

"I wish that I could explain."

"So do I, but you can't, can you? You have a plane to
catch."

She felt his hands on her shoulders and knew that he
intended to kiss her. "No, Jefferson," she pleaded.
"Don't." His lips found hers in a bruising kiss that stopped
all of her protests. She tried not to react, attempted to

show no emotion, but it was useless, and slowly her arms came up to entwine around his neck. They clung together for an endless moment before he slowly and determinedly pulled away from her.

"I'm glad you found me," he admitted earnestly. "I'll call you."

"You don't have to," she replied, fearing his response.

"I *want* to."

And then he was gone. He checked his watch and ran back to the waiting cab. Andrea stood on the porch and listened while the noisy yellow car ground its gears down the street and vanished into the darkness. Andrea had never felt more lonely in her life.

Three days after Jefferson had returned to California, Andrea could stand the emptiness no longer. He hadn't called. No one had, not even Bryce, and the calm that Andrea had hoped to find on her vacation eluded her. She attempted to renew her acquaintance with the city, but the quaint tea shops, the glistening antique stores, the open-air markets, held no interest for her. Instead of unwinding in the city, she found herself growing tired of her inactivity. She needed to *do* something—anything—to keep her mind off Jefferson and the few hours they had blissfully shared together.

Her worries wouldn't leave her alone, and by the end of the week she was tired of brooding over the problems of her job and daydreaming about Jefferson. She scanned the newspaper every day in hope that she might read something about him, and then felt guilty at being just like the rest of the public, hoping to catch a glimpse of him.

Her last suitcase was packed, and there was still a week remaining of her vacation. On sudden impulse, before buying her airplane ticket to Los Angeles, she tried one final time to reach her sister in Seattle. She let the telephone ring several times before hanging up. Her dark, arched brows drew together pensively. Although she had attempted to call her younger sister several times during the two weeks that she had stayed in Victoria, she had been unable to contact her. Once she had gotten hold of her brother-in-law, Doug, but never Gayla. Doug had promised to have Gayla return Andrea's call, but either Andrea had missed the call or her sister hadn't attempted to reach her.

Andrea couldn't help but feel uneasy about the entire situation, and she thought fleetingly of taking the ferry to Seattle and dropping in unannounced on her younger sister. There was something disturbingly out of character in her brother-in-law's voice—an uneasy restraint that was unlike Doug—which made Andrea discard the idea before it was completely hatched. Instead, she decided to try to reach her sister by phone once she was back on warm California soil.

Hurriedly, as if to ward off the chill of uneasiness that had begun to settle heavily on her shoulders, Andrea picked up her suitcase, marched out of the town house and locked the front door behind her. She huddled against the brisk northern wind as she waited watchfully on the porch for the taxicab that she had summoned. Pleasant memories of Jefferson kept filtering into her mind, but she resolutely tried to ignore them. Anxiously her eyes scanned the cross street for sign of the taxi. Suddenly she couldn't get out of Victoria quickly enough to suit her. She was fidgety by the time the yellow cab screeched around the corner, and she breathed a muted sigh of relief as the door swung open and she slid into the black interior of the cab.

"Where to, lady?" the portly cabby asked, turning to eye her appreciatively as he stubbed out his smoldering cigarette.

Anywhere, she thought to herself, but instead smiled and replied, "The airport."

Tires spun against the wet pavement as the driver shoved the car into gear and pushed against the throttle.

Puddles of water splashed nearly to the windows, and Andrea stared listlessly out into the approaching evening. She tried to convince herself that she was relieved to be leaving the stormy gray skies of Victoria behind her, but images of a warm November morning in Jefferson's arms wouldn't leave her restless mind.

It was over a week later that Andrea was back in the car driving on the concrete freeway network of Southern California. Her tired muscles rebelled at their cramped position in her tiny sports car. A week of cleaning, wallpapering and redecorating her small apartment in an effort to keep her mind from dwelling on Jefferson and the fact that he hadn't called left Andrea's muscles aching.

She had kept herself busy to the point of exhaustion during the final week of her vacation. Still, the nights of restless slumber were visible on her face. Her cheeks were more hollow than usual and dark circles under her eyes were evident despite her use of the most expensive cosmetics on the market.

The drive to Coral Productions was over too quickly. Although she was relieved to see the company was still functioning, and everything seemed "business as usual," she couldn't help but feel lingering wisps of dread tickle her spine. She thought it odd that Bryce hadn't telephoned her, and she wondered if Jefferson had explained his position about the interview to her boss. Chiding herself for her worries, she pushed open the plate-glass door. The entire interview with Jefferson was probably forgotten, she reasoned. No doubt Bryce had found a suitable replacement for Jefferson, a different subject for the lead-in interview of the series.

Most of the office personnel hadn't, as yet, arrived at the production company. Andrea sneaked a peek into Katie Argus's office and was disappointed to find that Katie was late, as usual. After grabbing a cup of black coffee at the kitchenette, Andrea made her way toward her own office and smiled ruefully to herself as she noticed the desk, which had been clean when she'd left, covered with memos, letters, reports and brochures. Her office, usually tidy, was cluttered with accumulated work. Thank God, she thought to herself as she began to sift through the paper. At least she would be too busy to think about Jefferson.

"Well, look who's back!" Jack Masters's voice caught Andrea unaware. She looked up to see him lounging against the doorframe, his tanned arms crossed over his chest.

"From the looks of it," Andrea retorted, her green eyes scanning the cluttered desk, "you missed me."

Jack's perfect smile extended to his eyes. "Of course we missed you—especially me!"

"Couldn't find anyone else gullible enough to get your coffee?" Andrea asked, lifting a dark brow.

"Are you insinuating that I take you for granted?"

"Me and the rest of the female population."

"Not fair, Andrea," Jack returned with an exaggerated wounded look. "I appreciate women—all of them."

"Sure you do," she agreed sarcastically. "What's been happening while I've been gone?" she asked.

Jack came into the office and sprawled into a chair near Andrea's desk. He reached for a paperweight on Andrea's desk and began rotating it nervously in his hands. He studied the hand-painted miniature carousel horse before lifting his eyes to search Andrea's perplexed face. His casual, lighthearted manner of a moment before had vanished, and his boyishly handsome face was set in stern, hard lines.

"I guess there's no reason to hide it from you. Things aren't going well here at all."

Jack's tension infected Andrea, and she felt her throat become dry. "Why not?"

"Did you happen to catch the last episode of *Pride's Power?*"

Andrea nodded thoughtfully as she mentally reviewed the episode that had aired the previous Saturday night.

"What did you think?" Jack's question was as penetrating as his guarded gaze.

"Well, it wasn't our best effort."

"It was rotten; a piece of garbage! And do you know why?" His brown eyes blazed furiously. "All because of Nicole Jamison! It galls me to the bone that she ever landed the part of Angela Pride."

Andrea sighed. They had been over this before.

"I don't think that solely Nicole can be blamed."

"Of course not. It's not her fault that she has no talent."

"Jack, don't you think you're placing too much of the blame on Nicole?"

"You saw Saturday night's program," he began slyly, sliding Andrea a sidelong look.

Andrea couldn't remember ever seeing Jack react so angrily. In Andrea's opinion he was usually too easygoing for his own good. But today, right now, he was barely in control of his simmering temper, and all of his hostility was aimed at Nicole Jamison. Andrea remembered that the story line for *Pride's Power* had originally been Jack's idea. Could it be that he was blaming the sultry actress as a scapegoat? Did he secretly feel that he was to blame for the poor ratings, and thus indirectly responsible for part of Coral Productions' financial problems?

Jack must have noticed the surprised, thoughtful look in Andrea's eyes, and some of his restrained anger seemed to ebb from him. "I'm sorry," he apologized, his affable smile neatly back in place. "I guess I'm overreacting."

Andrea's silence seemed to confirm this, and he felt a need to explain.

"It's just that it makes me so damn mad to see a good program scrapped, all because of a poor casting decision."

"Do you think that another actress could have saved the show?" she asked, eyeing Jack carefully.

"Maybe not. Who knows? But at least another actress—

one with just a modicum of talent—wouldn't have butch-
ered the part of Angela." He tapped his fingers nervously
on the edge of the desk. "What did you think of the long
speech—you remember, the first act, second scene—
where Angela discovers that her nephew is actually her
husband Justin's illegitimate son?"

"It was poor," Andrea was forced to admit honestly as
she remembered watching Nicole struggle with Angela's
lines of shock and dismay when confronted with the truth
that her sister's ten-year-old child had been fathered by
Justin.

The slim, fortyish actress with her hourglass figure,
long, raven hair and frosty blue eyes, just didn't come
across as the paragon of virtue that she was portraying.
The speech, designed to depict despair, disbelief and yet
compassion, was brittle and seemed insincere. Even with
flattering lighting, a decent script and hours with the best
makeup artist that money could buy, Nicole still seemed
harsh and waspish, not anything like the sensitive and
forgiving Angela Pride. Begrudgingly Andrea had reached
the same conclusion as Jack: Nicole Jamison was wrong for
the part of Angela.

"It wasn't poor, Andrea. It was a disaster!"

Andrea attempted to be equitable. "I don't think that
we can blame Nicole entirely."

"She certainly doesn't help matters!"

"Okay, granted that Nicole doesn't embellish the role,
what's the upshot of it all? You said that things weren't
going well. Just what did you mean?"

"All three shows, *Pride's Power*, *Night Sirens* and
Dangerous Games bit the dust. It's official."

Andrea sighed and leaned heavily back in her chair. She
bit her thumbnail and asked the next question with difficulty. "So where does that leave us with the interviews for
ITV?" The fears she had been propelling to the back of
her mind began to resurface.

Jack shook his blond head negatively, and with a frown, placed the paperweight back on Andrea's desk. "Even that doesn't look good," he conceded.

"Oh?" Andrea hoped she seemed only interested and detached, but she could feel her pulse beginning to jump.

"No. Bryce is absolutely adamant that we get Jefferson Harmon for an interview, but apparently the man in question has politely but effectively refused."

"Certainly there are other personalities—"

"You would think so, but Bryce is intent on getting Harmon." Jack's eyes narrowed thoughtfully. "I don't suppose that you've kept up on him?" Jack took Andrea's silence as confirmation of his opinion. "I didn't think so. Well, it appears that his wife has gotten herself into quite a mess."

"You mean his ex-wife," Andrea said, correcting him.

Jack nodded his head and apparently didn't notice the lack of color in Andrea's blanched face. "Yeah. It seems, according to the local gossip tabloids, that not only is she out drinking and partying with a new man every week, but now she's got herself tied up in some sort of lawsuit."

"You mean for custody of the child?" Andrea surmised, cautiously.

Jack nodded his head and waved his hand in the air dismissively. "That, too, of course. But there's something else. She was involved in a car accident a couple of weeks back." Andrea's mind whirled backward to the stormy night on Harmon Island and the soggy newspaper article on Lara.

"I read something about it," she responded calmly when Jack paused for a moment.

"Well, since then the occupants of the car that she hit are suing her."

"But I thought no one was injured," Andrea protested.

"It seems, or at least the other parties charge, that the car accident put a strain on an older passenger's heart. His subsequent heart attack, later that weekend, nearly killed him, and he is claiming the attack was the direct result of the car accident and Lara Harmon's negligence."

"But that's absurd!"

Jack shrugged. "People sue for almost any reason these days, you know." He surveyed Andrea with a sly gleam in his dark eyes. "Especially if they can blame a celebrity."

"Such as Jefferson Harmon's ex-wife?"

"Exactly."

"They can't possibly expect to win, can they?"

"Who knows? Harmon's got a lot of money, and he doesn't like publicity. Maybe the plaintiff's attorneys are banking on Harmon's privacy—hoping for a sizable, quiet, out-of-court settlement."

"I can't believe it," Andrea murmured. She hadn't been aware that she was holding her breath until it escaped in a trembling gust.

Jack noticed that Andrea was visibly shaken and pale. He hesitated only slightly before continuing the conversation, shrugging his broad shoulders as if to signify that what he was saying was inconsequential to him. "I'm only repeating what I've read recently," he said half-apologetically. "It looks like Harmon's newsworthy ex-wife is in more than a little hot water this time. The police report supposedly indicated that she was driving under the influence of alcohol at the time of the accident. Any way you look at it, the entire incident is a holy mess."

"I see," Andrea said, sighing wearily, only half-listening to Jack.

"Wait. You haven't heard the best part!"

Andrea's lowered head jerked upward, and she felt her heart miss a beat.

"It seems that his ex-wife wants Harmon to defend her. Can you beat that?"

Andrea swallowed with difficulty and twirled her pen nervously in the air. "This is all very interesting, I suppose," she whispered in what she hoped was a calm voice. "But I really don't see what it has to do with Coral Productions."

"Don't you?" Jack stood up and stared quizzically down at Andrea. "That's the reason that Bryce is so hot after Harmon. Between our infamous ex-governor and his beautiful lush of an ex-wife, we have one helluva story. A story no one really knows, but everyone is curious about. It seems that no matter how hard Jefferson Harmon tries, he just can't keep his name off the scandal sheets. And the public is begging for more!" Jack was swept up in his rhetoric, and Andrea felt as if a sinister shadow had crossed his intense brown eyes.

"Old questions and new ones center around the man. He's just mysterious enough to whet the public's appetite. Why did he resign the governorship? What is the *real* cause of his ex-wife's drinking problem? How does he feel about his kid—or his ex-wife's latest lover? Will he defend her if she goes to court? Why did their marriage break up? Does he still love her? What truth is there to the charges that he never really got over that college coed?"

The pen that Andrea had been twirling dropped noisily to the desk top as she watched Jack's animated face. "And you honestly expect Harmon to give you an in-depth interview?"

"That's what Bryce wants."

"But what Bryce wants and what Bryce gets are two different things sometimes," Bryce himself announced as he strode into Andrea's office and leaned his wiry body against the windowsill. His solemn brown eyes softened slightly as he peered over his bifocals, and a warm grin spread evenly over his face. "Glad to have you back, Andrea. We missed you."

"So I gathered," Andrea said with a wan smile. She was grateful for Bryce's intrusion and the change in the course of the conversation. "From the looks of this office, I would hazard a guess that anything not demanding immediate attention was shuffled in here to welcome me back."

"Would we do that to you?" Bryce teased. For a moment there was an awkward silence and Bryce rubbed his palm against his jeans. His jovial face sobered. "I assume that Jack told you about all of the fall shows."

The mood in the room was subtly changing, and Andrea felt the tension that was quietly gripping Bryce diffusing the comaraderie of a moment before. "He mentioned that all of the shows were canceled."

Bryce shook his head and pursed his thin lips together. "That's right . . . every last one of them. Even *Night Sirens* was axed, although it had climbed steadily in the ratings."

"Why?"

"Pardon me?" Bryce's eyes fixed on Andrea's hollow face, and she felt suddenly transparent. His brow furrowed, and she wondered if he considered her question impertinent.

"I just wanted to know why the broadcasting company cut *Night Sirens*, if it was moving up in the ratings. It's only been on for one season. I would think that the Powers That Be would give it at least one more chance to prove itself. Some of the longest-running programs on television got off to slow starts."

"My arguments exactly. But because of the shake-up in the management of the broadcasting company, the new president has decided to present a completely new lineup of shows to replace any that didn't break forty in the Nielsons."

"That's a tall order," Jack murmured. "They're going to need a bundle of replacement shows. And yet they didn't like any of our new ideas."

"Politics." Bryce squared his shoulders, and his lips thinned in determination. "For the past eight or nine months Coral has had a lousy track record, and the broadcasting company is edgy." He sighed wearily before continuing. "Well, there's no use beating a dead horse, is there? We've got to move ahead with our new ideas."

"That's what I was explaining to Andrea," Jack interjected. "I told her that we're all set with the interview series for ITV."

"Except for the fact that we haven't got our lead-in interview," Bryce reminded him.

Andrea could feel the muscles at the back of her neck begin to tighten and grow cold. "Harmon wouldn't do it?" she asked.

The lift of her eyebrows as she looked questioningly at Bryce and the question itself confused Jack Masters. He had just gotten through telling her about Harmon—why did she ask the same question of Bryce? He wondered. Suddenly, inexplicably, Jack felt himself an intruder in a very private conversation.

Bryce hesitated before answering, and Jack realized that this was his opportunity to exit from the suddenly tense room. He started to back toward the open door. "Yeah, I was telling Andrea how interesting a character this Harmon guy is, but I guess she isn't convinced. Maybe you can change her mind," he stated skeptically. As he reached the door he tossed out a final statement to Bryce. "I'll be down the hall in Katie's office if you need me. We're going to start working on a series of questions for Sondra Wickfield." With these final words Jack left the office.

Bryce quietly closed the door to ensure that his conversation with Andrea remain private. Andrea felt her breath constrict in her lungs—she guessed what was coming. Trying to seem professional and unrattled, she started the conversation where Jack had left off.

"So, you were able to get Sondra Wickfield to agree to an interview?" she asked, straightening the piles of paper on her desk.

"Her attorneys think that the interview will help her by swaying public opinion in her favor. Even though she's still serving time, her lawyers feel that if they expose her lover as some sort of sadist—a real psycho with his women— that it will be to her benefit."

"What will the interview do for her?"

"Spring her, the attorney's hope. With enough public sentiment in her favor, there's hope that she might be paroled early. From what I understand she's a model prisoner."

Andrea sucked in her breath. "And the other personalities? Have you talked to any of them?"

"Yeah, no problem. Everyone's willing to talk for the right price—with one exception." Bryce wiped his receding forehead and hoisted himself up on the corner of Andrea's desk.

"Jefferson Harmon," she said, hoping her assumption was wrong.

"That's right. It seems that no amount of money will sway him." His dark, probing eyes bore down on Andrea, and she knew that her stomach was fluttering, but she held Bryce's intimidating stare.

"A man of principle?"

"Why don't you answer that one?" Bryce suggested as he folded his arms across his chest.

"What do you mean?" Andrea felt her heart thudding, and her palms beginning to sweat.

Bryce's smile wasn't convincing. "Let's stop playing games, Andrea. I know that you knew Harmon in the past. That's why I called you in Victoria. You're the girl who was involved with him ten years ago. Good God, Andrea, were you actually an anti-war activist?"

"My brother was."

Bryce snapped his fingers together as if a thought had suddenly struck him. "That's the brother that was wounded in the war, right?" he asked, hopping off the desk and pacing restlessly between it and the window.

"Martin," Andrea answered, supplying Bryce with her brother's name. "How do you know so much about it?"

She leaned back in her desk chair and surveyed her boss speculatively. It was as if she were seeing Bryce Cawthorne for the first time. Had Jefferson been right about Bryce all along?

"Before you left on vacation three weeks ago, I noticed your reaction to the article in the paper about Harmon's divorce. I thought it odd at the time, but I never dreamed that you were the college girl from his past until I did some further digging."

Andrea's shoulders drooped, but still she held Bryce's gaze unwaveringly. Her voice was empty when she finally found her words. "You asked me to call Jefferson knowing what would happen, knowing about our past?" she accused.

"A little underhanded, wasn't it?" Bryce admitted with his most disarming grin.

Andrea's eyes sparked. "More than a little, I'd say."

Bryce held his palms outward. "All right, I should have leveled with you in the first place," he agreed. "But would you have done it? Would you have talked to Harmon . . . tried to persuade him?"

"I don't know. . . ."

Bryce cocked his head to one side and lifted his shoulders. "This way I knew that you would get to him. After all, what did it hurt?"

"What did it help? He hasn't agreed to the interview."

"Not yet."

"But you think he might?" Andrea asked, incredulously.

"Don't you?"

"No!"

"Why not?"

"Because he's not the kind of man who likes to have his personal life splashed across the headlines or paraded on national television. You know that."

"Don't you think you could change his mind?" Bryce asked, pulling thoughtfully on his lower lip.

"No!"

"No?"

"Bryce, I wouldn't, *couldn't*, ask him to do something he doesn't want to do!" Andrea's dismay was evident on her face and in the tone of her voice. What was Bryce asking her to do? Was it her imagination, or was he different than she had remembered? How desperate for the interview with Jefferson Harmon was Bryce?

"And I wouldn't expect you to," Bryce reaffirmed, but the rigidity of his spine didn't slacken.

"Then you don't expect him to come through," Andrea surmised, and a giant wave of relief began to cascade over her.

"I didn't say that. There's got to be a way to get to him."

"But he doesn't want to do it!"

"Not yet, but people have been known to change their minds—especially politicians." Bryce cocked his wrist and looked at his watch. "I've got to get to a meeting at ITV. We'll talk about this later in the week."

When the door to the office closed, Andrea felt a shudder of fear jolt her. You're imagining things, she told herself, but she couldn't help but feel a welling sense of dread spread through her. Why was Bryce so adamant about Jefferson?

Chapter 8

Two days after the confrontation with Bryce Andrea finally found time to have lunch with Katie Argus. The pile of work on Andrea's desk had prevented her from socializing, and the mood in the office was so tense that Andrea had difficult talking with the other employees at Coral Productions inside the building.

It was a warm day, warm enough to eat in the courtyard of the omelet house Katie had chosen. For the first time since returning to her job, Andrea felt the tension that had been building begin to dissolve with Katie's incessant chatter and sarcastic humor.

"I'm dying to hear all about your vacation," Katie said with a bright smile as they were seated at the parasoled tables in the brick courtyard. Although the walls of the adjacent buildings surrounded the courtyard, it was large enough to allow the winter sun to warm the backs of the patrons. Hanging baskets of flowers added just the right touch of fragrance and color, giving the enclosed patio a sense of privacy and casual charm.

"There's really not that much to tell," Andrea said.

"Don't hold out on me," Katie argued with a brilliant smile. "You've changed since you got back. My guess is it's a man!"

"You always have had an active imagination," Andrea

quipped back, and was relieved that the waiter came to take their orders.

Fortunately Katie was easily distracted, and Andrea took up the conversation, heading it in a different direction.

"So, how did things go at the office while I was gone?"

"Horrible," Katie admitted, pulling an exaggerated frown.

"Why?"

"Oh, who knows? Bryce was in one of his foul moods again and everybody suffered because of it."

"He's very worried about the company," Andrea suggested.

"I think there's more to it than that," Katie replied, accepting the plate that the waiter brought to her. She speared a piece of her mushroom omelet, dipped it in the sour-cream sauce and swallowed it. "If you ask me, he's bugged about Jefferson Harmon refusing to do the interview."

"Why is it so important to have Harmon?" Andrea asked casually.

"Not only does Bryce want Harmon, but apparently so do a couple of the guys at ITV. It's only gossip, but Sheryl, Bryce's secretary, told me that Bryce promised the cable company that he would be able to get Harmon for an interview. That's really something considering the fact that Jefferson Harmon hasn't given an official interview since he resigned as governor. At least, not a personal interview."

Katie continued to attack her omelet feverishly, but Andrea's appetite had slowly diminished. She pushed the remains of her shrimp salad around in her plate.

"Why did Bryce promise something he couldn't deliver? Harmon hasn't agreed to the interview."

Katie tossed her blond hair and shrugged. "Beats me. Maybe ITV wouldn't buy the package of programs without being assured of a celebrity of their choice." Katie looked up from her meal to study Andrea thoughtfully. "According to Sheryl, Bryce could persuade Harmon to go along with him. Bryce seems to think that he's got some special pull with our mysterious ex-governor. I can't for the life of me figure out what it might be." Katie set her fork down beside her plate and lifted her glass of wine, but her eyes never left Andrea's blanched face. "Hey, are you okay? You look a little pale."

"Do I? Oh . . . well. You have to remember that I've been away from the California sun for a couple of weeks," Andrea stammered, trying to regain some of her lost composure.

"You haven't touched your salad," Katie accused.

"I guess I'm not very hungry," Andrea suggested with what she hoped appeared to be a genuine smile for her friend. But Katie saw through the ruse.

"Something's wrong, isn't it?" the blonde charged emphatically. "Are you going to explain it to me, or brood over your problems all by yourself?"

"It's really nothing . . . a problem with my family while I was in Victoria," Andrea lied, wincing inwardly. Katie was a good friend, and Andrea would have liked to pour her heart out to her, but how could she even attempt to explain the depth of her feelings for Jefferson? The secret that she had hidden for ten years was not easy to confess, not even to her best friend. After concealing the truth for so long, it was impossible to let it out now, especially since nothing had changed between herself and Jefferson.

"I didn't mean to pry," Katie apologized as she witnessed a dark, incomprehensible cloud cross Andrea's delicate features.

"You haven't. I'm just a little concerned about my sister in Seattle, that's all." At least the lie wasn't entirely fabricated, Andrea thought grimly.

"Gayla?" Katie asked, her honey-blond eyebrows arching in dismay. "What's wrong with her?"

"I'm not really sure," Andrea sighed, and then

shrugged, as if to shake off her disconsolate mood. "It's just a feeling I have. I tried to reach her several times while I was in Victoria, and couldn't. I got through to Doug once, and even he seemed strange—uneasy. It's probably nothing," she admitted, but she didn't sound convincing.

"I wouldn't worry too much about Gayla if I were you. She's twenty-eight and can take care of herself. It sounds as if she and Doug just had some sort of marital tiff, if you ask me."

"I don't know," Andrea murmured.

"Don't worry about it. Now, let's get down to brass tacks. I don't buy the story that you're worried about your younger sister." Andrea began to protest and Katie amended her position. "I know, I know, you're concerned about Gayla, and you should be, but what's *really* bothering you?"

"I don't know what you mean."

"Sure you do," Katie pointed out. "We've worked together for a long time, been friends for years, and I know that there's a bigger problem eating at you. You've lost weight, color and apparently your appetite," Katie maintained, glancing at Andrea's plate. "If you don't want to talk about it, that's one thing, but don't try to lie to me with some overblown story about your sister."

Andrea had to smile in spite of herself. "You always could see right through me."

"It's easy, Andrea. You're transparent. You wear your heart on your sleeve. My guess is that you've got a new man in your life."

"I wish it were that easy," Andrea sighed, wondering if she was making a mistake as she began her story. "There is a man, but it's not a new one. You see, the man I was seeing was Jefferson Harmon."

"*What?*" The stricken look on Katie's face showed her obvious dismay. "You must be kidding."

Andrea's wistful smile convinced Katie that she was telling the truth. "No, I was the college girl that was involved with him ten years ago."

"Oh, Andrea. . . ."

"Bryce asked me to call Jefferson when I was in Victoria, but I couldn't find his number. Instead, I went to see him on his private island, the same island I visited years ago." Andrea sketched in the rest of the story, much of which Katie had read in the papers. Katie's expression darkened from shock to dismay and finally, to disbelief.

"You don't think that Bryce intends to use you to get at Harmon, do you? You aren't the special influence that he secretly holds?"

"I hope not," Andrea replied, still feeling vaguely uneasy. "Because even if I went along with any of Bryce's schemes, it wouldn't work. Jefferson's made up his mind."

Katie toyed with her napkin before lifting her eyes and giving Andrea a compassionate smile. "So, where does that leave you?"

"What do you mean?"

"I'm talking about you and Jefferson, for Pete's sake. Have you heard from him since you got back to L.A.?"

"I haven't seen him," Andrea hedged, but Katie was too quick to be put off.

"Has he called?"

Andrea bit at her lower lip before gently pushing aside her plate of uneaten salad. "Yes, he's called," she admitted sternly.

"And?"

"And *nothing!* He called twice, and it was very tense. He didn't ask to see me." Andrea pursed her lips together for a moment before tossing her napkin onto the table and rising from her chair. "Oh, he was polite, but it was very uncomfortable, and I felt worse after he called than before. It was almost as if he called me because he felt it was his *obligation!*" Andrea could feel the sting of tears biting at the back of her eyes, but she willed them back, refusing to break down in public over a man who thought so little of her.

"That doesn't sound like Jefferson Harmon to me," Katie observed as she rose from the table. "At least not the Harmon that I've read so much about. From what I understand of our ex-governor, he doesn't feel pressured into anything. That was why he was so popular as a politician. He was one man that stood up for what he believed, and couldn't be swayed by popular opinion or money."

Andrea couldn't trust herself to speak. Talking about Jefferson had only opened the wounds over her heart once again. With all of the feelings that she held for him, all of the love that welled within her, she wanted to believe everything that Katie was saying. Yet Andrea knew better than to be swayed by her emotions once again. Twice she had succumbed to her love for the man, and twice that love had been recklessly discarded by him.

Katie sensed Andrea's preoccupation and tried to turn the topic of conversation back to neutral territory, but Andrea only half-listened to her friend as the blonde rattled on about her latest romantic relationship with an up-and-coming producer. During the short drive back to the office Andrea's mind kept slipping back to Katie's earlier comments: *"Bryce seems to think that he's got some special pull over our mysterious ex-governor. . . . You don't think that Bryce intends to use you to get at Harmon, do you? You aren't the special influence that he secretly holds?"*

Andrea didn't want to believe that Bryce would stoop so low as to think that he could use her as a weapon against Jefferson. Would he? Andrea found the thought impossible, and yet the uneasy feeling burning in the pit of her stomach remained with her for the rest of the day.

The tension in the office continued to build, and when it was finally late Friday afternoon, Andrea couldn't wait to get home. Everyone in the office was on edge, including Jack Masters, whose usual affable grin had been replaced by a sour frown while he finished rewriting the final episode of *Pride's Power*.

Everything has changed, Andrea thought to herself as she locked her car and hurried up the short flight of steps to her second-story apartment. She kicked off her shoes and opened the sliding glass door to the redwood deck. It had been a warm, muggy day, and the promise of rain was thick in the air. The apartment seemed stagnant, and even the breathless air from outside helped cool Andrea's body against the stickiness of her clothing. After undressing she tossed her clothes into the hamper and started drawing a bath, hoping that the warm water would help wash away all of the tension from the office. The bath water lapped lazily around her and she closed her eyes before sinking up to her neck in the warm water. Her black hair was twisted onto the top of her head, allowing her to submerge herself to her neck. For the first time in over a week she felt at ease. The sleepless nights she had spent finally caught up with her, and she began to doze.

A short while later her eyelids fluttered open in response to some distant intrusion that had interrupted her catnap. Something had disturbed her, and she was surprised to find that she had actually fallen asleep in the soothingly warm water. She listened for a moment before the doorbell chimed a second time. The hot water had cooled and was barely tepid. She shivered as she rose and stepped out of the tub onto the bare, blue tile.

"Just a minute," she called as she hastily pulled on her velour bathrobe and hurried to the living room, leaving a wet trail where her feet touched the creamy white carpet. The doorbell rang again insistently, and Andrea, piqued by the intrusion, hastened her stride. "I'm coming," she called out again more impatiently. When she reached the door, she unlocked it and jerked it open.

Her heart turned over as she recognized Jefferson

standing on the porch, his shoulder propped against one of the black wrought-iron pillars that supported the roof. His burgundy-colored tie was askew, his sport jacket rumpled and the shadow of a beard darkened his jawline. He looked tired and disheveled as he leaned near the railing.

"Jefferson? What are you doing here?" she asked, astonished to see him. She hadn't heard from him in over three days. Their last telephone conversation had been so stilted and tense that she never would have expected to see him standing, alone and tired and looking as if he needed a friend, on her front doorstep.

His dark, hazel eyes traveled up her body, and his off-center smile, tired but amused, broke across his face. "You look great," he said simply, letting his eyes caress her. In the thickly piled, indigo-colored bathrobe, her black hair curling and studded with diamond-like droplets of moisture and her skin flushed from the warm water of the bath, Andrea appeared more desirable and provocative than Jefferson had remembered. Though she had haunted his nights, his dreams of her had never lived up to the innocently alluring woman she was as she stood before him. He didn't really understand why he had come to see her after his long airplane flight from Colorado, but instinctively he had sought her out for comfort and companionship.

Andrea, recovering from the shock of seeing him on her doorstep, opened the door a little farther as she found her voice. One hand clutched at her robe. "Please, come in," she whispered, stepping aside to allow him to enter her home. "I . . . I wasn't expecting anyone," she apologized.

"Obviously," was his dry retort as his eyes dropped to the gaping lapels of the deep blue robe.

She regarded him silently for a moment, her puzzled eyes seeking answers in the contours of his face. Why was he here? She could feel his intimate appraisal of her, and she knew that he guessed she was wearing nothing under the velour robe. Dewy droplets of moisture still ran down her legs. She shivered from the water beading on her skin . . . or did she shiver from Jefferson's searching, silent appraisal of her. Seeing him again made her feel more alive, more sensual, more womanly, than she had since leaving Victoria. His presence seemed to dominate everything in the small, intimate living room.

"Nice," he murmured as his eyes ran over the eclectic pieces of furniture and wall hangings in the room. His smile was sincere as he looked at the assortment of belongings that Andrea had collected over the past ten years. The rose-colored couch was faded, an antique found at an estate sale. The side chairs were modern, in bold burgundy-colored stripes. Woven baskets from India were filled with leafy green plants, and copper kettles overflowing with books and needlework, crowded the corners of the apartment. Open-weave linen draperies, the color of faded jute, covered the windows, which also were graced with deep maroon blinds.

As he looked at the room Andrea could sense him puzzling over the pieces of her life that he had missed. He was looking at the most private reaches of her, studying every little detail, and suddenly Andrea felt the intimacy between them grow. He was seeing too much of her life in his omniscient gaze. She had to break the spell.

"Jefferson, why are you here?" she asked impulsively. His eyes left the contents of the room to meet her gaze.

"I didn't think that our phone conversations were very satisfying—or conclusive."

Andrea smiled wryly. "Whose fault is that?"

Jefferson shrugged, and his shoulders sagged wearily. "I'm not blaming you. I should never have called you when I was so upset."

"Then why did you?"

"I told you I would call you in Victoria, didn't I?"

"So you phoned because you promised that you would, because you felt obligated?"

His expression changed, and his lips thinned into a tight,

uncompromising frown. "I called you because I wanted to, and for no other reason." Her black eyebrows lifted in an expression of doubt. "Oh, hell," he muttered, "I don't know why I'm trying to explain myself to you. My timing was poor. I shouldn't have called when I was so upset with the way things were working out with Megan. But damn it, Andrea, I just wanted to talk to you!" He bit out the last phrase as if it were an unwanted admission, and he dropped, without invitation, onto the faded, over-stuffed couch.

Something in the uncomfortable way he slouched on the sofa made Andrea smile in spite of herself. It was true that she had wanted to see him and had hoped to hear from him. But after the last tense telephone conversation, when he seemed more distant and remote from her than ever— as far away as the dark side of the moon—she had all but given up on ever seeing him again.

"I've been unfair to you," he stated as he looked up at her.

"What do you mean?"

"I've been selfish and self-centered."

"No—"

"Just listen, will you?" he cut in. "Can't you even accept an apology gracefully?"

Andrea pressed her lips together and sat in one of the contemporary chairs that faced the couch. She folded her hands together on her lap, leaned against the back of the chair and inclined her head toward him, encouraging him to continue.

"I'm not very good at apologies—I never have been— but I'm sorry about not coming to see you sooner. I've been up to my ears in business meetings. As a matter of fact, I just got in from Denver a little over an hour ago, and, well . . ." He closed his eyes and thought for a moment. When he opened them again, Andrea could sense a look of bewilderment and confusion in his gaze.

"How did everything get so fouled up?" he asked in a rough whisper. "Ten years ago everything seemed so simple."

"We were younger then," she said, thinking aloud.

"But not any smarter," he sighed. "We should never have allowed ourselves to get so far away from each other." He rubbed the back of his neck and again lowered his eyelids.

In the past Andrea had witnessed a dozen different sides to the complex personality of Jefferson Harmon. She had known him to be loving, gentle and kind; she had been aware of his soft persuasion or ruthless determination; she had seen him filled with rage or passion; but never had she witnessed the defeat that was now evident in his deep voice He looked older than he had on the island, though it had only been a few, short weeks ago.

"Jefferson, are you all right?" she asked quietly. Why did she feel compelled to soothe his worried brow?

His smile was grim. "I'm fine," he murmured sarcastically and looked at the ceiling. "I'm just fine."

"Is something wrong?"

His eyes narrowed. For a moment she saw a flash of anger as his jawline hardened. But just as rapidly it was gone, as if he had willed his anger away. "Nothing's wrong," he answered flatly.

"Are you sure? Maybe I could help," she offered.

"This is one battle that I have to handle myself!" He snapped the words out bitterly, and for a second Andrea sat frozen in the chair, holding on to her knees, which were tucked under her. What did he want from her? Did he expect something? Why was he here, and why in heaven's name was he so angry?

"Is there anything I can get you? A drink perhaps?" she asked as she rose from the chair and hurried into the kitchen. She had to move, to get away from him. She couldn't bear to watch him stare blankly up at the ceiling, lost in thoughts that excluded her. "Is brandy all right?" she called through the doorway to the kitchen. She didn't expect a response, and none came.

Andrea poured the drink just to keep herself busy. She wanted to help him, talk to him, ease his pain. But although he had come to her home looking for her, it was as if he had retreated from her into the dark thoughts that were clouding his mind.

When she returned to the small living room, she noticed that he had discarded his jacket and tossed it over the back of the couch. Gone too, was his tie. His shirt sleeves were rolled up to expose his forearms.

"Thanks," he said as she offered him the drink. His eyes touched her face and slid down the slender white column of her neck to rest on the overlapping lapels of the robe and the soft tops of her breasts as she leaned forward to hand him the brandy. He took a long, satisfying swallow, but his eyes never left her as they watched her over the rim of his glass.

Andrea felt the mood in the small room begin to shift and thicken as she stood near him. She noticed the smell of his cologne and the way his hair curled near the back of his ears.

Her voice became dry. "Excuse me," she whispered hoarsely, trying to break the seductive spell that was building in the living room.

"Where are you going?" he queried. His fingers reached up to slide against her forearm and touch the sensitive skin of her inner elbow.

Andrea swallowed the lump that was swelling in her throat. Her eyes lifted as she searched for the excuse to pull away from him. "It's beginning to rain. I thought I'd close the sliding door to the deck and change into my clothes."

"Not on my account."

She ignored the implication. "I don't want the draperies

or the carpet to get wet," she explained, knowing her excuse was feeble.

"Don't worry about that," he said, setting his drink on an antique end table. His voice was low and rough.

She ignored him and went over to the deck. The wind had picked up and was lifting the draperies to billow into the apartment. Small droplets of rain were running down the glass, staining the redwood slats of the deck. Andrea shuddered from the cool breath of the wind as it entered the room.

Just as she was pulling the door shut, she felt Jefferson's strong arms slide protectively around her waist. Her body responded to his touch, and her head fell backward as he began to kiss the wet tendrils of hair that surrounded her face and throat. Gently he pulled the pins from her hair, and it cascaded over her shoulders in soft waves of ebony silk. Andrea leaned against him as her skin came alive with his touch. The feel of his hands pulling her against him, the smell of the brandy on his breath as it whispered across her ear, and the warmth of his long, hard body next to hers, seemed to wrap Andrea in a magical cloak of seduction.

"Do you know how long I've waited to touch you?" Jefferson asked as his hands slid under her robe. Andrea sighed in contentment as his palm pressed warmly against the tight skin of her rib cage. Her heart skipped a beat when his fingers moved upward to caress her firm breast.

Warm, liquid sensations began to swirl within her, and her weak knees began to give way. She leaned against him, content to feel the gentle, insistent pressure of his hand under the folds of her robe. Slowly he untied the belt that held her garment together, and when it parted, he moved both of his hands to cup her breasts and hold her dear to him. In gentle, kneading strokes, his fingers embraced her breasts and his thumbs slid seductively over her nipples, sending waves of pleasure and desire through her body.

His hands dipped lower to run across her bare stomach. They pressed heatedly against her inner thighs, then pulled her roughly, insistently against him, allowing her to feel the desire that heated his loins and penetrated his heart. His hands were trembling as he turned her around to face him. Slowly he pushed the downy, indigo garment from her shoulders.

"How can any one woman be so beautiful?" he questioned as his finger traced an imaginary line from the tilt of her chin, down her throat, to linger at the swell of her breast. He closed his eyes against the passion rising within him. His fist clenched in frustration at his side. "Why can't I seem to get enough of you?"

Ignoring the questions that neither one of them could answer, he wrapped his arms around her naked form and pulled her close to him. His lips found hers in a protective, plundering kiss that sparked fires within her only he could ignite. She pressed her lips just as urgently against his, demanding as much as he could promise. When their anxious tongues met to dance in silent union, a shiver of anticipation raced up Andrea's spine as the heat within her ignited.

As he kissed her, Jefferson's fingers inched down her spine, gently touching each vertebra before they stopped to linger at the swell of her buttocks. While her lips were still locked in fevered embrace with his, she found the buttons of his shirt and nearly ripped them off in her pressing need to touch him. When at last the shirt lay crumpled on the floor, she stood on her toes and pressed herself more tightly against him, inviting his further exploration of her aroused body. She reveled in the pressure of his hardened chest against the soft contours of her breasts.

"I'm going to make love to you, Andrea," Jefferson whispered roughly against her ear. "And I'm never going to let you forget that you're mine—body and soul."

She thrilled at the protective, intense quality of his words. "I don't want to forget," she sighed before his hungry mouth captured hers and he pushed her gently onto the floor with the weight of his body. To ensure her comfort, he reached for a pillow from a chair and tucked it under her head. Once he had propped her against the pillow, he stood up, and lazily undid the belt to his trousers. His gaze never left hers as she watched his every move. She was content to witness the unveiling of his lean, hard legs as he stepped out of his pants. They were tanned and well-muscled and covered with the same dark hair that she saw on his chest.

Just as slowly, he slipped out of his underwear, and Andrea examined him boldly, unafraid to study all of him. He lay down beside her, and his fingers traced intricate patterns lightly against her shoulder. Shivers of delight sizzled through her body. "Make love to me," he commanded as he pressed his warm lips to her eyelids. "Make love to me as if this were our last night together."

Her hands, which had reached up to touch his chin, stopped, chilled by his words. "Is it?" she breathed, trying to ignore the welling sense of dread that his words had created.

His hands stopped their seductive movement. "Is it what?"

"Our last night together?" She couldn't hide the catch in her voice as fear settled upon her.

"Of course not," he sighed, nuzzling the soft skin of her neck. "I just thought it would be nice to let out all the stops." He paused for a second before repeating his throaty request. "Make love to me, Andrea."

Andrea slowly let out her breath and pushed any nagging doubts to the dark corners of her mind. She pulled herself onto him and rained kisses on his face and neck. A satisfied groan rumbled deep in his chest, and his fingers sank into the firm muscles of her back. Andrea's hands moved wildly through his hair as she boldly parted his lips with the sweet pressure of her tongue. Jefferson groaned again, and Andrea felt a shudder rip through the length of him. His hands slid caressingly down her body, rubbing her rib cage and hips in a gentle, persuasive motion that took hold of Andrea and warmed the deep core of her femininity.

Slowly she moved against him, allowing the feel of his soft chest hairs and light beard rub against her skin. She felt him sliding downward beneath her until his mouth found the supple mounds of her breasts. Lazily, he began to suckle, seeming to draw out all of her tension and fears. Instinctively she leaned over him, offering him the pleasure and comfort of her swollen breast. His mouth opened wider as she lay over him, and his tongue licked and caressed the smooth skin until she thought she would go mad with the longing that was spreading through her body. He murmured her name against the soft mounds, and his hands roved restlessly over the muscles of her back and hips, gently stroking her with sure, fluid movements.

A volcano was swelling within her, threatening to erupt at any moment. Warm, liquid lava was coursing through her veins, thundering in her ears. He slid beneath her once again, and his lips trailed hotly over her rib cage and smooth abdomen. She hugged the pillow more tightly to her as she felt his hot breath teasing her skin. His fingertips found the soft flesh of her inner thighs and he began touching her, petting her, exciting her, until she thought she would explode.

"Jefferson," she sighed. "Dear God, Jefferson, love me."

Her plea reached him. With a moan of pleasure, he pushed upward and spun her over onto her back. He moved against her and felt the dewy softness of her sweat mingling with his own. He was hot and fueled with desire. The ache in his loins was throbbing with need as a result of her gentle lovemaking. Nothing pleased him more than to hear the urgent, passionate cry that burst from her lips as he rolled over and felt her stretched out beneath him. His knee pressed her legs open insistently, and he lay upon her, touching each of her feminine muscles with their male counterparts. Knowing that she was as inflamed as he was, Jefferson let loose his passion and entered her with a wild, thrusting desire that was only equaled by the stormy lightning in Andrea's green eyes as she gazed up at him. Together they moved and blended in thunderous union, each igniting the other until the dam that had been holding them apart burst open and the shower of their love cascaded over them, sending them rolling in the after-washes of their combined passion.

"Andrea, I love you," Jefferson whispered as he tumbled beside her and kissed her quietly on the top of her forehead. "I always have." He held her tightly against him and snuggled with her on the carpet. "Let's go to bed," he suggested after a few minutes. "I want to show you how much you mean to me."

She sighed contentedly as he lifted her from the floor and carried her to the bedroom. Tonight, she thought to herself. At least we have tonight. I'll worry about tomorrow later.

Chapter 9

"I COULD GET VERY USED TO THIS," JEFFERSON DECLARED with a smile as he sat at the breakfast table in Andrea's apartment and finished his plate of French toast and sausage. He took a swallow of his coffee and leaned back in his chair. "You're as good in the kitchen as you are in the bedroom," he mused teasingly.

She smiled over her coffee cup and arched a doubting black eyebrow. "Am I?"

"Well, almost."

"Then why don't you get used to it?"

Jefferson suddenly sobered. "What do you mean? Do you want me to move in?"

"Why not?"

"It sounds great, but there's a hitch."

"An excuse, you mean."

Jefferson's eyes darkened. "Call it what you want, but it doesn't alter anything. I can't make any commitments to you until I find out about Megan."

"Her custody?"

Jefferson nodded and drained his cup. He rose from the table and put the empty cup in the sink. "Lara's very unpredictable. I can't do anything to rock the boat." Jefferson thought fleetingly about the negotiations with Lara. Could he explain to Andrea about the problems he was suffering at Lara's hand? Could he begin to explain to what lengths he would go to get back his child? Would Andrea possibly be able to understand? He looked into her eyes—wide, green and pleading to be a part of his life—and he denied himself. Until Megan was securely in his home, he couldn't trust anyone, including Andrea, with the knowledge of how he intended to get his child.

"I'd rather not talk about Megan or Lara right now," he said.

"Or us?" All the fears that Andrea had hidden in the night began to resurface in her mind.

"What do you mean?"

"I mean that I don't like the idea that I'm supposed to sit here and wait until you decide to see me again."

"What are you talking about? Did I say anything like that?"

She felt thankful that her fears were giving way to anger. "You didn't have to. I read between the lines."

His jaw hardened. "Well, once again you're reading more into this than there is."

"Am I?"

"Why do you insist on fighting with me?"

"And why do you lie to me and hide things from me, only to keep dropping back in my life?" She was trembling and tears began to collect in her eyes. "I didn't invite you here, you know."

"Just as I didn't invite you to the island! But you came, didn't you, for that damned interview! Don't accuse me of hiding things from you when you were the one that wanted to expose my life to the viewing public of America."

"Do we have to go through all of this again?" she asked.

His anger seemed to have simmered a little. "I hope not," he replied.

"Good."

There was an uncomfortable, weighty silence in the room. Jefferson leaned against the sink and stared at

Andrea, who feigned interest in her coffee. "I've got to go now," he said softly as he picked up his jacket from the back of the chair.

She didn't respond. She still heard the damning quality of his words as they rang in her ears. He still didn't trust her. That much was evident. She listened while he opened the front door, and mentally she counted his steps as he hurried down the stairs of the apartment complex. In a minute she heard a car engine sputter to life and then roar out of the parking lot. *He's gone,* she thought wearily, and the tears that had been burning at the back of her eyes began to slide down her cheeks.

The weekend without Jefferson loomed before her, and Andrea actually found herself looking forward to going back to work at Coral Productions on Monday. She told herself that all of her fears about Bryce and the interview were only ghosts. Bryce had probably come up with a dozen other names to headline the first interview of the ITV series.

The following week at work was tense but smooth. It was several days before Andrea realized just how desperate her boss had become. Just as she was beginning to relax and get back into the hectic routine of her job, the trouble began.

Bryce hadn't mentioned the Harmon interview, and Andrea assumed that her boss had finally admitted defeat. Jefferson had obviously convinced Bryce that he had no intention of making his personal life public, and the memo Andrea had received earlier in the week confirmed her thoughts. Bryce had requested that each member of the scriptwriting team come up with some alternate personalities for the ITV interviews, should any of the scheduled celebrities cancel at the last minute.

Most of the first five programs had confirmed guests, and Bryce was working on a list of celebrities for the additional ten shows. Andrea had researched the assignment and had come up with an idea for the show. In case Bryce didn't like her first choice, she also had a backup. She was grateful that the pressure was off about Jefferson Harmon. Sondra Wickfield, the imprisoned philanthropist, was slated for the first interview of the series, and for the first time since Jack had suggested Jefferson Harmon as a personality worthy of a television interview, Andrea breathed freely.

The door to Bryce's office was open, and Andrea hesitated slightly. Bryce had requested the meeting, but at the moment he was sitting back in his chair, looking out the window and listening raptly to someone on the other end of the telephone line. His balding head was bent to the side, and he cradled the phone between his ear and shoulder, leaving his hands free. He was busily scratching notes on a yellow legal pad as he listened. Apparently the person on the other end of the conversation was important. The words of encouragement that Bryce interjected into the one-sided conversation sounded reassuring, but the nervous twitch over his eye and the tightness of his skin, drawn over tense facial muscles, belied his calm.

"It will be no problem . . . just a few minor details to iron out. You know how it is with politicians, never able to pin them down. Don't worry about it. I'll take care of everything this afternoon." Sweat was beading on Bryce's head as he laughed hollowly at something that was uttered to him via the telephone. "Yeah, well, I'll talk to you later. *Ciao.*" Bryce slammed the receiver back into the cradle of the telephone, wiped his palm over his forehead and let his rigid shoulders slump. "Damn," he muttered to himself before raising his eyes to look into Andrea's questioning gaze.

A sad smile played on his lips as he waved her into his office. "Andrea . . . come in, come in. Sorry that I was tied up on the phone so long. I promise you that I haven't forgotten about our meeting."

Something in Bryce's gaze troubled Andrea, but she

tried to ignore it. "How's the interview series coming?" she asked, hoping to shake off the feeling of uneasiness that settled heavily upon her.

"Fine . . . fine," Bryce muttered as he scanned the notes he had written to himself on the legal pad and adjusted his glasses. "Sit down, Andrea. Now, tell me, have you come up with any ideas for the additional ten shows?" He held a pencil in his two hands and let his elbows rest on the table as he looked at her.

"I think so," she began. Why did she feel as if Bryce were scrutinizing her? Where was the easiness she usually felt in Bryce's modern office, filled with memorabilia from his successful television career? Everything looked the same—the tweed couch, plush charcoal carpet, cluttered desk—but nothing felt the same.

"So who have you come up with?" he asked with a smile that didn't quite make it to his probing brown eyes.

"I have a couple of suggestions, and I think that they would give a little meat to the series. I know that most of the guests we have slated are either television or movie people, stars with a flamboyant life-style."

Bryce nodded thoughtfully as he gazed over the pencil, encouraging her to continue. She did, although somehow she felt as if she was stepping onto shaky ground.

"A guy who has been getting a considerable amount of local press is Tom Reeves." Bryce's brows drew together, and Andrea continued to explain. "You know the man I'm talking about. He's a marine biologist who lives near Marina Del Ray. Lately he's been getting a lot of publicity due to his stand on preserving marine life, especially his concern about the whales."

"I know the man you mean," Bryce interrupted cuttingly. "But he's only a local hero for some of the residents of the coast. He has no *national appeal*."

"But—"

"Forget him, Andrea," Bryce retorted. "Who else do

you have in mind?" Bryce began to tap the pencil nervously on the desk. He was angry and agitated.

"I thought you might be interested in my brother, Martin."

"The ex-C.O.? Why do you think he would be interesting?"

"Certainly you've read of him," Andrea began. "He's California's spokesman for the rights of the Vietnam veterans. Because of him, and a few others like him, national attention has been given to the veterans: their disabilities, the social problems . . ."

"Who gives a damn!" Bryce asked, pulling a cigar from out of the box on his desk. He bit off the end and lit it.

"What?" Andrea asked, incredulous.

Bryce puffed furiously on the cigar until a cloud of blue smoke wafted over his head. "I said, who gives a damn about those crybabies? For Christ's sake, Andrea, men have been marching off to war since the beginning of time. Who the hell do these guys think they are to ask for special privileges? Their country called, and they answered. End of story."

"You can't be serious!"

Bryce rotated the cigar from one side of his mouth to the other. "Who the hell cares, Andrea? Certainly not *our* viewers! Do you think the same couple who watched an in-depth interview with Sondra Wickfield . . . or the pop singer, what's-his-name, Ricky Faith—the one who married the fifteen-year-old groupie—would be interested in watching a blind guy complaining about the way his country wronged him? Or some hillbilly of a marine biologist who spends his time worrying about whales and dolphins?" Bryce asked, brusquely. "No! Our markets center around the people between the ages of eighteen and twenty-eight who are either too young to remember the war, or had enough of it thrown at them ten years ago. What we need are topical, newsworthy personalities, stars that intrigue the public."

Andrea listened in silence, watching Bryce as he warmed to his subject. He got up from his chair and paced restlessly beside the desk, puffing angrily on the cigar.

"What you're saying is that you want only the most flamboyant, eye-catching celebrity willing to tell all, is that it?"

"Not quite." Bryce's eyes never wavered as he held Andrea's astonished gaze. "I'd settle for a respectable has-been politician with an active ex-wife and a scandal haunting him from the past!"

"You're still seriously considering Harmon?" she asked, and her stomach lurched uncontrollably.

"I'm not considering him, we're past that point. It's now just a matter of convincing him."

"I thought you already tried that."

"*I* did, but *you* haven't."

Andrea gasped, although she was trying desperately not to show her amazement. "You know I can't ask him."

"Why not?" Bryce sat down in his chair moodily. Once again he toyed with the pencil as he challenged Andrea with his blazing brown eyes.

"First, it wouldn't do any good. He's not going to listen to me any more than he listened to you."

"I wouldn't be so sure of that."

"But it's true! How could I convince him otherwise, even if I wanted to?"

"I'm sure you can be very persuasive when you have to be," Bryce intoned suggestively. "Use your imagination."

Andrea's eyes turned to green chips of ice. "What are you implying?"

"Look, Andrea," Bryce began, using a slightly more professional approach. He took the cigar from his mouth and let it burn, neglected, in the ashtray. "We're both adults. I know that you had an affair with Harmon ten years ago, and I'd be willing to bet that while you were on vacation, the two of you took up where you left off."

Andrea's back stiffened, and she swallowed with difficulty. She was silent as she listened to the end of Bryce's tirade.

"I don't expect much from you, just that you convince Harmon to talk to the public. That's not asking much. After all, they elected him; it's his duty to explain himself to them."

"I don't think so."

"What would it hurt?"

"I can't, Bryce, you know that."

Bryce pursed his lips firmly together, and his next words came out quickly and angrily. "Consider it part of your job."

Andrea felt sick to her stomach, but she wanted to be certain that she understood Bryce before leaving the room. "Are you suggesting that I sleep with Jefferson Harmon in return for his agreement to do the interview?"

Bryce frowned. "That's a callous way of putting it."

"But precise."

"Andrea, we're desperate. The bigwigs at ITV insist that Harmon be the lead-off story."

"Because you promised that he would," she guessed.

"It doesn't matter. The bottom line is that if we want to save the production company, we've got to get Harmon." Bryce's voice softened, and the hardness left his eyes. "I haven't asked much from you in the past, Andrea."

"What you're suggesting is illegal, Bryce."

The angry knot at the base of Bryce's jaw tightened, and the smile that covered his face was ruthlessly grim. "I don't think that you're willing to go to the Civil Liberties Union and tell them that I suggested that you sleep with Jefferson Harmon in order to keep your job. What would that accomplish? Exactly what you and Harmon are hoping to avoid—publicity. The scandal in the past, the divorce, your affair—everything that you and Harmon have worked so hard to keep private would be out in the open again."

Andrea felt backed into a corner, and a desperate

feeling of defeat encircled her. Bryce saw her vulnerability, and he pushed his point home.

"Come on, Andrea. We really need Jefferson Harmon for the interview. And maybe his ex-wife would be willing to be a guest at the same time. Just think of the public appeal that would hold, especially with all of the noise about her recent accident, and the fact that Harmon has agreed to defend her."

Andrea's lowered head snapped upward. "Jefferson is going to defend his ex-wife?"

"How about that!" Bryce smiled. "This is the kind of thing that will help our ratings rocket to the top."

Andrea's voice was calm when she found it. "I can't do anything that you're suggesting, Bryce."

"What?"

"I'm quitting. You'll have my official resignation within the hour."

"You're not serious."

"I am. I don't want to be a part of this."

Bryce's smirk became ragged. "Of course not, Andrea. You're a prima donna. I should have known I couldn't count on you when the chips were down."

Andrea left Bryce's office feeling suffocated from his taunts and the stale cigar smoke that had clouded her vision. Her chin was set in rigid determination as she cleaned out her desk and quickly typed her simple resignation.

"Andrea," Bryce called to her pleadingly. She felt all of her muscles tense at the sound. As her eyes moved up from the typewriter to the doorway where he was standing, she took in the beseeching look of pain in his eyes and the weary droop of his shoulders. She was still angry with him, but something in his dejected carriage made her anger slowly dissipate. "I'm sorry," Bryce apologized. "I shouldn't have jumped down your throat just because I'm having a bad day."

Andrea didn't move, but the challenge in her pale green eyes faded.

"I didn't mean half of the things I said."

"It's all right."

"No . . . no, it's not, and I hope that you'll reconsider resigning." He shrugged his shoulders awkwardly and pushed his hands into the tight pockets of his jeans. His eyebrows quirked nervously. "You and I, we've worked together a long time. I don't want to end it this way, when you're angry." He pulled the glasses from his face, folded them and tapped them against his chin.

"I think it would be best if I did leave," she sighed.

"We've had arguments before."

"Not like this. This is different, Bryce." Her voice was low and well-modulated, her opinion resolute.

"Things are different around here," Bryce explained.

"I know. That's why I think it would be best for me to leave."

"You don't approve of the changes I've made, do you?"

Andrea pursed her lips together thoughtfully. "No, I guess I don't."

"I had no choice. We had to go commercial in order to survive. This is a cutthroat business. You know that."

Andrea nodded and ripped the resignation from the typewriter. It was shaking in her hands when she gave it to Bryce. "I still think it would be best for all of us if I left now, today. The only thing I expect from you is a letter of recommendation."

"You won't reconsider?" Bryce asked tonelessly.

"No."

"All right. If it's what you want. But let me be the first to tell you, jobs aren't exactly plentiful these days."

"I realize that," was her clipped reply. The longer the conversation continued, the more uncertain she felt. For the first time in eight years she was giving up the security of a job, a good job.

Bryce turned on his heel and left her without so much as a good-bye. She wavered for an instant, but his taunts and mocking manner of only an hour before rang loudly in her ears. With quiet determination she slung her purse over her shoulder, picked up a small box of her personal belongings and headed out the door of Coral Productions for the last time.

Chapter 10

THE DAYS SLID INTO WEEKS FOR ANDREA. THOUGH SOUTHern California should have been abundant with employment for out-of-work scriptwriters, Andrea had no luck in finding a job. She hurried out of her apartment at eight thirty every morning, anxious to get to the next interview, and came home every evening discouraged and tired.

Every time the telephone rang, Andrea's heart stopped. Could it be Jefferson? Or could it possibly be a positive response to her most recent employment interview? Or, on the other side of the coin, might it be her parents asking about her life? So far she had been lucky. How could she explain to her soft-hearted mother and self-disciplined father that she had left a decent, well-paying job because of her involvement with Jefferson Harmon—the man they had openly denounced ten years ago?

Andrea was soaking in a warm bath when the telephone rang. Hurriedly she jumped out of the tub, wrapped a towel around her body and sprinted to the phone, leaving a wake of watery footsteps behind her.

"Hello," she called breathlessly into the phone.

"Andrea! God, I'm glad I caught you at home." Gayla's voice was a pleasant balm to Andrea's raw nerves. It had been ages since she had talked to her younger sister.

"You should talk," Andrea laughed back kiddingly as she adjusted the towel on her body and sank back onto the bed. "I've been trying to reach you for over a month and never gotten through."

Gayla's gaiety immediately subdued. "Yeah. Well, I haven't been around much."

"Not at all."

There was a long sigh on the other end of the wire. "I guess you're right. Doug and I were separated for a while. . . ."

"What?" Andrea's heart threatened to stop beating.

"It's a long story," Gayla admitted.

"I've got all night, if you want to talk about it."

"There's not much to talk about," Gayla sighed. "It's all so involved . . . a lot of emotions. I suppose I'm a lot to blame."

"I can't believe that!"

"Well, it's true. After Joey was born, things began to change for me. I didn't have my job anymore, finances were tight, and Joey hasn't been an easy child. Quite frankly, Andrea, I wasn't sure if I was cut out to be a mother."

"Of course you were."

"It's not that I don't love Joey," Gayla hastened to explain. "I love him more than I ever thought possible. It's just that it's hard, you know, being a wife to Doug, as well as a mother to Joey. I just didn't feel that I had any time left for *me!*"

"So you left Doug?"

"Only for a little while. Until I could sort things out," Gayla offered, and even over the long-distance wires, which spanned thousands of miles, Andrea knew that Gayla was crying.

"What about now? Are you happy now?"

For a moment there was a pensive silence as Gayla pulled herself together. "Things are better," she admitted. "Doug understands that I need more in my life than cleaning house and rinsing diapers. Recently I've been able to get out of the house a little more. I've found a relatively inexpensive exercise club that has a nice nursery for Joey, so I can go to exercise classes. I'm looking for a part-time job."

"That sounds encouraging," Andrea said, thinking aloud.

"It really is." There was more enthusiasm in Gayla's voice. "I guess my problem is that I want it all, Andrea— all life has to offer. I want to be a perfect mother, an understanding, caring, intelligent, sexy wife, *and* I want an interesting career. I don't want to miss out on anything— and that's impossible."

"How does Doug feel about all of this?"

"He's a very special man," Gayla admitted, and Andrea felt a little more at ease. "I think I really pushed him to the limit a couple of weeks ago, but I didn't understand all of the pressures he was coping with at his job." Her voice lowered slightly. "I'm surprised that he put up with me."

"Then you're telling me that I shouldn't worry about the two of you anymore, is that it?" Andrea asked.

"I think the worst is over. But, anyway, how about you? What have you been up to? I tried to reach you at the office today, but that flaky receptionist wouldn't give me any information other than the fact that you were, quote, 'no longer employed with Coral Productions.' What's it all about? Did you get another job? I never expected that you would leave Coral Productions or Bryce Cawthorne. The guy's practically a legend in TV land, isn't he?" Gayla's disconsolate tone had changed to one of enthusiasm.

"It wasn't an easy decision," Andrea hedged, sidestepping the real issue.

"But someone came along and offered you more money and a more prestigious position, right? You just couldn't refuse," Gayla surmised. Before Andrea could deny her sister's rosy-colored evaluation of her employment, Gayla continued. "You know that you've got a great career, don't you? I would give my eyeteeth to do the interesting things that you get to do. I saw *Pride's Power* a couple of weeks ago, and I thought it was great! I can't believe that it's being cancelled."

Andrea winced at her sister's opinion of her life, but then, even when she was younger, Gayla had always been a dreamer.

"Actually, *Pride's Power* never did all that well in the ratings," Andrea said, sighing.

"Who cares, now that you've got a better job? Who's it with? Some big-name production company?"

Andrea closed her eyes and tried to imagine Gayla's expectant face some two thousand miles away. "No, Gayla," she admitted hesitantly. "The fact is that right now I'm unemployed."

"What? But I thought—"

"I know what you thought, and I wish it were true, but the fact is that I quit Coral Productions a little over two weeks ago."

"Why?" Disbelief and concern rang in Gayla's question.

Andrea sucked in her breath. "I had become disenchanted with Coral, I guess, and then Bryce and I got into an argument."

"An *argument?"* Gayla echoed in disbelief. "You quit because of an *argument?"*

"It wasn't just an argument," Andrea conceded, aware that her sister thought she was covering something up. "It was an argument about Jefferson Harmon."

Andrea heard Gayla's sharp intake of breath. "Oh." There was a weighty pause before the younger woman continued. "What about Harmon? Have you seen him recently?"

"Yes."

"Oh God, Andrea, *why?* After the last time I thought you would never see that man again. Just because he divorced his wife—"

"The divorce had nothing to do with it. I went to see him because Bryce wanted him to do an interview for television. He refused, and Bryce got angry. I didn't want to be caught in the middle, so I quit."

"And what about Jefferson? Do you still see him?"

"He dropped by once, but it didn't work out," Andrea stated, but there was a trace of despair in her voice that Gayla detected.

"Have you talked to him since then?"

"A couple of times."

"And?"

"And nothing. We talked, that's all."

"But you would like there to be more between you, wouldn't you?" Gayla could always see right through her, Andrea mused to herself. She shifted restlessly on the bed.

"I guess so. I'm really not sure."

"That's your problem," Gayla stated flatly.

"What do you mean?" Andrea asked, almost fearful of her younger sister's candid response.

There was a resigned sigh on the other end of the wire. "If I've learned anything at all about myself during these past weeks when Doug and I were separated, I realized that I had to take charge of my life myself. No one else was going to do it for me. I had to let Doug know how I felt about him, and Joey, and, I guess, even myself. I couldn't hide inside myself and brood about my problems. And, Andrea, the same goes for you. If you really want Jefferson Harmon, then you have to let him know how you feel about him. Find out if he wants the same things in life that you want."

"It's a little more complicated than that."

"It's as simple as you want it to be," Gayla argued staunchly.

Andrea toyed with the edge of the pillowcase. "I thought you considered it a mistake for me to see Jefferson again," she accused.

"It doesn't matter what I think. I was only afraid that you might get hurt again," Gayla admitted. "*But*, you only have one life, Andrea, and you're the one who has to make the decisions about it. You can't hope to keep everyone happy. It just won't work!" Andrea could almost see her younger sister shaking her auburn head in frustration. "You can't sit around hoping that Jefferson will call you. If you want him, take the initiative for Pete's sake. This isn't the seventeenth century, you know."

Just as Gayla was about to continue, Andrea could hear a childish wail on the other end of the line. Suddenly Gayla's thoughts turned elsewhere.

"Look, Andrea," Gayla hurriedly added. "I've really got to go. Joey just tripped over the edge of the coffee table. I'll call you later."

"Sure," Andrea agreed with a smile. Gayla's motherly concern suggested that although she might have doubts about herself as a mother, she was indeed well-suited for the role. If nothing else, things seemed to be working themselves out in Seattle.

After replacing the receiver of the telephone, Andrea decided against renewing her now tepid bath water. Shivering slightly, she stepped into her favorite jeans and an orchid-colored cowl-necked pullover. As she tucked the light sweater into the waistband of her jeans, Gayla's well-meant advice echoed in Andrea's mind. *Take the initiative, Andrea. It's your life; you're the one that has to make the decisions concerning it.*

In some respects, Andrea begrudgingly admitted to herself, Gayla was probably right. But how could her younger sister, so far off and wrapped up in her own problems, analyze or even begin to understand the depth of Andrea's feelings for Jefferson, or the confusion that she experienced whenever she was near him. Sure, Andrea knew that Jefferson wanted her, at least physically, and she wasn't foolish enough not to realize that he cared for her. It was just that all of the misunderstandings of the past prevented him from allowing himself to *love* her. Even though he was divorced now, Andrea doubted that he could ever truly be free of his ex-wife, the mother of his child. Megan was the fragile link that would always bind Jefferson to Lara, regardless of any divorce-court agreement.

Andrea had begun to brush her long, onyx hair as her thoughts took hold of her, and though she stared into the mirror, her eyes didn't catch her reflection as she tugged the brush through her hair in furious strokes. She thought only of Jefferson—his dark, knowing eyes and familiar smile. Gayla had pierced to the heart of the matter in one respect, at least. Andrea wanted to be with him, *needed* to see him again.

It was true that Jefferson had called her twice in the past few weeks, and though the conversation had been stilted and uncomfortable, Andrea had known that, in a small way, Jefferson was attempting to reach out to her. It was true, also, that since that last night in Victoria, Andrea had willfully resisted any deep, feminine urge to contact him. Pursing her lips at the thought, Andrea mentally allowed that perhaps Jefferson's feelings of ambivalence toward her might have stemmed from the fact that she had not recently admitted her feelings for him. Perhaps he was as unsure of her as she was of him.

Andrea tossed the hairbrush onto the bureau with a sigh of disapproval. Then why hadn't he asked to see her? Why did she always imagine a rigid edge of wariness in his voice when he called? Why did she think that he was purposely holding something back from her—against her? *Why, damn it, hadn't he attempted to see her again?*

Angrily she pulled on her boots and sat for only a second on the edge of the bed, wondering if she was about to make a mistake that she would regret for the rest of her life. Preferring action to any further soul-searching, she marched out of the bedroom, snatched her purse from the couch and, with a jerk, pulled her leather jacket from the hall tree. She had decided to visit Jefferson, unannounced. He might not be at the address she had kept in her memory, there was always that chance, but Andrea didn't want to risk the confusion and disappointment of another tense, gut-wrenching telephone conversation. This time she wanted to look into the hazel depths of his eyes when she spoke to him.

The drive to the apartment building was a strain on her. As she wound her way in the clogged streets of the Southern California highway system, doubts crowded her mind. She gripped the steering wheel until her knuckles blanched. The music that blared from the radio didn't distract her, and she could feel her stomach beginning to churn at the thought of walking in on Jefferson Harmon unannounced. Would he be alone? Would he see her? What if he had company, perhaps his daughter, or worse yet, his ex-wife?

Quickly dousing any further conjecture about him, Andrea cranked the wheel of the car and ground to a halt in the parking lot of the high-rise modern apartment complex where Jefferson made his home. The antithesis of the grand old house on Harmon Island, the building was an imposing structure, composed of sand-colored stucco and splashes of rust-hued brick. To blend with the sunny, palm-lined surroundings, the architecture of the building was a modern blend of Spanish design. A large rock garden, nestled in a well-kept courtyard complete with wrought-iron gates, guarded the entrance to the building.

Ignoring her rapidly pounding pulse and the butterflies that were fluttering in her stomach, Andrea hurried through the courtyard and pushed open the hand-carved wooden doors of the building. Once inside she was given one last opportunity to retreat. A liveried security guard, wearing a smile that seemed as well-groomed as his clipped moustache, asked her politely to state her business.

Her voice faltered a little as she responded. "I'd like to see Jefferson Harmon. Is he in?"

The guard cocked a graying eyebrow condescendingly,

and his smile became routinely bored. "Are you expected?"

"No . . . no, I'm not," Andrea admitted reluctantly.

"I see."

Andrea squared her shoulders and tipped her chin upward in order to meet the security guard's assessing stare. "Would you please call Mr. Harmon and tell him that Andrea Monroe would like to see him?" she asked firmly.

While the corners of his mouth turned peevishly downward, the security guard did as he was bid, dialing Jefferson Harmon's floor from memory. As he relayed Andrea's message his sobered expression changed into surprise. Jefferson's response was not what he had expected.

"She'll be up right away, sir," the guard stated into the phone. With a face that had altered from bored indifference to genuine charm, the guard escorted Andrea to the elevator, instructing her to disembark on the eighth and uppermost floor of the building. As Andrea pushed the correct button, she wondered how often in the past the security guard had turned away inquisitive reporters who had hoped to get in to see Jefferson Harmon.

The elevator climbed smoothly upward to settle with a groan at the eighth floor. Andrea tried vainly to curb her growing anxiety and nervousness. Waiting for the unyielding doors to open, she unconsciously tapped her fingers against the brass rail that surrounded the interior of the elevator car. She tried to pull herself together, but found it impossible to appear outwardly calm when her nerves were twisted so tightly in apprehension.

The elevator doors parted silently, and after taking a deep breath, Andrea stepped onto the plush carpet of a short hallway. Before she reached the oaken door to his apartment, Jefferson unlocked the dead bolt. The door swung silently inward, inviting Andrea to enter Jefferson's private hideaway in the dusky California sky.

Jefferson stood near the door, and his demeanor was anything but warm. His dark, questioning hazel eyes studied Andrea with uncompromising intensity. Though he struggled to appear affable, Andrea could tell that he was as tense as she. His lips were pulled into a tight, unpleasant smile, and his hands were pushed deep into the pockets of his gray slacks. His torso was bare and rigid, all of the muscles straining in taut control. A pin-striped shirt was tossed carelessly over the back of a navy-blue sectional sofa, and Andrea guessed that Jefferson had just gotten home and was about to change his clothes before the security guard's untimely call had altered his plans.

"Come in," Jefferson invited tightly.

For a moment all of her determination fled Andrea. The look of foreboding in his eyes, the electricity that sparked in the air and his distracting, well-muscled chest, warned Andrea against entering Jefferson's apartment. "I . . . I didn't mean to disturb you. Are you busy?"

"If I had been busy, I wouldn't have let you in," he replied callously, and his unpleasant smile turned almost wicked as he recognized her discomfort.

Hesitantly Andrea stepped into the expansive living room of the apartment. The light that filtered into the room was from a long window that faced the western skyline and from skylights strategically placed over the sofa. Andrea's eyes roved anxiously over the dim interior and the furnishings. She noted a staid elegance in the blend of contemporary and antique chattels. Leather editions of law encyclopedias, original surrealistic paintings, elegant brass lamps, and modern sectional and period pieces that included leather wing chairs graced the room.

"Would you like a drink?" Jefferson asked smoothly as if to help ease the nervousness that she tried to hide. He stretched to put on his shirt and flicked on one of the lamps, intending to reduce the intimacy of the surroundings.

"Please," she responded, and crossed her arms involuntarily across her chest, as if to ward off a sudden chill in the air.

After casting a disdainful look in her direction, Jefferson strode over to the bar, pulled out an opened bottle of brandy and poured a drink into an empty snifter. Another drink, already half-consumed, was on the liquor cabinet. Andrea realized that Jefferson must have been drinking alone in the darkness, half-dressed, before she had arrived on his doorstep. The gnawing anxiety in her stomach began to grow.

As Jefferson offered her the drink, he spoke. "Well, to what, or *whom*, do I owe the honor of your presence?" he asked, hoisting his snifter into the air in a mock toast.

Andrea accepted the offered glass of brandy and took an experimental sip. "I came here on impulse," she replied, letting her eyes drift upward to meet his. Almost imperceptibly his jaw tightened.

"Is that right?" he mocked. Dark hazel eyes drove deeply into hers, challenging her.

Although she couldn't ignore the sarcasm in his words, she held her temper in check. "I just wanted to see you," she explained honestly.

The sincerity in her eyes reached out to him, and he had to caution himself against trusting her too completely. This time, whether she knew it or not, he was on to her game, and way ahead of her. Rather than feel rewarded in the knowledge, the thought gave him a sickly sensation. Undaunted, he continued. If she wanted to play out the charade for all it was worth, he would comply. "Just like you wanted to see me back on the island?" he asked. "About four weeks ago, right?" His eyes narrowed as he studied her response.

Andrea could feel his coiled tension. She knew he was baiting her, but she didn't understand why. "That was different."

"How?" His question stung the air with disbelief. The

anger that he had tried to conceal became unmasked in the starkness of his probing gaze. "Why was that any different? I thought that you came to see me on the island because you wanted to. Isn't that what you said?"

The sarcasm that tainted his words and the contempt in his disbelieving stare sparked Andrea's barely controlled temper. "You're twisting my words again, Jefferson," she accused. "Of course I wanted to see you on the island, you *know* that I wanted to be with you."

"But . . . ?" he coaxed, settling into the deep midnight-blue cushions of the couch and eyeing her speculatively. His shirt, still unbuttoned, opened slightly to reveal his tanned chest and rigid muscles.

"But," she began, picking up his cue, "it was more than just my curiosity to see you again, more than my need to be with you. I also came to the island as a favor to my boss. Is that what you're driving at?"

Jefferson ignored her question. "And this time is different, or so you claim. Do you honestly expect me to believe it?"

"Of course." Andrea was still standing as she looked down at Jefferson. Her eyes locked with his doubting gaze. "You obviously don't believe me. Why not?"

"Your boss tipped me off." He took a drink and emptied his snifter.

"What?" she demanded.

The edge of confusion and dismay in her voice caught Jefferson's attention. He could see that she was clearly perplexed and angry—angry enough to have been telling the truth. Jefferson could almost *feel* her confusion at his abrupt attitude toward her. He wondered fleetingly if he had been wrong about her, but discarded the traitorous idea. It would be too easy to trust Andrea again. Rather than look into her bewildered, misty eyes, he frowned in concentration at his empty glass.

"Look, Andrea," he sighed as he set the glass aside. "I

understand the reasons that you came here. . . ." His gaze lifted to meet the innocence of her eyes.

"You do?"

"Sure." His charming off-center smile, which had been a trademark during his successful political campaigns, fell neatly into place.

Andrea felt some of her anxiety ebb, just as he had anticipated. A small light of satisfaction entered his eyes, and Andrea knew that she should be wary. She waited, hoping that, given a little time, Jefferson would get to the point.

"Good. I'm glad you understand me." She forced herself to smile enigmatically as she took a seat opposite him. The stiff wing chair wasn't comfortable, but she attempted to appear casual as she sipped her drink.

Jefferson eyed her steadily. His pectoral flexed, belying his outward calm. "You can explain to your boss that my position hasn't changed," he announced evenly. His smile seemed tighter, his gaze more severe.

"What?" Andrea nearly spilled her drink at Jefferson's announcement. "What are you talking about?" Her glittering green eyes, filled with anger and confusion, dared him to continue.

"The interview," he snapped impatiently. "Don't bother to play dumb with me, Andrea. It belittles you. Cawthorne hasn't given me a minute's peace since I left the island!" Jefferson's voice lowered dangerously. "He threatened that he would send you—as some sort of sacrificial lamb, I suppose—but I didn't think that he—and least of all *you*—would go through with it! How could you stoop so low, Andrea?" His green eyes blazed in fury and disgust.

"Oh, my God," Andrea moaned, finally understanding Jefferson's uncompromising attitude. "You still don't trust me, do you? You honestly think that I'm involved in some sort of seduction that Bryce engineered! For God's sake,

Jefferson, give me some credit, will you?" The anger that had been rising in her throat quickly melted into bitter frustration and disappointment as her face drained of color. With hands that shook uncontrollably, she set her drink on the table near the chair. "I'm sorry," she apologized, whispering hoarsely. "I should never have come here. It was an unforgivable mistake."

She rose to leave but found that her knees seemed intent on buckling. Although she started for the door, Jefferson moved more quickly than she had anticipated. "There's no reason to play out this scene," he stated, capturing her upper arm in the strength of his insistent fingers. "Why can't you admit that Cawthorne sent you?" he demanded, giving her upper arm a painful squeeze.

"Don't touch me," she warned. "If you don't realize, if you don't *know*, that I wouldn't have anything to do with something as sordid as the scenario you're suggesting, I never want you to touch me again!"

Proudly she jerked away from him, unashamed of the tears that were building in the wide depths of her pale green eyes.

Jefferson wavered. Andrea's disdainful indignation and the pain in the shadows of her eyes were convincing, and there was more in her gaze as well. Disgust and contempt were thrust angrily in his direction through the sheen of unshed tears. Suddenly Jefferson realized that he had made a terrible mistake.

"Andrea, wait!" Again his arm reached for her, but she was already at the door. She grabbed for the handle and had opened the door a crack when he reached her and roughly slammed the door closed. "Don't go," he pleaded, pinning her against the polished oaken panels.

"I'm leaving, Jefferson," she hissed in response. "I didn't come here to listen to your insults and your lewd, imaginative fantasies." Her small fist clenched and pounded the door in frustration.

"Why did you come?"

"Oh, God," she cried, unable to hide the anguish in her voice. "I came here because I thought, or at least I hoped, that you and I had something worthwhile, something worth saving." Her voice lowered to a raw whisper. "I was wrong!"

"No . . . no! Don't ever say that." Jefferson's face twisted in a tormented display of the emotions that had ravaged him to the bone in the last four weeks. "You've got to believe that we do have something special, Andrea. We both know it." His hand, gently persuasive, moved upward to brush a tear off her cheek. She turned her head away from his touch and let the tears slide unrestrained from her eyes. "Andrea," Jefferson whispered, his fingers entwining in the soft strands of her ebony hair. "I love you."

She stiffened against the door, and a sob that had been building within her broke free. How long had she waited to hear just such a confession from him? Four weeks? Ten years? A lifetime? His thumb moved over the hill of her cheek, and she felt her body sag wearily against the door. "How can you say you love me," she asked, her voice and body trembling with savage emotion, "when you just accused me of trying to seduce you in order to please my boss?"

"I've always loved you, Andrea," he moaned. "Surely you must know that. Why else would you come back to me?"

"I think you already answered that a little earlier in the conversation. I can't understand how you expect me to believe that you could *love* a woman whom you thought capable of . . . of prostitution. Because that's what it all boils down to, you know. You just accused me of attempting to make love to you for personal gain. You were only one step away from calling me a *whore!*"

"Damn it, Andrea," Jefferson muttered, letting his head fall forward to rest next to hers against the door. His breath whispered raggedly against her hair as he spoke, and she smelled the sweet brandy mingled with his own woodsy-masculine cologne. His shirt draped open, and his firmly muscled chest pushed tightly against her body. He was too close . . . too near. His voice, hoarse and raw, seemed to touch the very soul of her being. "I never meant to hurt you. You've got to believe that much. I love you more than any man should love a woman. I always have."

"To the point of believing that I would actually seduce you, and *use* you for personal profit?" she hurled back at him. She tried to slide away from him, but his hands restrained her, pushing her against the door. She longed to believe him, yearned to fall victim to his touch once again, but the open wounds, still stinging from his earlier remarks, were too fresh.

"I didn't mean—"

"I know what you meant," she interrupted, aware that the rising and falling of her chest made her breasts touch his naked torso. "But I don't understand how you could believe it of me!"

Jefferson looked skyward for a moment. "I'm sorry. I know that an apology won't erase the words or the pain, but please accept it. It's just that your boss seems so adamant about that damned interview. He intimated that you felt the same."

"What? You talked to Bryce?"

"You know that I did," Jefferson snapped back. "You were in his office when he called yesterday." Jefferson's eyes searched Andrea's. "At least that's what he said."

"I wasn't there."

Jefferson tensed. His whole body became rigid. "You weren't in the room when Cawthorne called me?"

"No."

"But he said that you and he agreed that it would be best for everyone—you, me, the public, even Megan—if all the truth were out, all the skeletons hidden away in the closet were set free."

"And you believed him?" Andrea asked incredulously.

"Why wouldn't I? He asked you to come and see me in Victoria, and you agreed."

"I don't understand any of this, Jefferson. Bryce did ask me to do anything I could to make you do the interview. He even suggested that I . . . sleep with you," she admitted, and closed her eyes against the repulsive memory.

Jefferson's jaw squared. "And?"

"And I quit. I haven't worked for Coral Productions for over two weeks."

Jefferson took a step backward, putting distance between their bodies. His eyes held hers captive, and his hands were planted firmly on either side of her, preventing her escape.

"All right, I believe you. If you're not here because of the interview, why did you come?"

"I thought I explained that. I thought we had something to salvage."

"But why now—tonight?"

Andrea smiled in spite of herself. "Because I was tired of sitting around my apartment waiting for the phone to ring. I've been looking for a job, and it seems that I'm forever hoping that the phone will ring and that it will either be someone with a fantastic job offer, or . . ."

He nodded, encouraging her to go on.

". . . or that it would be you." Her eyes seemed to glaze with the mist from the sea. "I just wanted to be with you again." Slowly her hands moved upward and tentatively touched the exposed skin which covered his ribs. His eyes closed at the warmth of her touch, and he groaned.

For a moment he stood arrow straight, not moving, just letting himself enjoy the gentle persuasion of her soft hands. But when she pushed her body close to his, he could stand the bittersweet agony no longer. His arms wrapped possessively around her, and his fingers entwined in the rich thick curls of her hair. His lips, when they found hers, were insistent and full of promise. They parted willingly, and his supple tongue sought out and touched hers in flickering bursts of desire.

Andrea's pulse quickened, and her blood heated as it coursed through her veins. Her fingers kneaded the hard, inflexible flesh of his chest and a warm, growing ache spiraled within her body.

"You're a witch," he growled. "You know that, don't you?" Before she could answer, one arm curved under her knees and the other tightened around her back. Effortlessly he lifted her off the floor and, while hugging her close to him, carried her through a hallway toward the bedroom. She nestled against him and could hear his heart hammering heavily in his chest, echoing in the silence against the erratic thudding of her own heartbeat.

She ignored all thought of protest. For the moment she only wanted to be more intimate with him, to feel one with him. Her body ached for his touch. She closed her eyes and felt her eyelashes brush against the hard muscles of his chest. The love she felt for him was a desperate, passionate ache that controlled her thoughts and her body. His own words of love, whispered with such agony against the door, tore at her heart, but she tried not to think of them. Even in the warm embrace of his arms, she realized that too many years of treacherous misunderstanding had paled the meaning of his confession. But, despite all of the doubts that still plagued her, just as she had in the past, she would let her body rule her mind. Once again she would give in to the joy of expressing her love for him.

The bedroom was in shadows. Only a very dim moonglow and the frosted lights of the city entered the room to disturb the darkness. Andrea's eyes adjusted to the darkened interior and noticed that the pale stream of light from the moon entered through skylights positioned over the bed. The other furnishings in the room blended into the night, and Andrea was too caught up with

Jefferson's commanding virile presence to notice anything other than the soft feel of the bed on her back and the warm possession of the man lowering himself near her. His touch seemed electric, even through her clothes. His kisses were warm and erotic, seeming to explode with a passion that had been kept at bay for ten lost, lonely years.

His tongue rimmed her lips as if, by its touch, Jefferson could memorize the feel of the wet, supple softness of her mouth and the urgency of her desire. His hands caressed her lightly, stroking the soft fabric of her clothes to make her want more . . . all of him. Andrea closed her eyes against the dizzying, heady sensations that he evoked from her willing body, and her fingers massaged the firm, flat muscles of his chest and abdomen, eliciting the same pleasure in him that his fingers were arousing within her.

"You don't know how many nights I've dreamed of this," he whispered against the shell of her ear. "I thought I would go mad with the need of you."

"You should have told me."

"I couldn't," he groaned, and his lips captured hers once again. This time the gentle persuasion of his kisses had deepened into hungry demands. His hands pulled the hem of her sweater from her jeans and found the sensitive skin over her stomach. Involuntarily Andrea sucked in her breath, and Jefferson's fingers lightly skimmed the waistband of her jeans, softly brushing her hips.

Andrea sighed in contentment and wound her fingers in the thick, near-black waves of his hair. Urgently she pulled him against her, and with a groan he pulled her sweater over her head.

For a moment he stopped and stared down at her. Her raven-black hair was splayed in tousled curls against the light color of the bedspread, and her eyes, partially closed, reflected the silver moonglow in their misty green depths. Pupils, dilated from the darkness and the heat of passion, seemed almost iridescent as Andrea looked up at him. Her breasts, swollen in her need of him, strained against the lacy fabric of her bra, and the dark nipples waited expectantly for his expert touch.

Andrea felt drugged, and her eyelids half-closed as Jefferson took one supple breast in his warm hand and feathered his fingers across the taut, straining nipple. Andrea moaned with pleasure and arched upward against him. His fingers dipped beneath the flimsy barrier of the white silk, only to retreat and leave her aching for more of his sensitive touch. Slowly, as if with deliberate leisure to prolong her inflamed agony, his head descended, and in gentle strokes he licked her breast over the filmy bra, sending lightning bolts of passion through her blood and heating the molten desire in her body until she could stand no more of the sweet torture.

"Love me," she pleaded desperately, longingly. Her prayerful request made him groan in satisfaction. "Jefferson, please, make love to me as you never have before." In response he lifted his head and let his tongue rim the nipple before it slid over her breast to her collarbone. There he lingered, rimming the delicate bones in moist, sweet circles of desire that sent Andrea soaring to new heights of need and burning want. His tongue slowly climbed her throat until it found her parted lips. Slowly, lazily, he rimmed her mouth, deliberately ignoring the open invitation as she sighed.

He teased her, darting in and out of her mouth seeking a response. When at last he probed the furthest reaches of the dark, sweet cavern of her mouth, he let his tongue dance and mate with hers until she felt shudders of smoldering passion ripple through her.

His fingers toyed with the fragile, wispy bra until at last Andrea felt it part and her anxious, full breasts fall into Jefferson's waiting hands. With a groan of pleasure he pushed his fingers into the soft flesh and then lowered his head to take one nipple gently between his teeth. He tugged softly, and Andrea, overcome with the need of him, pushed his head into her so he could take all of the nipple in his mouth and end her torment. As he kissed and sucked at her breast, his hands found the waistband of her jeans and began to explore beneath the denim material. His hands touched her, stroking the most intimate parts of her until she felt as if she would be consumed in the fire of torment that was building.

When he pulled away from her, disappointment welled in her eyes, but he ignored it, and instead sat at the foot of the bed. Carefully he pulled off one of her boots, and then the other before sliding his hands caressingly up her calves under the legs of her jeans. His fingers reached upward, and she arched to meet him, frustrated that she was unable to feel the hardness of his muscles against her.

He inched the jeans downward, past her hips, and smiled wickedly when she lay on the bed waiting for him, wearing nothing but soft, lacy panties. His fingers played with the final barrier that stopped him from entering her. He seemed to delight in the hot whirlpool that was swirling inside her, running up her veins, giving her skin a rosy glow. "You are a sea witch, Andrea, but you're mine. My own."

With measured time he tugged at her panties, pulling them slowly over her hips and legs, letting his fingers touch each part of her leg as he removed the unwanted garment. His kisses started at her toes and moved upward, retracing the path that his fingers had blazed. Andrea felt the weight of his body as he lay on her, and she sighed in contentment.

"Undress me," he called into her sensitive ear. Quickly she responded, trying to restrain herself and bring as much pleasure to him as he had given her. She lowered his shirt from his shoulders and let her fingers graze the contour of his muscled arms. Before touching his pants she let her hands massage the flat muscles of his chest and abdomen, moving her fingers in loving circular patterns against the taut male nipples. Teasingly she put one in her mouth and felt Jefferson's groan of pleasure and satisfaction. The salty male flavor of his skin stayed upon her tongue and lips, and when he bent to kiss her, she felt as if she were drowning in the taste of him.

Her fingers touched the muscles of his back, his buttocks and his thighs as she pushed his slacks off his legs. When he was nude, lying near her, she touched his hot, naked skin in feather-light strokes until a thin layer of sweat gilded his body. His breathing became as labored and shallow as her own.

She continued to stroke him until with a groan of frustration he rolled over and lay upon her. His hands clasped over her forearms as he held her against the sheets. "You're a tease," he whispered, dipping his head to kiss her just beneath the ear.

"And so are you," she countered breathlessly, not listening to the conversation, concentrating instead on the small spot below her ear where Jefferson's tongue melted against her skin.

Slowly his arms folded and his weight settled firmly against the soft bed of her skin. Everywhere they touched Andrea felt warm needles of electricity piercing her skin, forcing her heart to beat more rapidly. He kissed all of her, leaving wet trails of fevered desire across her body. No part of her was unknown to him, and no part of her wanted for fulfillment. He loved her with the same desperate, driving need that was only matched by her own rapturous desires.

She lost herself to him and experienced the satisfaction and pleasure that only he could give. His hands molded her, teased her, and his lips and tongue pressed against her warm, salt-sweet skin. Her breasts were kneaded and kissed until they seemed engorged, and when he entered her, she willingly gave all of herself to him, melting against him with a gasp of surrender as she felt him join in ecstatic union with her. In her love-drugged mind, it seemed as if there had never been a time when they had been apart.

His flesh, her flesh, belonged together until the end of time.

She moved with him, found his rhythm and felt the hot throbbing force of his desire inside her. His hands and fingers guided her, touching her in all of the intimate places that pushed her to higher planes of sexual delight. The tension in her body began to coil and tighten until she finally burst in satiation. She felt shock waves of rapture race through her blood as his body pushed her into the final, shuddering explosion of long-denied passion, and the two of them blended together in a breathless union of flesh and spirit. Never had she felt so wanted. Never had she felt so free. Never had she loved him more than she did in those first few moments of afterglow.

His fingers caressed her skin, and his kisses continued until Andrea drifted off to a trouble-free sleep as she snuggled in the strong comfort of Jefferson's arms. How long had she dreamed of such blissful surrender? How many years had she waited to share just such a night with him?

Jefferson's passion seemed to feed upon itself. Later in the night, when both she and Jefferson had been sleeping, Andrea awoke to find Jefferson kissing her body. Her breasts were once again straining against him, asking for the sweet assuagement that only he could give. He suckled and held her close, as if he were drawing as much pleasure from her body as he were giving. Andrea held on to him, content to feel the gentle pressure of his mouth around her nipple, thrilled by the feel of his hands as they touched and petted her inner thigh, warmed by the feel of his kisses as they caressed her neck and shoulders. Once again they found each other, and warmth cascaded over Andrea when Jefferson lifted her on top of him, and encouraged her to move above him. Her black hair fell forward, and Jefferson ran his hands through the silken, raven tresses. Her breasts swayed above him as she moved her hips in rhythmic strokes, and Jefferson lifted his head to capture a dancing nipple in his mouth. The pressure of his lips pushed Andrea upward, higher and higher until with a shudder of rapture, she collapsed upon him in radiant pleasure.

The pleasure didn't stop. Once more before morning Jefferson awakened Andrea. She found herself dragged into consciousness by the erotic teasing of his lips brushing provocatively against the tip of her breast. His fingers touched her in feather-light caresses and aroused her until all desire for sleep left her and she longed for more intimate seduction and satisfaction from him.

It was near dawn when he finally wrapped his arms around her and settled into a deep, worry-free sleep. Andrea had never felt such utter contentment, not since the day she had first given herself to him ten years ago.

Chapter 11

ANDREA SQUINTED AGAINST THE OBTRUSIVE, BRIGHT SUN, and she tried to snuggle back into the peaceful slumber that slipped away as the sunlight settled boldly against her eyelids. It seemed that no matter how she turned on the large bed, the piercing light insisted upon disturbing her. Where was she, and why was the light so unyielding and bright?

The sudden realization that she had spent the night in the arms of Jefferson ran like ice water through her cloudy mind, and immediately she awakened. It was difficult to get her bearings in the strange room. The brilliant California sun impaled her from the skylight and didn't help clear the last remaining cobwebs in her groggy mind.

"So you decided to wake up after all." Jefferson was standing near an open window several feet from the bed and had turned to face her at the sound of her awakening.

Andrea pushed her hair away from her face and attempted to straighten the long ebony strands with her fingers. Her eyes became accustomed to the sunny interior of the room, and she stretched. "What time is it?"

Jefferson watched her unguardedly as the satin sheets slipped against her body and outlined the perfection of her slim figure. A smile crept onto his face for a moment. "Be careful," he warned as his hazel gaze drifted seductively over her body. "If you don't stop looking so damned provocative, I'll be tempted to climb back into bed with you and make last night look tame compared to what I intend to do to you."

She couldn't avoid the challenge. Seductively one of her black brows cocked over her heavy-lidded green eyes, and as she moved on the bed the sheet that had been draped over her breasts slipped just a fraction of an inch.

Jefferson's smile curved in wicked satisfaction. "I was right last night when I called you a witch. I'd like to—"

"What?" she asked in feigned innocence.

He hesitated for a moment, and then he shook his head in stiff determination. "You know damned well what I'd like to do to you, but it will have to wait. I'm late as it is."

"Late?"

"For work." He buttoned his shirt and slung a necktie under the collar. "Even ex-governers have to earn a living, you know," he stated as he knotted his tie and tucked the hem of his shirt into his pants.

"The law firm?" she asked.

"Yes." He nodded and straightened his tie. He hesitated for a moment, as if he wasn't sure how much he wanted to tell her about his work. His explanation was short and simple. "After a few months of restlessness, just after the resignation, I decided to re-establish my practice."

"Corporate law?" she asked, sensing that he was deliberately holding something back from her. She couldn't help but pursue the conversation. When he didn't immediately respond, she sat up in the bed and drew her knees to her chin, letting the sheet drape over her as she huddled on the bed and watched him. "That was your specialty, wasn't it?"

"Right."

He picked up his suit jacket and slung it over his shoulder. Although his stance appeared casual, Andrea felt an underlying chill to his curt replies. After the passion of the night before, she refused to be shut out. He must have guessed her thoughts, and with a sigh he dropped the jacket and came over to sit on the edge of the bed.

Jefferson's eyebrows drew together to form one dark, angry line, and his lips pulled into a tight, grim frown. Restlessly he racked his fingers through his dark hair. "For the most part, I work in corporate law," he conceded. Then, as if to change the course of the conversation, he picked up his watch from the nightstand and slipped it on to his wrist. "It's nearly noon," he announced, almost as if talking to himself.

"No!" Andrea jumped out of bed and began gathering her clothes. "I've got an interview across town at one thirty. I'll never make it!" She tugged on her jeans and as hurriedly as possible pulled her sweater over her head. Jefferson stood and watched her as she got dressed, bending down to pick up her boots and hand them to her as she needed them. He wrestled with a decision in his mind and wondered just how much of his life he wanted to share with Andrea. One part of him wanted all of her, every bit of her life, to blend with his, but another, more wary side of his being reminded him of the pain he had borne in the past at her hand, and noted that any further involvement with her might cause more agony to not only him and Megan, but Andrea as well.

Andrea eyed Jefferson curiously as she slipped into one boot. It was obvious he was wrestling with a weighty decision.

"Well, are you going to tell me what's going on in your mind?" she asked. His eyes asked an unspoken question. "It's obvious that you want to tell me something, but feel, for God only knows what reason, that you can't." She crossed her legs and looked upward at him. "Don't you think it's time we stopped playing games with each other? If you have something to say to me, say it."

"You're not the only one who's late," he admitted. He came nearer to her, and his hand reached out to cup her chin and force her eyes to hold his. "I have a client who, no doubt at this very moment, is pacing the reception area of my office." His voice was low and somber, and his eyes darkened as he searched Andrea's face. A scene from the night before flashed in her memory—Jefferson drinking alone in the dark.

"Someone important, I gather," she said lightly as she pushed a clinging strand of hair out of the neck of her sweater.

"You might say that," he agreed vaguely, teetering between holding his silence and confiding all of the secrets of his life to the petite woman he couldn't drive from his mind.

"Who?" she asked. Her voice was off-hand and casual, but she felt a tension beginning to contract within her. She reached for her other boot and began to pull it on.

"Lara."

Andrea let the boot fall to the floor, and her green eyes swept upward to study Jefferson's grim face. She let her teeth sink painfully into her lower lip before she could trust herself to speak. "So it's true. I had heard that you were going to defend her."

Jefferson's fist clenched, and he ground his teeth together in frustration. "It's true, but it wasn't by choice!"

Suddenly she didn't want to see any more clearly into what had been his marriage. She felt herself an unwanted intruder in a life she hadn't shared with him. Another woman had first claim on him. Her voice was surprisingly even when she responded. "It doesn't matter. It's really none of my business. . . ."

"It is your business, damn it!" He sat beside her on the edge of the bed and rubbed his hand over his forehead. His shoulders sagged wearily. "I know that this is probably hard for you to understand, but right now, with things as they are, I can't make a commitment to you."

She felt as if a cold, sharp knife had been thrust in her back. "I haven't asked you for one," she reminded him.

"But you deserve one, don't you see," he hurled back at her. "Look." He stood up and began pacing at the foot of the bed, his hands pushed into his pockets. "You know how important it is that I gain custody of Megan?"

She nodded silently, never letting her eyes off of his worried, strained face. Thoughts raced through her head. He was going to reject her again; she could almost feel the cruel sting of his words before they were uttered. Holding her emotions at bay, she dug her fingers into the bed and listened while silent dread overcame her.

He continued, and his pacing never slackened. "Then you understand that I would prefer not to drag her through the torture of a messy custody hearing? I don't want her to ever feel that she's a possession that Lara and I have to fight over. I hope that somehow we'll be able to avoid hurting Megan any further. A custody battle made public by the press is something I want to avoid. However, I am willing to take my chances with the court if nothing else works."

"I know," she whispered, almost inaudibly.

He paused for a moment and cast a stern look in her direction. "Lara seemed determined to fight me for Megan," he began, his hazel eyes darkening. "And I accepted the fact that without a doubt we would have our day before the judge." His eyes narrowed thoughtfully, and a sinister smile twisted on his lips. "But that was before my ex-wife broadsided a car while intoxicated. Now one of the passengers is suing her, and she's in serious trouble. Fortunately Lara realizes what kind of trouble she's facing."

"So she asked you to defend her?" Andrea guessed.

"And I refused." The pacing stopped.

"But I thought you just said—"

"I know what I said. Just listen for a moment. I told Lara no flat out, and she became desperate. It seems that no other attorney worth his salt would risk his reputation on her case. She had no choice but to ask me."

"But I thought you weren't available."

"I wasn't. Not until Lara made an offer."

"An offer?"

"Think of it as a deal. We struck a bargain." His jaw tensed with the disgust that he so obviously felt.

Andrea's green eyes widened in horror as the meaning of Jefferson's words became clear to her. "You bargained for your daughter?"

"Sounds a little callous, doesn't it?"

"Jefferson, how could you *bargain* over an innocent child? You said you didn't want her thought of as a possession, but it seems to me you treated her as if she was some sort of commodity. You used your wife's misfortune to get her to agree to give up her daughter. Good God, Jefferson, that's right out of *Rumpelstiltskin!*" Andrea blanched, shock and disbelief cascading over her.

Jefferson's eyes glittered mercilessly as he disagreed. "Not quite. You're forgetting that I'm Megan's father, and that her mother is a neglectful alcoholic. Megan has to get away from Lara!" His features softened slightly. "You know that I would be willing to let Lara retain partial custody if and when she successfully wins her battle with alcohol. But until that time I'll stop at nothing to see that my daughter is safe and cared for!"

"I still think it's cruel," Andrea said, sighing.

"To whom?"

"Megan, for one."

"How? She's too young to understand right now. And when she's older, she'll respect my point of view."

"You're sure?"

"Nothing's certain except that I have to do what I think is best. And just think about the scandal and problems a custody hearing will cause." Jefferson shook his head thoughtfully. "No, I've considered all of the alternatives, and as far as I'm concerned, I've come up with the best solution for Megan's welfare, and that's really what custody is all about, isn't it? If I honestly thought that Megan would be better off with Lara, I would let her stay with her mother. But it's obvious that my child is being neglected, and I won't stand for it! Nothing . . . no one . . . will stop me from doing what I feel is best for Megan. *No one!*" The severity of his gaze and the brittle harsh sound of his voice startled Andrea. His words could only be construed as a warning to her.

Andrea wet her lips anxiously. "Jefferson, are you suggesting that I'm a threat to your relationship with Megan?" she asked, puzzling over the dark shift in his attitude.

His face softened slightly, and he put a comforting hand on her shoulder. "Of course not," he murmured earnestly, and bent down to place a kiss on her forehead. Andrea thought she would melt with relief.

"But you were including me when you said that no one would stop you from doing what's best for Megan, weren't you?"

His eyes clouded, and the corners of his mouth lifted into a grim smile of self-defeat. "I know that you wouldn't consciously do anything that might jeopardize my chances for custody of Megan."

"Of course not!"

"But I don't trust Lara. Just because she's agreed tentatively to give me guardianship of Megan doesn't mean a damned thing. It's not as if I can draw up a legal document stating that in exchange for my legal fees I expect to become Megan's guardian. The law doesn't work that way."

"Thank goodness!"

"Touché." His smile became wistful. "But the point is that Lara hasn't signed the change of guardianship papers I gave her, as yet, and I'm only giving her till the end of next week to do it."

"Why?"

"What if she doesn't sign?" Jefferson countered. "How would it look if, on the one hand, I'm in a custody battle with my ex-wife, claiming that I'm more fit than she to take care of my daughter, and on the other hand, I'm defending her against someone who might well have a legitimate claim against her?" Once again Jefferson raked his fingers through his hair. "I think the term most commonly used in a case such as this is conflict of interest."

"Then you may not be able to defend her anyway."

"Right. If the prosecuting attorney for the victims of the automobile accident cries 'foul,' then I'll have to drop the case. And," he admitted raggedly, "I'll be back to square one."

"A custody hearing?"

"And fight."

"Then what have you gained?" Andrea asked. "And what does all of this have to do with me?"

"You're one of the reasons I'd rather not wind up in a custody battle. If Lara decides to fight me for Megan, she'll try to paint a very black image of me to the judge. It could get very ugly."

"And she could dredge up all of the scandal about us from the past?"

Jefferson's repressed anger flashed in his eyes. "For starters, yes. And then she'll claim that I never got over you, and that I failed her, and probably that we—you and I—were having an affair during the entire duration of my marriage to her."

"But that's a lie!" Andrea nearly shouted.

"You know it, and I know it, but the judge doesn't," Jefferson conceded.

Suddenly everything that Jefferson was saying made sense, and she finally understood his point. "Oh, dear God," Andrea whispered desperately. An invisible leaden weight settled on her slim shoulders. "I shouldn't have come here," she thought aloud.

"Don't be ridiculous."

"I'm not! Don't you see? If she finds out, Lara will crucify you. If she knows that we're seeing each other, she'll use it against you!" A new horror, deep and filled with pangs of twisted guilt and anguish, buried itself in her heart. "We can't see each other again . . . not until you have your daughter." Tears threatened her eyes and burned in her throat, but she refused to break down and cry.

"That may be a long time. I don't want to lose you, not again." Jefferson thought for a moment, and sat down on the bed next to Andrea. "If Lara signs over the guardianship papers, everything will work out. A custody battle won't be necessary, nor will a hearing. No judge will argue with the parents' mutual consent. If that's the case—" he placed a comforting arm over her shoulders—"we could be married."

"Married?" Andrea repeated, stunned.

"Of course. Andrea, we should have been married ten years ago."

Andrea shook her head, and her black hair swept across her shoulders. "And what if Lara doesn't agree?" she asked, thinking about the future. Dread steadily inched up her spine and her green eyes, filled with both love and regret, drove into Jefferson's, demanding an answer.

He frowned. "Then we'll just have to be discreet until everything is settled. Once it is, we'll get married."

The silence and tension that were building between them was heavy and oppressive. The joy that should have erupted in Andrea at the prospect of marrying Jefferson was killed by the knowledge that the future with him was only a dim hope, an elusive quest. Too many obstacles stood in the way of their happiness.

Jefferson looked at his watch, shook his head and reached for the jacket. "What's wrong?" he asked, touching her lightly on the knee.

"You make it sound so simple."

"It's not simple," he admitted, "but we can work it out." He helped her to her feet and guided her by the elbow out of the bedroom.

Her mind was whirling with vague thoughts of the past blending unevenly with hopes of the future. As she reached for her purse and jacket, Jefferson took hold of her shoulder and gently turned her around to face him. "All I want from this life is to have you as my wife and to live with both you and Megan. That's not really so much to ask, is it?" His head lowered, and his lips found hers before she could answer. His kiss was warm and enticing, touching the very core of Andrea's soul. Jefferson's hands, broad and strong, pushed against the small of her back, forcing her body to mold uniquely to his. A sob broke in her throat, and tears pooled in her eyes.

When he pulled himself from her embrace, it was to look down upon her with eyes firm with resolve. "We just have to be patient a little while longer. That's all we need . . . a little time."

Andrea shook her head in despair. "I don't know if I can wait any longer, Jefferson. It's been over ten years."

"I know." He kissed her lightly on the forehead, and his lips lingered on the smooth surface of her brow. "A little longer won't hurt."

Why was the pain twisting inside her like a cold, silver dagger? Andrea didn't think she could bear any more of the agony. "I think it would be best for everyone concerned if we, you and I, didn't see each other again. At least not for a while," she stated in a voice that trembled from her emotions.

"No!" Jefferson's denial was vehement, and his eyes began to blaze dangerously.

"I don't see how it can be any other way. At least not until you have custody of Megan."

"Don't worry about the custody, or anything else. I can handle all that. As I said before, by the end of next week I should know where I stand with Lara and whether she'll grant me custody without a battle." He unlocked the door of the apartment and propelled her by the elbow toward the elevator. They stepped inside, and as the elevator car groaned into motion, Jefferson continued. "The only reason that you and I have to be discreet is because of the past. Since I knew you before I met Lara, and because of all of the publicity and scandal that was involved ten years ago, we have to be careful. Although Lara and I have been separated for several years, the divorce was final only a couple of months ago. I can't do anything that might look bad before the court."

"You're saying that we'll have to act as if we're ashamed." She pulled her arm away from him gently and continued. "I don't think I can do that. I don't think I can continue seeing you in the dark, always looking over my shoulder, afraid of who might be watching, on the lookout for the press or your ex-wife." She shook her head firmly, and her eyes glittered with determination. "I can't hide in the shadows, Jefferson, while you put on a public facade."

"That's not what I'm asking."

"Think about it! You expect me to hide my love for you, don't you? Well, I've hidden it for ten years, and I don't think I have the strength to do it any longer! Besides which, I don't care to be put in the middle, between your daughter and your ex-wife.

"I want what's best for you, Jefferson, and right now, things being what they are, the best thing for you is to find a way to get control of Megan. Everything else, including me, has to be secondary, which I'm willing to accept, but I can't hide, damn it! I won't!" The tears that had been threatening to spill began to slide down her cheeks. Her voice, rough with emotion, failed her, and she whirled away from him to stride through the elevator doors as they parted.

Jefferson was on her heels, and when she reached the parking lot he caught her arm and whirled her around to face him. She began to lose her balance and fell against the hood of her car. "I'm not letting you go, damn it!" he bellowed, emotion ravaging his face. So loud was his proclamation that an elderly couple turned to see who was making the commotion.

"You're not giving me much of a choice," she countered, and added with a hissing whisper, "Don't you see that?" She struggled to break free of his uncompromising grasp.

"What I see is a ten-year-old scene being replayed by a woman who hasn't really grown up!"

"What?" she gasped, her eyes brilliant with indignation.

"Isn't this exactly what happened ten years ago, Andrea?" His voice was as raw and savage as the fury that flamed in his eyes. "Things got a little rough for you then—the water too deep—and you ran away!"

"No!" She raised her arm as if to strike him, but his furious gaze restrained her.

His grip on her arm tightened. "You ran out on me ten years ago, when the press and your family were ready to nail me to the wall, and you're doing it again! Your excuses might have changed, but the result is the same. Well, this time I'm not going to let you have the privilege of hiding from the truth!"

"Don't use your courtroom tactics on me, Jefferson. I know you too well, and I won't let you twist my words with your convoluted logic!" Haughtily she raised her head and her eyes over the sarcasm and mockery in his words.

"I don't have to twist your words, Andrea. What you're attempting to say is coming out loud and clear. Why don't you, with your straightforward, common-sense approach, explain to me why it is that each time we get close together, each time I think we're falling in love, you run out on me like a frightened animal. Is it me you're afraid of? Yourself? Or the commitment of love that terrifies you?" The sarcasm in his words was reflected in his eyes, which were as cold and hard as green stones as they pinned her against the car.

"You seem to forget that I was the one who came to you

last night. Just as I was the one who visited you on the island." Her trembling lips pulled into a grimace as she jeered, "I don't recall that you made much of an effort to see me!"

He twisted her arm slightly in his anger. "I searched everywhere I could to find you ten years ago! And as for recently, I only wanted to wait until I had everything straightened out with Lara concerning Megan before I saw you again!" He released her arm and shook his open palms skyward in exasperation. "I was only trying to avoid another misunderstanding with you, Andrea."

"And you did a great job, didn't you," she taunted, sarcastically.

"Damn it, woman! Can't you understand? Don't you know what torture I've put myself through because of all of this?"

"Torture? Torture? Don't use your courtroom theatrics to gain my sympathy. The reason you never came to see me in L.A. is much easier to explain. You told me so yourself last night. You thought that I was working with Bryce Cawthorne in order to get an interview for the television program, remember? Last night you accused me of offering my body to you in order to get a story!"

Jefferson stepped backward as if he had been struck. "There's no reasoning with you!"

"That works two ways, Jefferson," she replied hotly, fumbling in her purse for her keys. Her heart wrenched at the painful words they had thrown at each other, and her fingers quivered as she unlocked the car door and settled inside. Tears were streaming down her face, and quiet sobs escaped from her throat as she started the car, put it into gear and roared out of the parking lot. She didn't look backward and avoided the image in the rearview mirror. She didn't have the strength to cope with even one last fleeting glimpse of the man she loved.

Chapter 12

As the 747 jet increased in speed to take flight Andrea's anxiety increased. The huge jet lifted upward, but Andrea's stomach seemed to stay on the ground. Only after the jet had leveled did Andrea's tense fingers release their white-knuckled hold on the armrests. She watched the earth below her, studying the countryside until a thick bank of clouds obstructed her view and the only image visible in the small window of the plane was the reflection of her own pale face.

Even though earlier in the day she had taken pains with her makeup, the strain in her weary eyes was beginning to surface, and the color of her skin, usually rosy and slightly tanned, was now morbidly white. Dark circles were evident under her eyes, and her full cheeks had hollowed. Her appetite had become minimal, and even the expensive weave of her heather-colored wool suit couldn't hide the fact that she had lost nearly five pounds in the past six weeks. She recognized the symptoms for what they were. Hadn't the same malady ailed her ten years ago? But knowing what the cause of her problem was couldn't give her back her usual zest for life. No, once again she would have to rely on time to heal her wounds.

As if to dislodge the thoughts beginning to take hold of her, she reached under her seat and pulled out her leather briefcase. Quickly she pulled out a neat stack of typed correspondence. Though she had read the letters from Carolyn Benedict at least a dozen times in the past week, she once again studied the request that had prompted her sudden trip to New York.

Carolyn Benedict was the producer of *Days of Promise*, a New York based, mediocre daytime soap opera. The ratings for the show had been slipping, and Ms. Benedict was looking for several fresh writers. She had learned of Andrea from some discreet checking concerning the writing staff of *Pride's Power*, cagily deducing that with the cancellation of the night soap, possibly a few writers would lose their jobs. Carolyn was a cunning woman and realized that what couldn't hold a viewer's attention during prime time, might well be a success during the early afternoons. Hence the letter to Andrea.

After nearly two months of job-hunting, it looked as if Andrea might be offered decent employment. Thoughtfully Andrea tapped the letters from Ms. Benedict against her skirt. When she had first received them, Andrea had been hesitant to accept the invitation to New York. But the other job offers she had received had been poor and few. After her initial ambivalence about moving to New York had subsided, Andrea reasoned that a move might be the best thing for her at this point in her life. A change of scenery might be the only thing that could snap her out of her recent depression.

After all, Andrea had asked herself, what held her so passionately to California? Without a job and without Jefferson there was nothing in California that couldn't be found elsewhere. She bit her lip at the thought and continued tapping the letters against her knees.

Since her last quarrel with Jefferson, Andrea had replayed the damning scene over in her mind so often that it haunted her nights and nagged at her during the day. Pieces of the heated argument lodged themselves in her mind, and she had trouble ignoring them. The hot words, Jefferson's savagely angry face, her own unfair and cruel words, wouldn't leave her a minute's peace. To make matters worse, a day hadn't passed without seeing something to remind her of Jefferson and what he must be going through. Stories about him, some true and some outrageously false, occupied the headlines of all the local scandal sheets. Even the more reputable tabloids had tidbits of his life to fill leftover space on the social pages.

The news that Jefferson Harmon, California's exgovernor, had agreed to defend his wife in a scandalous lawsuit had hit the newsstands full force. And then, when two weeks later it was rumored that Harmon had resigned as Lara's attorney, the fires of gossip flamed to new heights. Rumors concerning the once-popular politician and his socialite wife spread, and all of the interest in Jefferson Harmon's stormy marriage rekindled.

The custody battle over Megan, once discreetly avoided by the press, was now the subject on the cover of most of the weekly gossip tabloids. Even Andrea's name had crept into the copy of some of the stories, and the anonymity of an unlisted telephone number hadn't deterred a few persistent reporters. More than once in the last two weeks Andrea had slammed the receiver of the phone down in anger when an inquisitive reporter had called and asked her galling questions about Jefferson, if she was, indeed, the Andrea Monroe who had once been involved with the man.

Dinner was served by an efficient stewardess, and for a short time Andrea was distracted by the meal. Just as she had for the last six long weeks, she attempted vainly to push thoughts of Jefferson from her mind.

The flight was long and tedious. When at last the plane touched down and sped along the lighted runway of JFK International, Andrea let out a sigh of relief. Though only seven o'clock in L.A., the three-hour time difference took hold of Andrea, and she felt as if it were, indeed, ten. Andrea disembarked as quickly as possible, waited for her luggage and hailed a cab. It had been several years since she had last visited Manhattan, but tonight the excitement and electricity of New York held no fascination for her.

The hotel was located not far from the studio, and the room assigned to her was clean, if not inviting. After a long, hot bath, she pulled on her robe and turned on the late news to take her mind off her worries concerning the interview that was scheduled for early the next morning. Though she was tired, the night stretched before her, and she wanted to fill as many hours as she could so she would be tired enough to fall into a deep sleep.

The anchorman was discussing the President's most recent peace-keeping trip to the Middle East when the picture on the television became clear. Andrea listened to the story with interest, and when the commercial break came, she began leafing through a magazine that had been left on the nightstand.

Perhaps it was the brawny anchorman's lead-in line or the more personal tone his well-modulated voice assumed, but whatever the reason, Andrea dropped the magazine to stare at the television.

"Unfortunately, today a glamorous life, once the envy of most Californians, has ended in tragedy." Andrea's eyes widened in horror and her throat became raw when a recent still photograph of a beautiful, slightly wistful Lara Harmon flashed on to the screen.

"This afternoon Lara Whitney Harmon was pronounced dead on arrival at Mercy Hospital in suburban Los Angeles. Cause of death is uncertain at this time, although there is speculation that Mrs. Harmon's death might be alcohol-related." The picture on the television changed to show an older photograph of Lara standing beside Jefferson during the inauguration ceremony while he took the oath of office as governor of California. Jefferson looked younger and less haggard than he did now, but even then, some five years ago, there was a haunting, savage cast to the clean, even lines of his face. The newscaster continued with the story.

"Mrs. Harmon, considered at one time to be San Francisco's most eligible banking heiress, was married for eight years to California's ex-governor, Jefferson Harmon. Governor Harmon resigned his position before completing his term, citing 'personal reasons' as explanation for his hasty retreat from public office. At the time there was speculation that the cause of the governor's resignation was related to Mrs. Harmon's rumored alcoholism. That rumor was firmly denied by Mr. Harmon's press agent."

The photograph of Jefferson and Lara was replaced by live coverage of the apartment building that Andrea recognized as Jefferson's California residence. Jefferson, appearing haggard, lean and worried was clutching a frail-looking child to his chest and pushing through an insistent throng of reporters who had gathered near the entrance to the building. Questions were shouted at his retreating figure, but he ignored them all, only pausing once to hurl a look of frustration and annoyance toward an intruding camera. Then he disappeared into the guarded building, and the reporter began to speculate further into the personal, mysterious life of Jefferson Harmon.

"Oh, dear God," Andrea moaned as she lay on the bed and clasped her hands over her mouth. She closed her eyes and listened while once again Jefferson's life was rehashed by the local reporter and the anchorman summed up the events leading to Lara Harmon's untimely death.

Andrea felt as if she should run from the room, scream the anger and confusion boiling within her out of her lungs and attempt to find a way to comfort Jefferson and his daughter. Jefferson's agonized face, captured by the television camera, vividly burned in Andrea's mind. And the image of the child, small and distraught, clinging to Jefferson in a death grip, tore at Andrea's heart. She wanted to cry, she wanted to shout, she wanted to ease the pain of both Jefferson and his young child.

Instead, still holding her hand against her mouth, she got up, snapped off the television and went into the small bathroom. She stood over the sink to douse cold water on her skin and after the first icy splash looked dubiously into the mirror at her ashen image. Lara was dead! The thought drove thin needles of disbelief into her mind. Dead! How could it be? Andrea sat down heavily on the edge of the bathtub and rolled her head in her hands. "No," she whispered to herself. "No . . . no. . . ."

A half an hour must have passed before Andrea found the strength to make her way back to the bed and collapse heavily upon it. She was surprised at her reaction to Lara's death and tried to think rationally about it. Although she had never met Jefferson's ex-wife, she felt as if she had known her, at least vaguely. Lara Whitney Harmon had always graced the headlines of the social pages, and there was something elusively beautiful about her that had made her the darling of the press. Even when her alcoholism was suspected, the press, and therefore the rest of the world, considered it more Jefferson's failing than Lara's problem. Even Jefferson himself admitted as much.

Andrea slipped under the covers and felt a chill pass through her body. How was Jefferson handling Lara's death? Was he able to cope with Megan? Was the child old enough to understand what was happening? Tears welled in Andrea's eyes and slid backward toward the pillow as Andrea wondered dismally about Jefferson, thousands of miles away from her.

The telephone sat invitingly close to the bed. Jefferson's telephone number blazed in Andrea's mind, and after a moment's hesitation she picked up the receiver. She started to dial, but quickly changed her mind and hung up vehemently. What could she say? It probably would be impossible to get through to him anyway. Dear God, was he all right?

Andrea flipped off the light near the bed and shut her eyes. She tried to concentrate on anything other than Jefferson or Lara, but no matter how sincerely she tried to erase the painful picture from her mind, the haunting image of Jefferson, his dark hair disheveled and his suit wrinkled, remained as if frozen in her mind's eye. She tossed and turned in the bed as she replayed the scene of Jefferson shoving his way through the unyielding crowd of reporters. And then there was Megan, so small and frail-looking, clinging to Jefferson.

Sleep remained elusive for the rest of the night. It was just as well, because any moment that Andrea did doze, bizarre nightmares of Jefferson and Megan would permeate her thoughts and awaken her. Each time she awoke, Andrea found relief in the knowledge that she had only been dreaming, until she realized that Lara Harmon was, in fact, dead. Jefferson's ex-wife, the mother of his little girl, was gone forever.

An intense, dull, throbbing headache pounded relentlessly in Andrea's mind throughout the night, and by the time that the first slanting rays of dawn crept through the crack in the drapes, Andrea was glad for the excuse to get out of bed and away from her miserable thoughts.

She dressed more hurriedly than she normally would have, but suddenly her appearance didn't seem important. The smart, ebony suit appeared professional. Its tailored lines accentuated the turquoise silk blouse and its bow, which tied around Andrea's throat. She took some care with her hair, pinning it carefully to the back of her head into a loose coil, and she used more color on her cheeks than she normally did. It wasn't a very good disguise. The ashen color of her face and the dark circles under her eyes were still evident.

Andrea still had over an hour before the interview. She hurried to the lobby of the hotel and located a small restaurant near the entrance of the building. She didn't feel like eating, but she knew that it might be hours before the opportunity for a meal arose again, and somehow she had to try and calm her queasy, churning stomach.

The cup of tea didn't calm her nerves, nor did the toast

and jam settle her stomach. She found herself ignoring the hasty breakfast to stare at the clock or a copy of a newspaper that some patron had left on a nearby table.

Telling herself that it was a mistake, she reached for the paper lying open to the sports section. She refolded the paper and found the front page. In the lower corner of the front page was a picture of Lara Harmon—the same wistful portrait that had flashed on the television screen only hours before. Steadying herself with a swallow of tepid tea, Andrea read the article. A picture of Jefferson and his daughter accompanied the article located in the midsection of the paper.

The story was essentially the same as had been reported the night before, but speculation had apparently grown that Lara Harmon's death was suicide. Whether intentional or not, authorities had determined that the lethal combination of alcohol and sleeping pills had cost Lara her life.

The picture of Jefferson and his child wasn't clear, and yet Andrea saw through the anger in his eyes as the photographer had caught his attention. There was more than fury on his glowering face—it seemed to Andrea that there was desperation in his eyes. Once again Andrea thought of calling him, but she didn't. No doubt he'd had a restless night himself, and there was a three-hour time difference to consider. It wasn't even five o'clock in L.A.

After tossing the paper aside, Andrea stared into her teacup. What was she going to do? Should she call Jefferson, give him words of sympathy and comfort, or would he think she was once again intruding into his private life? What was he doing? What was he thinking? How was he coping with his child? The questions came so quickly into her mind, and she couldn't find answers to any of them.

Disgusted with herself for dwelling on something she couldn't alter, she decided to walk the seven blocks to the studio and wait there until the time of her appointment. Perhaps the bustle of activity on the set of *Days of Promise* would take her mind off of Jefferson and his child.

To say that the studio was busy would have been a gross understatement. Although Andrea had spent the last eight years writing for Coral Productions, nothing that Coral had done could come close to the level of activity that accompanied the rehearsal in progress on the set of *Days of Promise*. It seemed as if the entire thirty-person cast was scrambling around the studio rehearsing lines or waiting for the sets to be complete or studying last-minute changes to the script. The cameramen, lighting technicians and production crew added to the confusion.

A secretary led Andrea to another area of the building to wait in Carolyn Benedict's office.

"Ms. Benedict will be here shortly," the redhead explained apologetically. "Could I get you a cup of coffee while you wait?"

"Yes, thank you," Andrea murmured, and the secretary hurried out of the office. Andrea was still standing in the middle of the room, looking at the various pictures adorning the walls. She recognized several movie and prime-time actresses that at one time or another had played a role on the twenty-year-old *Days of Promise*. Andrea couldn't help but smile when she recognized a much younger Nicole Jamison in one of the photos.

"Here you go," the secretary said as she entered the room with two steaming cups. "Do you take anything in your coffee?"

"No, black is fine."

A smile spread on the secretary's impish face. "Good. I just saw Carolyn. She's on her way."

"Thanks." Andrea took an experimental sip and continued to peruse the old photographs. At the sound of Carolyn Benedict's entrance Andrea turned to face the door.

"See anyone you recognize?" the smiling, gray-haired woman asked.

"A few." Andrea returned the smile.

"Did you notice Bryce Cawthorne?" At the surprised look on Andrea's face Carolyn continued. "Down there on the left . . . in the black and white. Bryce was in the original cast, twenty years ago."

Andrea had to bend over to look at the slightly faded photograph. There were several members of the cast assembled, and one was indeed Bryce Cawthorne. "I didn't know he worked on *Days of Promise*," Andrea explained, lifting her eyes from the photograph to study Carolyn's face.

Carolyn waved in the air as if to brush Andrea's statement aside. "Most of the actors in the business have been on a soap at one time in their lives. Of course I wasn't here at the time, but Bryce Cawthorne was the original Andre Van Cleave," Carolyn explained. "But enough of that. I guess by now you know that I'm Carolyn Benedict."

Andrea's smile widened. There was something forthright and personable about the middle-aged woman. "I guessed as much."

"You got my letters, obviously, or you wouldn't be here." Carolyn sat behind a desk and pulled out a file from her drawer. "Sit down, sit down," she said with a wave of her plump hands.

Andrea took a sip of her coffee while Carolyn adjusted her reading glasses and studied the papers in the file. "By the way, I talked with Bryce Cawthorne about you."

Andrea swallowed with difficulty.

"He seems to have the highest regard for you." Carolyn's deep brown eyes looked over the top of her glasses and found Andrea's expression to have changed from pleasant to shocked. It took Andrea a minute to recover her professional poise. The last thing she expected was praise from Bryce.

"I worked with Mr. Cawthorne for eight years," Andrea said weakly.

"And you quit because of the cancellation of *Pride's Power?*"

"It was time for a change."

Carolyn's eyes narrowed speculatively. "Yes, well, I guess it was." She lit a cigarette and blew a blue stream of smoke upward in the air. "Let's get right to the point, shall we?"

"Fine with me."

"*Days of Promise* is having problems of its own, and our ratings have begun to slip. Part of the problem lies with the fact that ABS has rescheduled their afternoon lineup, and the show playing opposite *Days of Promise* has a lot of viewer appeal. What we've decided to do is change the direction of our story line and beef up the script. We're going to add three new writers and introduce several new, young characters. By summer, when the teen viewing audience peaks, we hope to have story lines centering around the new, younger characters."

Carolyn had stopped, as if she expected Andrea to comment, and Andrea quickly nodded her agreement.

"You realize that this is quite a bit different from writing for prime time?"

"Yes."

"Then you know that we churn out four times the scripts that you're used to. And that's on a daily basis, and doesn't include the rewrites." She stubbed out her cigarette as she eyed Andrea. "Do you think that you can handle that?"

"I'm sure of it," Andrea said.

"And you wouldn't mind moving to New York?"

"Not at all." Andrea felt her heart twist at the false words, but she attempted to maintain her composure.

"All right, let's go down to the set and I'll show you around. . . . You can meet a couple of the other writers and the director, and we'll discuss the salary we're offering." Carolyn got up from the desk, tucked the file folder neatly away and led Andrea out of the office. "And before any decisions are made, I think you'll be interested in seeing how we get through each tear-jerking episode of *Days of Promise.*" The short producer gave Andrea an exaggerated wink as they walked down the hallway toward the studio.

Chapter 13

WHEN ANDREA ARRIVED HOME THE NEXT DAY ALL SHE wanted to do was hide in her bed. She knew that the interview had gone worse than it should have, due largely to the fact that she couldn't take her mind off of Jefferson. Wherever she went it seemed that his name appeared. On television, in the papers, or as the subject of idle conversation, Lara Harmon's death was *news*.

For the next few days she kept herself busy by visiting friends and relatives. She went shopping, had lunch with Katie, walked in the park and still hunted down jobs. She avoided staying home alone in her apartment, and installed a tape-recording machine to answer her calls. She didn't want to miss any job offers that might come over the phone, and yet she couldn't stick around her apartment. If she had experienced phone calls from nosy reporters before Lara Harmon's death, they had doubled since the tragedy. She felt visible and vulnerable. There was no place to escape.

She had tried to get through to Jefferson, but it was useless. The recorded message left on his telephone indicated that he was indisposed for several days. Feeling as if she had to let him know how she felt, she had written him a quick note of sympathy and then mailed it before she could tear it to shreds. There was nothing she could say that would even hint at her true feelings. How could she explain that she loved him, desperately, passionately, and yet felt a deep, welling sense of remorse—or was it guilt—at his ex-wife's untimely death. How could she say that she wanted to be with him every moment of his life, and yet felt that she couldn't?

It was late Friday evening by the time that she returned home from the shopping mall. She was empty-handed but weary, and she hoped that she would be able to fall into a deep and dreamless sleep. Lara's funeral, a private ceremony, had been held on the previous day, and since then much of the publicity concerning her death had quieted.

After kicking off her shoes Andrea absently flipped on the recording machine, intending to listen to the messages as she got ready for a long hot bath. For the first time in a week there were only a few messages, and only one from one of the more persistent reporters.

The call that surprised Andrea was from Carolyn Benedict. It was simple and to the point. The producer of *Days of Promise* wanted to offer Andrea a job as a scriptwriter for the soap opera. She left the number of the studio on the machine, with instructions for Andrea to call her to work out the terms of employment.

Andrea glanced at her watch. It was eight o'clock in the evening, eleven in New York. She hesitated a moment, bit her lower lip and dialed the number. It was unlikely, but perhaps someone might be working late. Andrea's throat went dry when her call was answered, but her expectations were short-lived as she listened to a recorded message explaining about the studio's regular hours of business. Somehow Andrea was relieved. Although she had tried to convince herself that the best thing for her would be moving to Manhattan, thousands of miles away from Jefferson, a small part of her had argued against her logic. As a sigh of relief passed over her lips she placed the receiver back on the telephone and turned the recorder off for the night.

She had just gotten out of the bath and settled into bed

with a best seller when the phone rang. She waited for the machine to answer the call before realizing that she had turned it off. Her stomach knotted as she reached for the phone near the bed. What if it was another reporter?

With false confidence and a slightly irritated tone she answered the phone on the fourth ring. "Hello?"

"Andrea?" Jefferson's voice asked. Andrea felt herself tremble at the familiar sound of his voice. In her mind she pictured him, and saw his dark eyes and noble face.

"Hello, Jefferson," she whispered. All of the emotion that she should have hidden from him surfaced in her words. Her throat became constricted, and she found it difficult to speak. For no reason other than that he was on the other end of the line, tears began to well in her eyes. "I . . . I want you to know how sorry I am about Lara," Andrea managed to say, though choking.

"I know. . . . I got your card."

"Oh, Jefferson . . . why? What happened?" she asked, her voice ragged and raw.

"I don't know, no one does, not even her latest boyfriend. Or if he does, he's not saying."

"Are you all right?"

"Fine."

"And Megan?" Andrea asked, hardly daring to breathe, afraid that the sobs building in her throat might surface. Slowly she attempted to regain a modicum of her composure.

"It's been difficult," he admitted. His voice sounded strained and tired. "But I think it will get better," he added flatly.

Though tears were spilling from Andrea's eyes, she kept her voice steady. "I'm sure it will." *Oh, God, Jefferson,* Andrea thought to herself as she clutched the receiver, afraid to lose him, afraid of breaking the frail connection that held them so fragilely together. *What can I do for you . . . for your child? If you only loved me the way I love*

*you, I would touch you, caress you, make love to you, until
the pain went away. If you only knew how much I need
you, how much I want to take care of you and Megan.*

There was an unsteady silence, but Andrea couldn't
bring herself to end the conversation. Finally, in a tight
voice, Jefferson attempted to ring off. "I just wanted to
thank you . . . for the card. Good night."

"No!" Andrea blurted, and a sob erupted in her throat.
"Don't hang up!"

Again the silence.

Andrea pulled in a ragged breath and wished that she
could control her emotions.

"What?" he asked severely.

"I . . . I just want you to know that I care," she
breathed.

"Oh, Andrea," he sighed, and hesitated. "I wish that I
could believe you."

"But I do. I always have."

"There are so many things . . ." His voice lowered and
became distant. "I would like you to meet Megan," he
said at last.

"I want to."

"She's still up. . . ." Was it an invitation?

"Now?" Andrea asked. "You want me to meet her
now?"

"If you would." His voice seemed empty.

"But don't you think it's too soon after . . ."

"Life goes on, Andrea."

"But . . ."

His voice had become severe, the edge of his words
bitter. "But what? What kind of an excuse can you come
up with this time, Andrea? You always have a reason to
push me away, each time that I try to touch you!"

"No!" she cried, attempting to defend herself. The
sound of a receiver being shoved back into its cradle
echoed in Andrea's mind, and the flat buzzing to remind

her to hang up filled the silence of the room before Andrea could find the strength to disconnect her end of the conversation.

Was he right? Was she running from him again? That was ridiculous! She loved him with such passion that it sometimes scared her. She talked angrily to herself; she told herself that it was all his fault. He was the one who continued to distort everything she said.

When the phone rang again, Andrea jumped to answer it. It had to be Jefferson, repentant over his hasty harsh words. Andrea was ready to forgive him, to be with him, to somehow make things right between them.

"Hello," she answered breathlessly.

"Hi," Martin called back to her. "You must have been sitting on the phone! How are you?"

"Fine," Andrea responded weakly.

"Well, aren't you going to fill me in on the job in New York? Gayla just called me last night and told me about it. The least you could do is keep me informed. I'm still your brother, you know."

Her spirits lifted slightly at the sound of Martin's warm voice. "All right, all right. It wasn't that I was hiding anything from you, it's just that until a few minutes ago I really didn't know anything."

"But you do now?"

"Yeah. Carolyn Benedict, producer of *Days of Promise*, left a message for me on my answering machine just tonight."

"And . . . ?" he asked expectantly.

"She offered me the job."

"How about that! Are you really going to move to New York? I can't believe it!" He sounded oddly relieved.

"I . . . I don't know," she admitted.

"Why not? Something wrong with the pay or the hours?"

"No, it's not that," she tried to explain, feeling suddenly

caged. "It's just that I haven't had a lot of time to think about it."

"What do you mean? Wasn't your interview with that producer over a week ago?"

"Yes, but . . ."

"But what? You have a better offer in L.A.?"

Andrea let out her breath. "Don't I wish," she sighed.

Martin's voice turned frigid. "I bet this has something to do with Jefferson Harmon, doesn't it?"

"Why?"

Martin snorted. "Gayla told me you were seeing him again, and I really couldn't believe it. Not after the way he ran out on you the last time."

"He didn't run out on me."

"No? Then why was it that you moped around for him for a couple of years? Why did he marry that other woman? Hmm?"

Andrea's nerves had already been stretched by Jefferson's call. Now, with Martin's needling, she felt even worse. It was with difficulty that she held on to her composure. "That was a long time ago. We all did things, said things, that we didn't really mean."

"Come off it, Andrea. Harmon dumped on you. He'll do it again."

Andrea's temper snapped. "You had a little to do with it, as I recall. All those horrid stories you told your friend at the campus paper . . . and he printed them all!"

"We've been through this before," Martin muttered.

"I know."

"But if Harmon had really wanted to find you and keep in touch with you, he could have. He didn't have to wait for ten years."

"Drop it, Martin," Andrea said.

"Don't you like being reminded of the way Harmon treated you ten years ago?" he taunted.

"I don't like being reminded of the way that you treated me!" she bit out.

"I've paid my dues, Andrea, and then some," he retorted hotly. Once again Andrea was reminded of the agony that Martin had suffered—the physical torture of his wounds and sightlessness and the mental pain of a sister who couldn't find the forgiveness in her heart to write him one letter while he was fighting for his country. Pain, anger and humiliation washed over Andrea.

"Let's not fight," she whispered. "It's so pointless."

Martin sighed. "You're right," he admitted. "I'm sorry I got so mad. It's just that I can't stand Jefferson Harmon. Maybe it wasn't his fault, but I can't forget about the way he turned his back on me, and the pain he caused you."

A protesting noise began in Andrea's throat, but Martin ignored it as he continued. "I know I hurt you too, sis, and you know that I didn't mean to, but—oh, hell! Let's not go into all of that, not now. I just called to check up on you, to see if you were serious about moving to New York."

"I'm considering it."

"Good."

"Sounds like you're trying to get rid of me," she joked, but the humor fell flat.

"You know that's not it. I've just been worried about you, ever since Gayla told me that you were seeing Harmon again. That man's trouble, Andrea, you've got to realize that. Look what happened to that ex-wife of his. There's talk that she committed suicide, for God's sake. You can't tell me that her problems didn't stem from being married to Jefferson Harmon."

"You don't know that."

"It's a good guess."

"I don't think so!" Once again Andrea's voice had a razor sharp edge to it.

"Okay, okay," Martin said reluctantly. "I'm sorry I brought the subject up. Just be careful, okay?"

"I will." Some of her temper ebbed.

"I wish I could talk some sense into you, but then I never have been able to," he muttered.

"Don't worry," she pleaded.

Martin hung up, and Andrea set the receiver back down gently. Martin's worries haunted her; they were the same doubts that she had felt but hadn't admitted. Could he possibly be right about Jefferson? Or was he still holding a grudge that he couldn't dismiss because of the bitterness of the war in Vietnam?

Jefferson's words came into her mind: "I would like you to meet Megan. She's still up."

Silently she began to get dressed, never actually making the mental decision to visit him. How many times must *I* go to him? she asked herself. Why is it always me that is knocking on his door?

Not fair. He had called several times and visited her after her return from Victoria, and every time they had separated, it was because she walked away from him, or his proposals for their future. This is the last time, she swore to herself. I will never go crawling to him again.

It was raining and dark as she headed her car out of the parking lot and onto the busy freeway. With her visibility curbed and the hazard of slick streets after a long dry spell, Andrea felt as if she were indeed crawling—at a snail's pace—to find Jefferson.

Jefferson's apartment house was well lit. The wind whistled through the giant palms, and the tall, spindly trees moved in the night to make dark, eerie shadows on the tall apartment building. The rain that had only been a drizzle when Andrea had left her apartment had increased in volume, and by the time Andrea parked the car, the wind was carrying sheets of rain to the earth.

Andrea steadied herself for a moment in the parked car. In the solitude and darkness of the small automobile she looked up toward Jefferson's apartment on the top floor of the building. It was dark except for a feeble light coming from the window that she guessed to be the living room. *What am I doing here?* she asked herself, and a cold tingle of apprehension spread across her shoulders and skittered down her spine.

Her determination faltered only slightly, and with a mumbled oath at herself for being such a fool where Jefferson was concerned, she slid out of the car, slammed the door shut and ran toward the building. The tempo of the wind increased, and she was reminded of another stormy night—which seemed to be years ago—on the island.

Andrea shook the raindrops from her hair as she entered the lobby. The guard at the desk was the same man she had encountered on her visit several weeks in the past. His unyielding and stern smile at her entrance softened in recognition as she walked toward the desk.

"You're here to see Mr. Harmon," he guessed.

"That's right," she agreed, forcing a smile.

"You're expected?"

Her mouth twisted into a thoughtful smile. "I don't think so; no." She shook her head with her admission, and her black hair brushed against the light fabric of her coat.

"Then I'll have to call Mr. Harmon," the guard said apologetically.

"That's fine. I'll wait."

It took only a few minutes before the guard hung up and escorted Andrea to the elevator. "I'm sorry you had to wait."

"No problem." She smiled at the kindly old man until the elevator doors closed and she was once again alone.

Jefferson hung up the phone and flung himself down on the couch. Andrea had decided to come after all. He slammed his fist against the edge of the navy-blue sectional and whispered a stream of invectives, largely aimed at himself.

After she had refused to come to see him earlier, he had put Megan to bed and decided that no matter what, he would shove Andrea Monroe out of his life forever. And now all she had to do was waltz back into the building, have the security guard announce that she had come to visit him and all of his resolve had melted. Damn him! Damn her! Damn the whole ridiculous situation that pulled them apart and thrust them together. He cursed the day that he had ever laid eyes upon Andrea Monroe, but even now, as he conjured in his mind the first time he had seen her, innocent and wise, beautiful and young, trusting and independent, he knew that he was lost to her forever. He had never loved a woman so fervently, never felt the pain of loss or anguish that she could instill in him with only the disdainful arch of an exquisite black eyebrow. Damn it all! Damn it all to hell!

Jefferson poured himself a quick jigger of Scotch and downed it quickly. He was about to pour another when the knock at his door stopped him. He held the liquor bottle in midair for a moment, hesitating. *Let her wait,* he thought to himself. His mouth twisted into a mirthless smile as he poured the second drink and took his time savoring it.

The second time she knocked, more sharply, it seemed, the sound was louder, more insistent. His angry smile pulled more tightly at the corners of his mouth. Still, he lingered at the bar. *It served her right. Let her find out what it feels like to always be begging and never receiving. Let her see for herself how it is to be on the other side of the door.*

The knocking subsided. Her voice, full, rich and obviously concerned, finally compelled him to answer the door. It was as clear and sweet as he remembered, the same voice that called to him in the middle of the night when he was alone in his bed. His smile faded as he strode across the dimly lit room.

"Jefferson," Andrea called anxiously against the hard wood of the door. "Jefferson, are you all right? Jefferson?"

Just as Andrea was about to knock again, the oaken door swung silently inward. Andrea held her breath for a

moment as she came face to face with Jefferson and his
condemning stare. His eyes were as cold as stones, and as
she lifted her face to meet his hardened gaze, she involuntarily trembled. He looked tired and angry.

"Thank God you're all right," she breathed, stiffening
her shoulders for the impending attack she could see
developing in Jefferson's savage eyes. "I was beginning to
worry about you." Her voice echoed the relief she felt at
the sight of him.

"You don't have to worry about me, Andrea," he
replied, his mouth set in a grim, hard line. "I can take care
of myself." He shifted to lean against the door. "So you
changed your mind and decided to come over here after
all," he said tonelessly. "How nice. Come in," he invited
in the same cold, flat voice.

Andrea moved from the security of the brightly lit
hallway into the darkened interior of Jefferson's apartment. Only one small reading lamp in a far corner of the
room was lit, but even in the shadows Andrea could see
that the room had become cluttered. All of the tidiness of
the roomy apartment was gone, and it appeared disorga-
nized and unkept. If Jefferson noticed Andrea's quiet
appraisal of the room, he didn't show it. Instead, he
looked steadily at her, adding to the uneasy feeling that
was growing within her.

"How about a drink?" he asked suddenly, but his severe
expression didn't change.

"I don't think so." His barely restrained hostility and
the scathing mockery in his voice shocked her. She realized that his anger was directed at her, and she didn't
understand why. He was the one who had invited her over
to meet his daughter, and once she had come he was
barely civil to her. Had she unwittingly intruded into a
crisis with his daughter? Where was Megan?

Jefferson ignored Andrea's wishes and poured her a stiff
drink, along with another for himself. It was unlike him to

rely on alcohol for any source of comfort or strength, but Andrea's unexpected presence unnerved him. Part of him wanted to toss her out of the apartment and tell her in no uncertain terms that he had no use for a woman who couldn't make an honest decision and stick by it. She had spurned his proposal the last time she'd been alone with him, and now she was back—just to taunt him. He was angry with himself and his weakness for her. He should never have let her back into his home, and yet a traitorous male part of him still wanted her, both physically and mentally. Just the sight of her made vivid pictures of her naked body and pleading eyes flash into his mind's eye. He felt a need to hold her, caress her, protect her forever. The thought of his weakness and need for her made him tighten his jaw in determination. With effort he willed his trembling hands to still as he poured the stiff, amber-colored Scotch.

Andrea watched Jefferson in silence as she stood in the middle of the room still wearing her coat. She didn't know if she should stay or flee. She could feel the tension in the room as sure as if it had been a visible barrier between them. She was both afraid and angry, confused and determined, torn and whole. She wanted Jefferson, needed him, but she couldn't understand him. Suddenly she wondered if she ever had.

It was obvious that Jefferson, too, was torn with conflicting emotions. He was dressed more carelessly than she had ever seen him. His dress shirt was rolled up at the sleeves and pulled out of the waistband of his jeans. His hair was so rough and disheveled, he would have appeared boyish, had it not been for the savage look to his eyes. Though years had passed, Andrea was reminded of the dashing young California senator who had stolen her heart ten years ago. Even with the angles of his face hardened in anger, Andrea could see in him the air of charm and warmth that had captivated the Californian voters. He was enigmatic, frightening, mysterious and yet loving. If only she could get past his cold, biting words. If only he would love her again.

When he crossed the darkened room and walked to within inches of her, Andrea held his cold, arrogant gaze. His eyes swept her body, and for a fleeting moment Andrea recognized the raw and persistent passion that still burned silently, hungrily, beneath the facade of ice.

"So why are you here?" he asked, with only the merest trace of interest. He handed her the drink and took a long swallow of his as he sat back on the couch to study her.

"I came to meet Megan, as you suggested," she replied. Wasn't it obvious?

"Megan's been asleep for over an hour."

"You told me she was awake."

"She was *then,* but when you said you weren't coming, I put her to bed."

"I guess I should have called," she said, testing the water. Why was he so angry?

"That would have been nice."

"But I got tied up. Martin called."

Jefferson stiffened at the mention of Andrea's brother. He set his drink aside and smiled wryly to himself. "Your brother, Martin? He called you?" His bitter sense of humor surfaced. "Oh, I get it, Martin talked you into coming and seeing me, right?"

Andrea felt the deep pang of pain at the mockery in his words as surely as if Jefferson had stabbed her. She shook her head and pursed her lips. "No, as a matter of fact he thought it was a bad idea."

"Wonderful guy."

"You don't even know him."

"I don't want to!" Jefferson reached for his drink and finished it in one deep swallow. "I had enough of your brother to last me a lifetime."

"He's changed!"

"Just like you have?"

Andrea's eyes blazed. "Damn you, Jefferson, I came over here willing to apologize for the last time we were together." Her voice began to quiver, and she could feel her body beginning to tremble. "I came here because I thought you wanted me to."

"So you could meet Megan?"

"Yes!" she cried desperately. Tentatively Andrea sat on the couch next to him. "Jefferson, I do want to meet your daughter." Her green eyes were pleading with honesty, and her hand came out to rest upon his knee.

Jefferson closed his eyes at her touch. He tried not to think of the warm, enticing pressure of Andrea's fingers against the light fabric that covered his thighs. "Megan has been through a helluva lot," he said, rubbing his forehead with his hand. Good God, would the heat that Andrea was causing in his legs stop before it traveled upward and he was lost to her and his own blinding passion?

"I know it must be hard on her," Andrea whispered.

With a groan Jefferson slid away from her, and his eyes narrowed skeptically. "You can't even begin to imagine," he snapped. He moved over, hoping to put some distance between them and cool his heated blood. She leaned seductively closer to him, hoping to catch hold of that part of him that wanted her so desperately.

"I thought you wanted me to come here."

Jefferson made a deprecating sound. "And I thought you were too busy."

"That's not what I said."

He crossed his arms over his chest, causing the muscles to bulge on his shoulders and upper arms. "Then what exactly is it that you did say?" he asked rhetorically before answering himself. "Something to the effect that you needed a little more time?"

"Not me, Jefferson—Megan. She's only five and probably doesn't understand death, especially not her mother's. I thought she might need a little more time to adjust to the change and emptiness in her life. She just lost her mother, for God's sake, and now she's living alone with you. The poor thing must be confused and lonely."

"Don't preach to me, Andrea. I live here, remember? I see everyday what my daughter is going through. I'm here at night to witness the nightmares!" His words were hot and venomous, but something in his face changed, and he raked an impatient hand through his thick, near-black hair.

"Look, Jefferson," Andrea began, not knowing exactly how to deal with him. He didn't want her, at least he didn't want to want her. That much was clearly evident, and maybe he was right. Maybe there never could be another time for the two of them. What they had in the past might never again be relived. "I just came over to see you and to meet Megan. Obviously you don't want me here . . . and . . . and I can deal with that." Contrary to her bold words, the rejection began to burn in her throat, and she knew that if she didn't leave soon, all of her pride and dignity would crumble. She would break down in front of him. She couldn't allow that to happen, not now, when he had almost cringed when she touched him. Jefferson's head snapped up at the catch in her voice. Confusion paled his eyes. Her voice sounded nearly dead when she continued. "I've been offered a job in New York." A small, betraying smile played upon her white lips.

"What?" he asked hoarsely.

"And I've decided to take it." Her last words had spilled from her lips in an unconscious tumble of feelings. She stood up and walked hurriedly toward the door. She wanted to leave as quickly as she could, before her ragged emotions got the better of her. She didn't look at him, couldn't bear to see his condemning face another moment, as she reached for the doorknob. The small, frail, frightened voice of a child stopped her.

"Daddy! Daddy!" The high-pitched voice grew louder and more fearful. "Daddy?"

"Andrea, wait. Please stay," Jefferson said as he dashed

from the room. There was an urgency to his words that compelled her to hesitate. *Go. Leave while you have the chance,* a voice inside her mind commanded. *Don't stay!* She sagged heavily against the door, her hand still clutching the knob. Her ears heard, over the wind that whistled outside, the sound of a door opening just as the child began to scream frantically at the top of her lungs.

"Daddy . . . Mommy . . . Mommy, where are you? Mommy, I want Mommy!" Sobs erupted in the small, frightened voice.

Andrea felt her knees buckle in compassion for the child she had never met, and tears began to slide down her cheeks. The sobbing grew quieter, and Jefferson's voice, soft and reassuring, whispered words of comfort to his child. Not taking the time to understand her own motive, Andrea moved and followed the direction of the sound. It was dark in the hallway, but a shadowy light from a bedroom guided her. In the small room, on the single canopy bed, Jefferson sat rocking his daughter. He was holding her as tightly as she was clutching him, and softly intoning comforting words.

The child had her arms draped around his neck. Her thin, pale skin contrasted to the dark, curling hairs on the back of Jefferson's head.

"It's all right, sweetheart. Daddy's here, and I'll never leave you. Everything is all right."

"But Mommy . . . where's Mommy?" the little girl asked more quietly, and Andrea's heart wrenched in sympathy with the pain the small child must be suffering.

She didn't hear Jefferson's quiet response, but when he shifted his position on the bed, Andrea saw Megan's face for the first time. Her large, luminous eyes, lighter than Jefferson's, were shimmering with pooled tears. Her blond hair cascaded to her slim shoulders, which tightened as Megan attempted to stifle her remaining sobs against her father's chest. The comforting words continued as Jefferson tucked the child snugly into her bed.

Andrea backed down the hall, letting her hands guide her in the darkness. She was afraid to take her eyes off the intimate scene of father and child and yet fearful of being caught intruding on a private moment.

Once she was back in the living room, Andrea waited, pacing the room, while Jefferson continued to calm Megan. Images reeled mercilessly in her head as she paced: Jefferson comforting his daughter; Jefferson as a young, captivating senator; Jefferson laying over her, naked in the bright Pacific sun; Jefferson holding her hand while they walked barefoot in the tide.

The images flashed faster and faster with the increased tempo of her pacing. The tears that she had attempted to keep at bay were cascading freely down from her eyes to stream down her face. So caught up was she in her vivid, heart-wrenching memories that she didn't notice when Jefferson's voice had stopped soothing his child, nor when he had entered the room to stand and watch her.

Suddenly Andrea realized that she wasn't alone. A small tingling sensation in the small of her back made her whirl about to face the hallway where Jefferson was standing. She blinked back her tears and looked into Jefferson's confused face. The questions in his eyes demanded answers.

"I came to the bedroom. . . . I saw you with Megan," Andrea stammered, hoping somehow to explain herself. "Oh, Jefferson, I didn't mean to intrude."

"You didn't."

"I'm just so sorry about all of this," she whispered.

"It's not your fault," he assured her, walking over to her.

"But I wish there was something I could do." She turned her eyes upward to seek his.

He closed his eyes as if afraid of his own suggestion. "There is something you could do."

"What?"

His fingers reached out and touched the edge of her jaw.

They stroked her skin for a second as hesitation wavered in his eyes. "I've asked you before, and I want you to think about it again. Marry me, Andrea."

"Oh, Jefferson, why?" she asked, letting herself fall against him. "You can't expect me to fill Megan's empty heart. She needs Lara, not me."

"I'm not asking you for Megan," he whispered into her hair. His warm breath seemed to caress her skin. "I'm asking you for me . . . for *us*. Damn it, woman, I'm trying to tell you I love you!"

His arms encircled her and pulled her tightly against him. "I'm not setting down any rules this time. We can get married immediately or we can wait, but for God's sake woman, let's do it!"

Andrea pulled herself away from him, but he drew her closer. "When I came into this room," she stated, "I knew that you wished you had never laid eyes upon me."

"That's because I thought you would come into my life fleetingly and then be off. I can't stand being toyed with."

"I never intended to play games with you."

"Just drive me insane!"

"Never."

"But you did . . . for ten years. And I can't stand it any longer. I want you to marry me, and I want to go back to Victoria. Let's leave California."

"But my work. . . ."

"And forget about New York, too! If they want you so desperately, you can free-lance."

"Oh, Jefferson," she sighed, resting her head against his broad chest. She could hear his thundering heart, and she felt nearly weak at his touch. "What about Martin . . . and my family?"

"Let's not worry about them. For once let's just think about ourselves."

"And Megan?"

"Of course Megan. What is it, Andrea? Don't you want to marry me?"

She was compelled to honesty. "I've wanted to marry you for over ten years."

A smile, radiant and warm, spread over his lips. It was off-center and boyish, the smile she remembered from his youth. "Well, ma'am," he drawled, "looks like this is your lucky day."

Silhouette Intimate Moments

more romance, more excitement
$2.25 each

1 ☐ DREAMS OF EVENING
Kristin James

2 ☐ ONCE MORE WITH FEELING
Nora Roberts

3 ☐ EMERALDS IN THE DARK
Beverly Bird

4 ☐ SWEETHEART CONTRACT
Pat Wallace

5 ☐ WIND SONG
Parris Afton Bonds

6 ☐ ISLAND HERITAGE
Monica Barrie

7 ☐ A DISTANT CASTLE
Sue Ellen Cole

8 ☐ LOVE EVERLASTING
Möeth Allison

9 ☐ SERPENT IN PARADISE
Stephanie James

#10 ☐ A SEASON OF RAINBOWS
Jennifer West

#11 ☐ UNTIL THE END OF TIME
June Trevor

#12 ☐ TONIGHT AND ALWAYS
Nora Roberts

#13 ☐ EDGE OF LOVE
Anna James

#14 ☐ RECKLESS SURRENDER
Jeanne Stephens

#15 ☐ SHADOW DANCE
Lorraine Sellers

#16 ☐ THE PROMISE OF SUMMER
Barbara Faith

#17 ☐ THE AMBER SKY
Kristin James

#18 ☐ THE DANVERS TOUCH
Elizabeth Lowell

#19 ☐ ANOTHER KIND OF LOVE
Mary Lynn Baxter

#20 ☐ THE GENTLE WINDS
Monica Barrie

#21 ☐ RAVEN'S PREY
Stephanie James

#22 ☐ AGAINST THE RULES
Linda Howard

#23 ☐ THE FIRES OF WINTER
Beverly Bird

#24 ☐ FANTASIES
Pamela Wallace

#25 ☐ THIS MAGIC MOMENT
Nora Roberts

#26 ☐ OLD LOVE, NEW LOVE
Jane Clare

#27 ☐ DIANA'S FOLLY
Jillian Blake

#28 ☐ WALTZ IN SCARLET
Muriel Bradley

Silhouette Intimate Moments

more romance, more excitement